The Fate Between Us

The Fate Between Us

Margaret Emerson

images & adjectives
PUBLISHING, LLC

ISBN: 979-8-9880125-0-4

This is a work of fiction. Names, characters, events and incidents are the products of the author's imagination. Any resemblance to actual persons, living or dead, or actual events is purely coincidental.

Book design by Margaret Emerson

Printed in the United States of America.

First printing edition 2023.

Images and Adjectives Publishing, LLC
2119 County Road 1A
Montrose, CO 81403

www.ridgwaywritingworkshops.com

To anyone who's ever loved and lost, and found love again.

1

∾

Saving My Life

December, 1999

It's been almost a year since I stepped foot on American soil. Two weeks to the day, as a matter of fact. I have sat here looking out at this azure ocean almost every morning. On days when the thunderheads hover threateningly, it's the color of brushed platinum. Most mornings, though, it's the color of your eyes.

I still remember the first time I looked into them. I felt that same vastness I feel now as I look out onto the Pacific. It is the color of the horizon where the sea meets the sky. It is the color of forever.

There are quite a few things I miss about the States, about my life back in California. Mostly, though, I miss you—even though in all the time we've known each other we were only together a couple days.

The sun rises on this side of the island, a few minutes earlier or later every day. I'm usually up before the horizon spills its light. I haven't been sleeping well since I got here. My dreams keep me in a restless, semi-awake state half the night, the heat and humidity the other half. Looking out my window at two in the morning, I marvel at how there are more stars here than in California—more than I've ever seen in my life. They keep me company as I lay awake, beckoning sleep to take me again. Always it's the same routine: nightmares at one thirty, awake at two, asleep again by four. Then I'm here on the beach with my notebook when the sun is rising.

I often wonder what you are doing now. Are you still married? How is little Pete? I've been writing you every day, you know—in my notebook. Every day I ask the same questions and wonder the same things. Every day I am answered with silence. That's not your fault, of course. I know you're probably thinking and going through the same thing since you know I can't mail you anything, and since you really don't know how to get in touch with me, either. Because of everything that happened and everything we said to each other when I left, I decided it would be better if we didn't communicate for a while.

I looked up from the laptop and thought about the last sentence of my email. Had I been wrong about that? That it was better that I didn't try to get in touch with the woman I thought was the love of my life?

That's the question that's been nagging at me for months now. And so, last week while serving drinks to an overweight, sunburned tourist from the Midwest with his face buried in some Excel document on his laptop, I did something impulsive. I offered him five thousand dollars for it. He looked me up and down, snickered, and went back to the remnants of his fruity cocktail.

"That thing have a modem on it?" I asked.

"Yeah," he answered, his voice like a rumble from a nearby thunderhead.

"You have some ISP software set up on it too?"

"Yes, but what do you want with my laptop? Five thousand dollars? C'mon."

"I'm serious. Give me twenty minutes and I'll be back here with five thousand dollars. Cash. For your laptop."

"I'll tell you, buddy, you can get one of these a lot cheaper than five g's. I bought this one about six months ago for about fifteen hundred."

"Yeah, but you see any CompUSA's around here?"

He went back to his drink and almost dismissed me, until a half hour later when I showed up with a small plastic bag full of hundreds. He fingered the money with his hairy, fat knuckles and blew out a long whistle.

"Shit buddy, you've been getting some great tips serving up the Mai Tais, haven't you?"

"Do we have a deal or not?"

"You're gonna have to let me put some stuff on a disk. Do a little clean up first." His voice had that restrained excitement that fat, middle-aged men get when they know they bagged a sucker and want to hurry up and get the hell out of there before the sucker changes his mind.

"That's fine. Come back later this afternoon."

He came back an hour later.

Anyway, I managed to buy a laptop off a tourist for cash and that's how I'm writing this email to you. I even gave the guy a little extra to pay for the internet service for a few months until I figure out how to get it myself without a credit card. The money I spent on the laptop was the most impulsive and frivolous I've allowed myself to be with the money since I arrived on the island.

It was dangerous perhaps, but somehow I doubt Mr. Hairy Knuckles will be compromising me. He'll probably go back home to Michigan or somewhere and hoot it up with his pasty middle-aged co-workers over a pitcher of cheap beer at Friday Happy Hour—How Some Dumb American Schmuck Hippy Loser Blew a Year's Worth of Bar Tips On My Old Laptop.

Whatever.

He'll be working quite a few years before he can make enough salary to match what I have in cash. Even then, it may take him a lifetime to realize that money is almost a worthless commodity when it comes to putting to rest what is eating away at your soul.

I rub my eyes and save the file I've been composing now for the past hour. I am a little nervous about sending this letter. I have no way of knowing if she still keeps up this email address, or if she'll want to hear from me. My fears are getting the better of me, I know, and I start digging my heels into the sand to fight the sinking feeling in the pit of my stomach. I consider shortening the letter, perhaps to just a few sentences:

How are you? I'm doing okay. Things here are better than I expected they'd be. Do you still think about me every single day like you used to? Because I'm dying over here, missing you terribly. The weather is good, though. Better than back home.

There's no way around it, I know. I can't pretend I'm just sending some silly Christmas greeting while downing a doughnut before the boss gets into the office that morning. This is serious. What it was between us—it meant something. I have to cut the crap and just write the letter. I've been wanting to for as long as I've been here.

In the distance I see my friend Adelle running up the shoreline, his tan torso bobbing up and down as he jogs his daily five miles. He's been living here about seven years. He owns the resort and the bar where I serve drinks to the tourists. I met him shortly after I arrived on this island. I was sitting at the counter of a fish shack down the street, admiring the deeply tanned strip of belly peeking out beneath the short T-shirt of the girl serving up the food. I asked her where I could look to find rooms for rent, and she wrote down an address for me in her child-like scrawl. A friend of hers owned a place, she had chirped, and there was a recent vacancy.

The waitress turned out to be Adelle's girlfriend, one of a few regulars. Adelle is very non-committal when it comes to women. He likes it that way, he tells me. It goes along with his plan to uncomplicate his life.

He jogs by in front of me and does a quick salute, his tempo uninterrupted. I put my hand up in return. "I'm going to be over a little later this morning to use your phone!" I yell across the sand.

He nods slightly without missing a beat. Adelle's expensive running sneakers kick up chunks of sand behind him as he takes the beach in long strides. He moved here to save his life, he often tells me. He doesn't know I came here for the same reason, although in his mind the meaning of that phrase is altogether different. Adelle once showed me a photo of himself from when he was still living in the States. He was almost 150 pounds overweight. He smoked, he drank to excess. I almost couldn't recognize him as the same person from that old photo.

But now, every morning, Adelle starts his day with this long run on the beach, rain or shine. He has foregone many things from his former life, but his energy and his need for discipline have turned into a daily obsession with exercise. He never had the time or the inclination to lose the weight, until he started living here. Here, there is a lot of time, too much time, nothing *but* time. It can be a dangerous thing if one isn't careful, so much time. Your life can slip through your fingers before you know it.

I continued the email:

A few days after I arrived here, I began working at a small tourist bar bussing tables and serving drinks. The owner hired me because I spoke English fluently, and unlike some of the places where I had gone looking for work, he didn't ask me why I wanted a job in Fiji or what I was running away from. He agreed to pay a small salary in cash but pointed out that I would have to earn most of it through tips. He is also my landlord and gives me a break on rent because I am fixing up the house where I'm living. So, in an ironic sort of way, I'm still a sort of a property manager.

I don't know how long I'm going to be here. I try to make the best of it, although some days it feels like I'm just floundering or on some permanent vacation or something. I know a lot of people are thinking of me and worried about me. I can't help that, but at the same time I know that this is better than the alternative.

I hope that I can still reach you this way. I tried to call your work number one night, but your desk has evidently become someone else's. I am almost afraid that in waiting so long to write, I have missed my chance. I hope you're well, Ellen.

I take a deep breath and click the send button. I'm aware that perhaps

I've been a little too paranoid for too long, but it was for good reason, I think. That one split-second decision I made a year ago has haunted me ever since. It's the reason why I've been so tortured about writing Ellen, the woman I think about every day. It's the reason my life today is nothing like what I imagined it would be when I was living in San Diego. I would make that decision again, despite what I've lost.

I don't know what will happen after Ellen reads my email. I don't know if she still loves me. I don't know if she's still married to her husband. I don't know how long I'll have to be a bartender or if I'll ever get back to the U.S. I don't know what happened to my wife, Dana.

The truth is, the uncertainty of my life *now* scares me so much less the certainty of my life *before*. I dread the idea of what my life would have been if nothing in my circumstances had ever changed.

2

Ellen

November, 1998

Ellen and I met online about two years ago. She had read a critical note I had posted on a message board for Contemporary Fiction. I had slammed the "sugary genre" of a particular novelist named Jerry Roth and had gone on to point out the ridiculousness of romance novels in general. She had written a funny and thoughtful reply. The author I had slammed, she wrote, was her brother-in-law.

Immediately my interest was piqued, but I also felt embarrassed to be confronted by someone who knew the author I had criticized. Jerry didn't always write such sugary nonsense, apparently. He had spent five years as a field reporter for Newsweek and Time, and spent a quite a few months scrounging around Yugoslavia, covering the atrocities there. He had been holed up in a small village one month, unable to leave or even make contact with anyone because the Serbs had bombed the shit out of the place. Every day, he and the villagers would have to move in and out of the woods, waiting for the Serbs to give up and leave. Every day they would find more and more bodies littering the streets in the morning. Under the cover of darkness, they would dart in and out of houses, looking for food and supplies.

They hovelled in the forest for days, in small groups. They were afraid to ignite fires that would heat the water or cook the food for fear the smoke or flames would give away their hiding spot. Jerry found a family that had been in the middle of a wedding when the Serbs fell on the village. The groom had been executed in cold blood, as were several other adult men. It was there that he had met his wife, a beautiful woman named Halina. He stayed with Halina and her family until they were able to relocate to a town some fifty miles away that was tentatively safe. It wasn't long after that he had lost interest in writing about the war and instead developed an obsession of getting Halina out of the country.

Soon after he had succeeded in aiding Halina's emigration to the states, they got married in Chicago. Jerry had put in his resignation as a field reporter and had willingly and excitedly accepted his new roles: husband and father-to-be. But his passion for writing hadn't abated. Using the new energy and inspiration he had found through Halina, he began a series of short romance novels.

Ellen wasn't really defending her brother-in-law's style of writing; she was explaining the reason for it. She normally doesn't reply to Internet message boards, but she couldn't resist this time because the criticism hit so close to home.

I had been both amused and fascinated by Ellen's letter. She was able to tell a story with such clarity and humor that I asked if she was a writer. She wasn't, but she was an avid reader, she replied. One of her favorite things was browsing the bookstore for books with original plots and an odd sense of humor. Since she loved to read and I loved to write, we found ourselves unable to resist corresponding.

We wrote almost every day, bouncing around ideas and thoughts about writing, our jobs, our marriages. We laughed about ourselves. We encouraged each other. She encouraged me to stay optimistic about my life and I encouraged her to work her way toward her dream job. At the time I met her, Ellen was completing a master's in marketing and working for an insurance company in Connecticut. She had been married for five years and had a four-year-old son named Pete. She was hoping that her master's would enable her to find a more rewarding job, perhaps even allowing her to venture out on her own as a business consultant.

Almost immediately, it seemed, I began to look forward to Ellen's emails more than anything else. My life at the time had started fluctuating between mind numbing and intolerable. I was the property manager of a large self-storage in San Diego, a path that I had stumbled onto a few years after graduating with a bachelor's in English. Managing a self-storage certainly wasn't what I had gone to school for. But when I first started the job, I wasn't expecting that I would still be working there four years later. I was so exhausted by the new responsibility in the beginning, that I kept putting off looking for work as a writer. Before long, I had become too lazy to keep up my daily routine of writing. The need to write became just one more nagging chore in the back of my mind. I spent more time feeling guilty than actually sitting down at the computer.

After I met Ellen, it all changed. I would start composing letters to her all day in my mind, even away from the computer. I would remember an incident in my past and would have half a letter composed in my mind before my fingers even touched the keyboard. I looked forward to her reactions, to her thoughts. I found myself paying close attention to making my letters interesting and surprising.

I hadn't felt so excited about writing since college, and I found myself suddenly inspired and full of ideas. I began to formulate and conceive complex plots after hearing about something on the radio or on TV. I would meet an eccentric customer at the self-storage and a character for a book would form in my mind.

Ellen's personality slowly began to take shape in my mind and heart too, becoming almost an addiction. It wasn't just that I raced to the computer every morning to see how she'd responded to my ramblings; it was that I needed to know what was happening in her life, what she was feeling, what she was thinking. At first I would mention Ellen's letters to my wife Dana, and we would occasionally use Ellen's letters as a starting point to a discussion on current events. But as the months went by, Ellen would be in my thoughts more, and I stopped talking about her altogether. Perhaps it was out of guilt, or perhaps I was simply being careful not to say too much to Dana and make her suspicious.

I wanted to know what she looked like, but at the same time I was afraid to ask. What if she was this awful, pasty frump? My brain wanted to know, but my heart didn't because it was clinging to the picture I had formed of her in my mind. There, she was tall and beautiful, with wild, red hair that she had to constantly fight with in order to look professional. She had a small sprinkling of pale freckles on her nose and cheeks, and full, plump lips that would spread wonderfully across her teeth when she smiled. Her eyes were as green as a freshly mowed oval of grass on the putting green of the eighteenth hole.

These were the thoughts clouding my brain one Sunday morning as I sat at the computer, watching the steady blinking of the I-beam over the glare of the monitor. I considered asking what she looked like, if we could exchange pictures, then almost retched after reading what I had written. I sounded like an eighth grader.

"David? Are you at the computer?" Dana's voice snapped me out of my haze.

"What?" Exasperated, knowing what she wanted, I saved my half-finished letter and shut the computer off.

"What the hell are you doing? It's almost ten o'clock. We have to go soon."

Every Sunday we made a thirty-mile drive across the city to Dana's parents' house for brunch. My stomach turned. This was the hardest part of the week for me. I tried to talk myself into a better mood, but it was no use. I considered feigning illness, perhaps playing up my sudden need to retch, but I knew that Dana would see right through that excuse.

I heard her rummaging around the junk drawer in the kitchen as I made my way down the stairs. Like clockwork, I thought. Next, she would open the cupboards one by one, slamming each one harder as her search proved futile.

"Dammit, David, where in the hell are my parents' house keys?"

I made my way into the kitchen and saw her jabbing through her purse. I almost laughed out loud but thought better of it.

"They're in the center console of the car, hon."

Dana looked up at me and squinted. "What are they doing in there? I don't remember leaving them in there."

I bit back a sarcastic comment. I was growing tired of this routine. Dana had the worst short-term memory of anyone I had ever known. This amazed me, because I always thought women were the sticklers for detail and men were the ones who couldn't find their own ass with *Rand McNally* heading a search party. I often wondered if Dana's parents didn't drop her when she was an infant or if she had secretly smoked too much pot in college and never told me.

When we visited her parents, we always let ourselves in with a spare set of keys. Her parents claimed they couldn't hear the doorbell if they were in the yard or on the deck, which either implied they were deaf or they lived on an estate, neither of which was true.

Dana was the youngest, and in my opinion, the favorite of three siblings. She was a big part of the reason why Frank and Susan had decided to move out of St. Louis and purchase their retirement home in the suburbs of San Diego.

Today, I was silent during the drive, my mind humming on a pleasant idle. I should write Ellen and tell her about my in-laws, I thought. They're condescending and snobby, but hell, at least they're interesting. What was it that Ellen had written? It was true that the two extremes are always worth a story—the brilliantly wonderful and the awfully horrid—but it was the truly talented writer who could make the mediocre fascinating. I felt up to the challenge.

"You're quiet today." Dana's voice felt like a splash of cold water on my Ellen-fevered brain.

"I'm just tired. That's all." I shifted in my seat.

"That's what you get for staying up so late last night."

"I was on a roll with the book, I told you," I said.

"Still. Until 3 a.m., David?" Dana's tone was bordering whiny.

For the past three years I had been trying to get through a novel I was writing about an Illinois farmer's journey through a series of financial and emotional hardships. Every time I got back to it I kept changing the details and thus would have to rewrite dozens of paragraphs. I was starting to think I would never finish the thing, and lately I wanted to scrap it altogether and start a new story. I was growing bored with the main character and I had come up on a dead end in the plot. I knew that I had the motivation to finish a book because I certainly got a high from telling a story. Unfortunately, the story I started three years ago was the wrong one.

Dana's acceptance of the time I spent working on my book was all but gone, too. I would be at the keyboard no more than an hour before she started popping her head into the room, asking me what I was doing, how long would I be? Often I could hear her downstairs, flipping through the channels on the television or on the phone with her sister or mother. "Yes," she would sigh, "he's at it again. Don't ask me. I don't know when he's ever gonna finish that stupid thing."

She didn't think I could hear her, or maybe she didn't care. Sometimes I would catch myself staring at the monitor for what seemed like an hour, struggling against feeling demoralized.

Actually, I was lying to Dana about the previous night's writing frenzy. I hadn't been working on my book. I had been chatting with Ellen online.

"I don't want to get into this right now, Dana. I don't want to be in a middle of a fight when we get to your parents' house."

"Why not? Isn't that the way it always is?"

"The way what always is?" I asked.

"You're always in a bad mood on Sundays. Bringing you out to my mom and dad's is like pulling teeth. Maybe next week you should stay home."

"I'd love to, but then I'd have to put up with your foul mood the rest of the day when you get home. Fuck that."

I ground the palm of my hand into the steering wheel, forcing myself not to say anything more. The silence in the car was unbroken the rest of the way there.

3

I Only Came for the Food

Frank and Susan live in a five-bedroom red brick house overlooking the fourth hole of a private golf course. The house is nestled within a half dozen mature eucalyptus trees. A redwood deck sprawls from the French doors in the back of the house. They had bought the place when Frank retired from the CEO position of a large Midwestern bank. Susan had been the typical corporate wife, coordinating all the details of Frank's life outside the office.

When we found them outside on the deck, Frank was leaning against the rail wearing his green and white plaid golf slacks and gripping a glass of orange juice, which was undoubtedly spiked with vodka. Susan was fussing with a flower arrangement in the center of a brightly set patio table.

"How was your golf game this morning, dad?" Dana kissed her father on the cheek.

"Wonderful, honey. Hi David. How's things?" Frank asked.

"Things are good," I replied.

Dana followed her mother into the house to help her bring out the food. I walked over to the outdoor refrigerated bar and poured a beer into a chilled glass. I usually didn't drink that early in the morning, but for some reason, that morning it seemed necessary.

Frank's gaze fell on my heady glass of Heineken as I plopped down on a chaise lounge and stretched out.

"How's the handicap coming along?" I asked him.

"Improving. Although today my game wasn't all there. I think I may have sprained my back a little last time, so my swing was strained this morning."

"Ah." I didn't have much to add. I was just being polite. I didn't play golf.

"You sure you wouldn't want to join me next weekend? Seven a.m. tee time. It'll get your blood flowing."

"I appreciate the invitation, Frank, but I wouldn't want to drag you down. I'd probably be all over the course and it would take me all day to get through it."

"That's how you learn. You have to start somewhere," Frank offered.

I had no interest in learning how to hit a small ball around twenty acres of freshly mowed grass. "That's okay, really."

"I'm sure it won't kill you to get up before nine a.m. on a Sunday, David."

I glared up at him and took a long swallow of the beer.

***

Susan had outdone herself as usual with the food. Eating my mother-in-law's gourmet meals was always my favorite part of the visit. I picked at the rich brandy cake she'd sliced out for dessert. Everything was laid out on matching china and expensive silverware. The coffee was brewed with an expensive German appliance, the name of which I had never heard before. I thought about our own TargetWare at home. Dana and I never had a formal wedding, and thus didn't have cupboards full of hundred-dollar plates bought for us as wedding gifts. That was fine with me. We didn't exactly have hundred-dollar-plate dinners. Dana and I usually ate fast food or rotated the same ten quick-fix menus.

I showered Susan with compliments, hoping to end the visit on a good note. She was gracious about them. Dana was more relaxed than I had seen her all week. I was almost beginning to relax myself, until Susan brought up Dana's sister, Kelley.

"Oh, I almost forgot, honey. Kelley sent pictures of the baby yesterday. He is so adorable! I can't wait for you to see them. You're just going to want to eat him up." She placed her napkin gingerly on the table and disappeared inside the house. I looked at Dana, who sagged a little bit, pushing a chunk of papaya around her plate with a fork. I wanted to follow Susan into the house and tell her not to bring the pictures, to just forget the whole thing.

Susan placed the deck of photos on the table and began cooing at the pictures of Kelley's five-month-old baby. "Look at him here, with that rattle stuffed in his mouth. Isn't he cute? Doesn't it just make you want a baby, too? It just has to."

Dana gripped her coffee cup with both hands, trying to keep them from shaking. "We can't afford a baby right now, Mom."

Susan looked at me from above her reading glasses. "David! Really, you have to think about getting a better paying job or something. What are they paying you over there at the self-storage? Every time I bring up kids to Dana it's always the same thing: 'We can't afford it, we have no money.' Hogwash! I say."

I didn't answer. Frank cleared his throat and went to the bar to officially pour himself another screwdriver. It was now past noon.

"Well, David?" Susan asked.

"Well, what?" I said, feeling tired suddenly.

"Mom, leave him alone," Dana interjected.

"Is this what I'm going to keep hearing over and over again until I'm ninety years old and on my deathbed? That you can't do this and you can't do that because you didn't make enough money? That you wasted your entire life and wasted my daughter's life as well? I want to know! Am I?"

"I don't know, Mrs. Hughes. Maybe. Unless your daughter comes to her senses and marries a real man." I felt a rush of anger, but my voice stayed calm. Dana stood up and started clearing the table.

"You ready to go?" Dana asked me. From the corner of my eye, I could still see Susan's mouth forming a small oval, her reading glasses swaying back and forth in the grip of her forefinger and thumb.

"Wait, now, just a minute!" Susan cried.

"No Mom, we have to go. I've got some stuff I have to do." Dana stacked another plate on her arm and started walking away. When I reached in to take some of the dishes off her hands, I could see her eyes were welling up with tears behind her sunglasses.

"Thanks again for lunch." I nodded toward Frank.

When I walked into the kitchen Dana was already gone. She had rushed out to the car and left the front door wide open behind her. On the drive home I shut the radio off and spent the entire forty minutes directing and redirecting the air conditioning to get comfortable. I couldn't see what Dana was thinking because she turned her shoulder away from me and stared out the side window, grumbling.

When we got home Dana and I drew the shades in the bedroom and sprawled out on the bed, not even bothering to take our shoes off. She scooted over to my side, and as soon as I pulled her head to my chest, she began sobbing.

"I'm sorry."

I caressed her head and face. "Shhhh. There's nothing to be sorry about. If your mom knew, she wouldn't have said all those things."

Her body shook and I pulled the covers up over her shoulder. I held her for a long time, my own chest pent up in a dark, tangled wad.

4

∽

A Problem With Rats

"Do you air condition the buildings?"

The woman was in her late fifties with a tightly curled head of brown, thinning hair. A vague sweaty odor wafted from her. I placed my feet on the floor in front of the swivel chair and rolled back a little, trying to get as far away as I possibly could from the smell. It was too damn early in the morning for this.

"No," I replied. "The buildings aren't air conditioned."

"Well do you offer any refrigerated units?"

"Ma'am, we do not. May I ask what you're storing?"

She looked down at the counter where she had been filling out a contract. She resumed writing, ignoring my question.

"We don't recommend you store any food items or anything that is perishable. As a matter of fact, we don't allow that."

Not looking up from her paperwork, she added, "You don't have a problem with rats, do you?" She emphasized the word rats, almost shouting it.

The phone rang and I lunged for it. Rats? What was this woman going to store? Her deceased husband's body?

"Coastal Storage, may I help you?" I suddenly felt uneasy about turning my back to her. I rotated my chair a little so I could talk on the phone and watch her at the same time. She stopped writing and was staring at me, unmoving.

"Do you have units large enough to store a car?" A man's voice buzzed into my ear.

"Sure, we have garage-sized units. They're two hundred dollars a month. We have about five available right now."

"What kind of security do you have there?" The male voice had a hint of an accent, but I couldn't quite place it. The caller was either trying to fake one or was working hard to smooth one out.

"We've got sensors on every unit. An alarm goes off here in the office if a unit is accessed without a passcode at the gate. The facility is open from seven a.m. until seven p.m. daily. You get in by punching in your code on the keypad at the gate."

"You got someone there on site at all times for security?"

This guy is storing a car? What kind of car is it? A Lamborghini? I thought.

"I live on site, and the security system is on twenty-four hours a day."

The freaky woman was still staring at me, except now her mouth hung open and she looked like she was going to start drooling soon if she didn't snap out of it.

"What happens when you're away from the facility after business hours?"

"I have a pager I take with me that is tied into the security system. Usually I call the police or just return to the facility if the pager goes off, depending on where I am."

"You guys got a regular Fort Knox over there, huh?" The man chuckled.

"We have a good record." I am always leery when I get calls like this. I wonder if it's in fact a potential customer or if someone is casing the place, looking for a security loophole.

"Sir?" The woman was now waving her contract at me from the counter. I held up my hand and nodded.

I returned my attention to the caller, but he had hung up.

"Sir, you never answered my question about the rats."

I took a deep breath. It was going to be one of those days.

***

I led Mrs. Vaughn to her unit—a ten- by five-foot space on the second floor of one of the back buildings. She inspected it thoroughly, checking along the walls and looking up at the unfinished ceiling. Again, I warned her she couldn't store anything perishable. Again, she ignored me and then poked her head out into the hallway where I was standing, looking down both directions.

"Almost all the units have padlocks on them. How often do the owners come to visit their things?" she asked.

"Hardly ever. Most of them just come twice. To store and to retrieve. Why?"

"No reason."

Mrs. Vaughn was beginning to worry me. It didn't elude me that she had come to the facility on foot and that, other than her small white, vinyl handbag, she didn't bring anything to store. I stood in front of her with my arms crossed. Then again, she might come back later with her junk. Some people did that.

"This will do, I suppose." She sniffed, nodded her head, and followed me back out of the building. The hall echoed our footsteps.

Afterwards, I decided to take a break and check my email. Dana and I lived in a two-bedroom manager's apartment above the office of the self storage. Part of the reason I had taken this job was the free apartment. My salary wasn't bad, but by far the best benefit was living this close to the beach rent-free, in a nice apartment with a balcony and a view of the ocean half a mile away. The facility itself was the largest in Southern California, and since the gates were locked down after seven p.m. it felt almost like living on a huge, private estate. I often would jog around the maze of two-story buildings at night—my own private running track.

The biggest drawback to living where I worked was that I was on-call constantly. A few times in the middle of the night we had been jolted awake by the alarm, a loud electronic beep that would sound in the office below us. I would pull on a pair of sweatpants and a T-shirt and go investigate outside. Even though I was prepared to confront an intruder, inevitably the alarm would turn out to be nothing more than heavy fog clouding the laser sensors on the perimeter, or once, a huge tiger moth tripping the motion detectors in the office.

I flipped on the monitor to my computer and dialed up the Internet. After almost a year of hinting around about her looks, Ellen had promised to get me an actual photo of herself this week. She had been wanting to send one earlier but had been waiting for the right time to ask the graphics department at her company for the favor of scanning it in for her. As I waited for the modem to connect, I felt queasy. I wasn't sure if I wanted to know what she really looked like. I was afraid of spoiling my fantasy image of her. The fact that I would have to reciprocate and find a way to send her my photo crossed my mind, too.

The mailbox flag was up. I violently clicked the mouse, rolling the cursor to the READ MAIL button and watched the spinning wheel as it processed my impatience.

Her note was uncharacteristically short.

> *Well, here it is. I had to bribe the graphics manager with a cup of latte this morning to get her to scan this for me. It's a picture of me and Petey eating ice cream. I don't want to hear any comments from the peanut gallery on our matching outfits. It was a coincidence, I swear. My husband had dressed him that morning while I was in the shower! Really!*

The photo started downloading and rendering on my screen from the top down. I looked out the window for a few seconds while it finished. *Please be decent looking, Ellen,* I thought. *I don't want to see lumpy features or blotchy skin or thinning hair. Please have nice knees and a cute butt. I don't mind some cleavage. Just not so much that it's spilling out of your chest and into your lap. That's all I ask.*

I looked at the image filling the screen and sighed a breath of relief. She was beautiful. My first thought was that she looked a little like Courtney

Cox. Her hair was pulled back in a ponytail and she was smiling ear to ear with her arm around her son, his face smeared in pink ice cream. They were both wearing white short-sleeved shirts and navy shorts. She had great eyes—I thought they must have been blue or very light green because they highly contrasted her tan complexion and dark hair. The photo was cropped above their waists and she was squatted down close to her son. As far as I could see, she had a nice body too.

I hit the reply button on her note.

> *Dammit, why do you have to be so attractive? You're scaring me, Ellen. You're smart, you're funny, you're fun; and now I see that you're gorgeous. If you keep up this campaign, I might just have to fall in love with you. So do me a favor, will you? Write me back and tell me that you have hideous warts all over that wonderful body of yours or tell me that you have this high-pitched Disney voice or maybe that you have chronic halitosis or that you're an incessant nag or something. Please, burst my bubble, Ellen. I need the reality check.*
> *David*

My smile stretched out wider with each sentence. I was trying to be funny, but I felt there was a bit of truth to what I was writing. I hadn't felt this giddy about a woman since I met Dana. All the old, familiar feelings were beginning to stir inside me. I was more distracted at work. I was more and more anxious to hear from her. I was even starting to have sexual fantasies about her, which seemed ludicrous to me up until this point since I didn't know what she looked like. That had been all the more reason for me to want her to be good looking.

Fighting back the urge to work out the ache that had started forming in my crotch, I got myself a glass of water and headed back down to the office.

5

Quittin' Time

Dana got home from work an hour earlier than usual, popped her head into the office and declared that she was too tired to think about what to cook. I looked up from a stack of contracts I was sorting through and before I could answer she grumbled that she was going out for fast food.

"Get me some fish tacos. I don't want burgers," I said.

"Alright." After changing into some shorts, she headed back out to her Honda.

"She's home early." Hans, my assistant manager, put an unlit cigarette into his mouth and stood in the middle of the office, sucking on it. I didn't allow smoking anywhere near the office, and he was often too lazy to walk the few yards away from the building to light up. The thing dangled from his lips when he spoke. "And she seems in a bad mood."

I followed his gaze as he craned his head to watch Dana walk by outside the office window.

"Her boss gets on her nerves. She probably faked some doctor's appointment and took off early," I said.

I think Hans is enamored with my wife. He often seems to get fidgety —nervously pacing the counter when he sees her car pulling into the driveway every day after work. I told Dana about it once and she nearly choked on a chip she had been munching on, she laughed so hard.

"Jesus, David," Dana hooted, "that man is the creepiest thing this side of Mississippi. Did you notice how much hair he's got growing from his knuckles? And that strange way he walks, all stiff and sucking in that fat gut of his. I swear to you the man is a closet pedophile."

"How do the hairy knuckles and the stiff walk relate to being a pedophile?" I asked her.

"I don't know. They just do."

"Well then that explains why he likes *you* so much, you being the nubile young age of twenty-eight."

"What the hell is that supposed to mean?" Dana threw a tortilla chip at me.

I remembered how we had spent that evening speculating on what Hans did in the evenings and on his days off. "Probably sits on some crusty old couch, jacking off to old reruns of the Little Rascals or something," she snorted.

"That's pretty rude."

"I know. I'm sorry. I know he's your employee and you like him. But he just creeps me out."

When I looked up again, Hans was facing away from me, his hands in his pockets. His oversized jeans were sagging off his butt, the seam a full six inches lower than his waistline.

"I saw that old lady you told me about this morning," Hans said. "What was her name?"

"Mrs. Vaughn?"

"Yeah, her. I saw her come back a little later with some stuff."

"What kind of stuff?" I asked.

"I don't know. It looked like some clothes and one of those portable closet things."

"Did she come in a car?"

"Yeah, I think so."

"Okay. Let's just keep an eye on her. She was asking some really funny questions."

"She came in to use the office bathroom later and asked if I could re-fill the soap dispenser. I was with a customer and couldn't get to it right away, so she stood there, staring at me until I went to the storage closet to get some."

"I hope she took full advantage of that soap. She needed a good wash."

When Dana returned, she had a large plastic bag with the Kentucky Fried Chicken logo on it. I heard her tromp up the stairs with it in a heavy, irritated way. The wall between our apartment stairwell and the office was thin.

"Hans, do you mind if I knock off early today? I gotta go see what's going on with her."

"Sure, Dave. Let me know what she says."

Like it's any of your business, I thought, and made my way up to the apartment.

***

Dana sat on the floor in front of the coffee table, where she had hap-hazardly laid out the contents of the KFC bag. After licking the chicken grease from her fingers, she opened up a can of coke and poured it quickly into a glass of ice. The fizz from the soda made a ring of moisture on the table.

"Aren't you going to have any chicken?" she asked.

"Not right now. I had a late lunch." Actually, I had really hoped she would have gotten some fish tacos. Greasy chicken just didn't appeal to me just then. "So, what's going on? How come you're home early?"

"I couldn't take one more minute today at work. So I just took off."

"Why, what happened?"

"The dumb bitch went off on me again today. It's a long story. I don't want to go into it right now."

"So what did you tell her?"

"What do you mean?"

"Why you were leaving work early."

"I didn't say shit. I just fucking left."

I went to the refrigerator for a beer. I felt the beginnings of a headache forming around the base of my skull.

Dana worked as an administrative assistant for the Vice President of Operations at a software company, a job she had had for about six months. This was at least a full month longer than her previous five jobs, all of which had been similar low-paying secretarial positions. Each time she started a job, she would go about a month before the complaining would start. The co-workers were too nosey, the building was too stuffy, the pay plan wasn't that good, it was too far to drive, the hours sucked. Eventually, she would quit or get fired.

I came back to the couch and sat down, grabbing the TV remote. I watched the back of Dana's head as she ate. There was too much hairspray in her hair, I noticed. It resembled a tangled thicket of brown twigs.

"Maybe you should call Marilyn and tell her you weren't feeling well and had to leave. Why don't you call her right now?"

We needed Dana's paycheck. The last time she quit her job it had taken her three months to find something she liked. Meanwhile we had racked up hefty charges on our credit cards. Some of those charges had been necessary to pay some bills, but most of them were the result of Dana's boredom. She needed a better wardrobe to land a better job, she had said.

"I can't," she said while chewing a mouthful.

"Why not?"

"Because I don't want to."

"Are you kidding me?" I almost laughed out loud but stifled it.

"I don't want to talk about this right now."

"Dana, you can't afford to lose this job."

"Don't tell me what I can and cannot do!" She slapped her hand on the table for emphasis.

"I can't talk to you when you're like this." Not in the mood to go back to the office, I threw on some shorts and sneakers, got the car keys, and left. I would go for a long jog on the beach to work this out of my mind for a while.

On the way out to my car, I noticed Mrs. Vaughn on the way to her storage unit. She was wearing a plum-colored dress that was a size too small for her and a ridiculous white hat with white netting. When she saw me she quickened her pace, clutching a small stack of paperbacks to her chest.

***

When I returned home that evening, Dana was gone. She didn't leave a note and I assumed she had gone to her parents' house. That's where she always went when she was upset with me. It was just as well, I thought. I didn't want to talk to her yet. The run on the beach didn't help any; I was still furious with her.

I fired up the computer and logged online. Ellen hadn't written me back. I wondered if she had read my letter and put the wrong inflection on it. *If you keep up this campaign, I might just have to fall in love with you.* Why had I written that? Jesus. She probably thought I was getting carried away and decided to let me chill for a while.

Just as I was about to log off, I saw her screen name pop up on my buddy list, indicating she had just gotten online. I drew in a quick breath and went to message her. She beat me to it.

> *Hi David. This is my first chance today to get on. How are you?*

> *Boy, am I glad to see a friendly face! You're a sight for sore eyes.*

> *Bad day?*

> *You could say that. I'm here by myself for a while, I just got home from a long run. How about you?*

> *Hang on, let me read your note first...*

Oh crap, I thought. Was it too late to click the Unsend button? The seconds ticked by in my brain like a detonation timer.

You're such a charmer.

Whew, I thought. She was cool with what I wrote. I responded:

You deserve to be charmed.

I have a reality check for you, if you want one.

Hit me with it!

I'm a lazy couch potato. My idea of exercise is running around the house scrounging for matches so I can light candles, read, and eat chocolate ice cream.

You don't look like a couch potato. You look pretty fit.

Thanks. So why are you having a bad day?

I think my wife quit her job.

You think?

Well, I'm not sure yet. I went out for a run and when I got back she was gone.

Why did she quit her job?

Who knows? She's had a hard time finding something that she likes. I don't know.

I'm sorry that you're stressing out, David.

Let's change the subject. How was your day? How's Pete? How's that husband of yours?

Let's see. My day was great. I gave a presentation at work that I had been working on for the past two months and it was a great success.

Ooo...good for you!

Thanks. It will be good for me. I think I might have the promotion I've been vying for after this.

I'm proud of you.

And Pete is doing fine. He painted a nice little landscape for me today in daycare.

Budding young artist.

Yes, just like his grandfather. How is your writing coming along?

It's not. I have writer's block.

You need a change of scenery.

In more ways than one, I'm afraid. I need to scrap what I'm doing and start over. The story is going nowhere. What started out as a good idea has turned out to be pretty drab.

Sounds like you need a little inspiration for a new story. How 'bout if I come over there and give you one?

Would you sitting on my lap help me think clearer? Hardly.

Who said anything about sitting on your lap?

I didn't know whether she was being playful or whether I had offended her. I decided to change the subject.

I noticed you didn't answer my question about how your hubby is doing.

I guess he's doing fine. He's not here. He's finishing up some business in Dallas.

Wasn't he in New York the other day?

He was. And somewhere else before that. I can't even remember where.

He's been away more than he's been home for a long time now.

I noticed you don't mention him much anymore.

There's nothing to mention. He's never here.

If you were my wife, you'd have to peel me off you every day so you could get to work.

Stop it, I'm still blushing from your email.

I wish I could see that.

You know, I just had a thought.

Yes?

What if I called you tonight? It's a great time since neither Dana nor Jack is home. I want to hear your voice. I want to hear what you sound like.

I felt hot. I felt the beginning of a hard on. This certainly didn't feel quite on the up and up. I didn't care.

Well?

I typed out a sentence and poised my cursor over the SEND button, thinking.

I would love that. Call me.

I typed in my phone number and signed off, then waited impatiently during the five seconds before the phone rang. I picked up and breathed a slow, sensuous, "Hello" into the mouthpiece.

"David, you sound funny. Were you sleeping?" It was Dana.

"Wh— No. Uh, where are you?"

Shit!

"I went back to the office to get the rest of my stuff out of my desk. I still had the keys. I'm still here. David, you'll never guess what I found in Marilyn's office."

"Oh God, Dana, don't tell me you've been snooping in her desk!"

"Yeah, but don't worry. Listen, I'll be home in twenty minutes. I'll talk to you then."

6

∽

Compromising Positions

She must have been speeding, because no more than fifteen minutes after I hung up with her, she was bounding up the stairs. She saw me on the couch and smiled, swaying her hips exaggeratedly in a mock dance and waving a white manila envelope at me, her eyes gleaming.

"Marilyn is going to have a stroke when she can't find this." She threw the envelope into my lap but as I reached down for it, she snatched it back, waving her index finger at me. "Wait! I have to tell you the story first."

"By all means."

"A couple months ago I noticed Marilyn was starting to do some weird stuff in the office that she never did before."

"Like?"

"Like, she would lock her door and close the mini blinds so no one could see into her office, in these fifteen-, twenty-minute stretches throughout the day. It was weird. I would go up to her door to see if I could hear what she doing, and all I could make out was that she was talking on the phone. And it sounded like a personal call."

"I'm not surprised she locked her door and closed the blinds with snoops like you around."

Dana picked up the sofa pillow and playfully swung it at the side of my head. She missed.

"Anyway! Ugh! Then I noticed, once in a while when she'd come back from a long lunch, the first thing she'd do was go into her filing cabinet next to her desk and transfer something from her purse to the cabinet. Actually those were the lunches some of the people in the office were gossiping about. They were long—very long lunches—sometimes as long as two, two and a half hours. She would go with Chuck, the V.P. of Finance. Some people were saying that it was probably just business, but I always suspected there was something going on with those two. Like, once when she locked herself in the office I called Sylvia, who worked in accounting, and asked her if Chuck was on the phone too. She said that not only was he on the phone, but that he had locked his office as well."

I was beginning to see why Marilyn was always on Dana's case about her productivity. It seemed to me that Dana was confused about her job description. Not wanting to risk getting bopped on the side of the head again if I made a sarcastic remark, I nodded in agreement and continued to listen.

"So one time, I saw Marilyn pull this envelope out of her purse, fiddle with it for a few minutes, then stash it her file cabinet, locking it. This time, I paid close attention to where she was hiding the key. She stuck it under the phone. She had this weird look on her face when she did it, like the cat that ate the bird or something."

Dana watched my face carefully, checking to see if I understood where this was heading. I had an idea, but I wanted to hear the rest of her adventures in amateur sleuthing.

"A couple of weeks ago, when Chuck's wife brought their three-week-old baby boy into the office for everyone to see, Marilyn was in a really pissy mood. Mrs. Magruder came over to my desk and I was cooing at the baby and Marilyn just stormed right up to my desk and demanded a bunch of files. She was being a real bitch, and I remember thinking that there was something for sure going on with her and Chuck. She was acting totally jealous."

"So how did you get into her office today?"

"No big deal. None of the V.P.s keep any company secrets in their office, so they're not locked up after hours. I just waltzed in and went right to her filing cabinet. The envelope was buried on the bottom, under all the hanging files." She handed it back to me. I knew right away by the weight and shape of the contents what Dana had found, even though I already had a suspicion—photos. Slightly squishy photos. So I knew even before I took them out that they were Polaroids.

"Holy shit." I was blasted with the image of a pale, over-made-up middle-aged woman with her blood red lips wrapped around a penis. Her hair was sticking out in frizzy clumps, her eyeliner slightly smeared in the grooves of the crow's feet around her eyes. The second photo was similar, except in this one she was looking directly into the camera and her tongue was forming a slug-like adhesion to the man's shaft. The next series was from Marilyn's eye-view, showing a man's head between her two rather large and butter-colored thighs, the lower half of his face obscured by her dark pubic hair—a rather bushy tuft of it, as a matter of fact.

I flipped quickly through the stack, which were progressively worse. I handed the photos back to Dana. "I don't want to look anymore. It's revolting. That man, Chuck? He's gruesome. You'd think he'd at least take his glasses off."

"You have no idea how nasty that guy is. A regular mouth-breather."

Dana continued to look at the Polaroids, biting her lower lip and grunting quietly.

"What's going to happen when she finds out you took these?" I asked.

"That's the beauty of it." Dana looked up at me.

"What do you mean?"

"She won't know *who* took them. Lots of people have access to her office. Hell, pretty much anybody in the company. She hasn't been out for a long lunch with Chuck for a couple of weeks, so I don't even think she's looked at the envelope lately."

"As far as you know."

"Yeah, but think about this: I don't have the keys to the cabinet. So why would she suspect me?"

"You put the keys back?"

"Yep, wiped 'em down first, too. In case."

"In case what? In case Inspector Clouseau dusts for prints?"

"Whatever."

"So what are you going to do, blackmail her?"

"Nope. I'm just going to keep them. Like an insurance policy of sorts. Marilyn will eventually discover they're gone and panic. She won't know who took them. She's not about to start asking too many questions about it. Think about it. She may or may not suspect I have them. Of course I'll deny it, if she asks. At least now I can be sure she'll give me a good recommendation."

"Because you're going to play on her paranoia?"

"Exactly. Every day when she gets home from work she's going to wonder if her husband got any anonymously-mailed parcels. Her heart is going to bust out of her chest every time he gives her a dirty look, thinking he knows."

"You really hate the woman that much?" The image of a large, floppy breast flashed across my brain, and I felt pity for Marilyn. "Dana, does she really deserve this?"

"Hell yeah, she does." Her voice went up a pitch but she looked away from me. "Why are you always judging me?"

"I'm not judging you. I'm just saying that maybe your neat little plan might blow up in your face. Maybe it's not worth it."

"How's that gonna happen?"

"I don't know. But sometimes even the best laid out plans get screwed up by some unforeseen thing. I'm just saying...be careful."

She shook her head and clucked her tongue in disgust. "Jesus, you're such a killjoy." Getting up off the couch, she went to the bedroom, slamming the door behind her. I noticed she had taken the photos with her.

I retreated to the office and logged back online. There was an email from Ellen waiting for me.

What happened? I tried your number and got a busy signal. Did you change your mind about talking to me?

Hoping that she would get back online while I replied, I wrote:

No, as a matter of fact, I was so anxious to talk to you, when Dana called at exactly the same time you were trying to get through! What timing, eh?

Apparently, she wasn't at her parents' house as I originally thought. Instead, she had gone back to her office to retrieve her things. She's quitting for sure. This worries me, as I told you earlier, but not as much as what she did when she let herself back into the building. She snooped around her boss's desk and found some very compromising photos of her and another married co-worker. Dana says she's not going to do anything with the photos, just keep them for 'insurance'. That's not the point, and it's not what worries me.

What worries me is that she's getting more and more out of control. She hasn't been able to keep a job longer than six months ever since her miscarriage. I'm not sure how much that has anything to do with it. She says she simply hasn't found a job she likes as much as she liked the one she had when she lost the baby.

She's plowing through people like she plows through her jobs— without regard for the longterm consequences of her actions and words. I've been on the receiving end of her starchy sarcasm and dark moods too many times in the last couple of years. It's starting to wear on my nerves.

Part of the problem is that she blames me for the miscarriage because she blames me for the pregnancy to begin with. Since she was afraid to tell her parents about any of it (and still is), there is this tension now between the three of them. Guess who she blames for that?

I've been droning on, I know. I'm sorry, Ellen. It's just that I feel like things are sinking quickly into a void. My book, my marriage, my career. I don't know how to get them back, or, if I even want to.

I sent the letter and remained logged on while I opened up my writing file. I scrolled down to the very bottom, and the program told me I was on page 221. I re-read the last paragraph I had written, when I heard the computer chime. It was Ellen, online, and sending me an instant message.

You sound terrible! Is that really all that happened between you and Dana from an hour ago?

I'm sorry about the phone call. We should try again soon.

I wish you could call now; it's a good time. I'm sitting here with a cup of tea, some nice music in the background, feeling particularly lonely tonight. But of course I understand it's lousy timing.

You know what? Not at all. Why don't you give me your number and I'll go downstairs to the office and call you from there.

You sure?

Absolutely. I could use a friendly voice right now.

I scribbled her number in a notebook that was lying on the desk and took the whole thing with me downstairs. I knew that Dana wouldn't be able to hear what I was saying unless she stuck her ear right to the door of the office. I considered turning on the radio to mask my conversation but decided that it would be better to keep things quiet so that I could instead hear her coming down the stairs.

Ellen let the phone ring twice before picking up.

"Hello?" Her voice was natural, as if she wasn't expecting me.

"Hey beautiful. Guess who."

She laughed softly. I immediately loved her laugh.

"Hi. You sound exactly like I thought."

"You're smart not to answer the phone like I did when I expected it was you but got Dana instead."

"Which was?"

"Oh, you know, as if I was about to lick the mouthpiece."

"You didn't!"

"I did. I almost blew it—I came this close to answering, 'Hi Ellen.' Can you imagine?"

"I can, but the kicker would be that you're not doing anything wrong. Not really. Are you?"

"Yeah, sure, tell that to Dana."

We chuckled a little, then there was a brief pause. Ellen's voice was strong but feminine. I sighed.

"I'm sorry you're feeling so down tonight, David. I know how it is, these ups and downs. It feels like you're never going to get out of your rut. But you will, believe me. It'll happen when you least expect it. Something will inspire you."

"So how's that cup of tea taste?"

"Tangy. I spiked it."

"You boozer."

"I know. I was so depressed earlier when you blew me off."

"I know, I'm sorry. It won't happen again, I promise."

"Isn't that just like a man? Here we are, only a minute into our first real conversation and already he's making promises he can't keep."

"Keep talking, I think I'm starting to feel my dick again."

"I didn't know you had trouble with numbness. You never told me!" She started laughing again.

"I'm glad I've managed to make you laugh. I just don't want to be complaining to you all the time."

"All the time? Tonight is the first time I've heard you complain about anything. What kind of friend would I be if you couldn't tell me what's on your mind?"

"Like all the other friends I have?" I snickered, but something about her tone made me put my head in my hand and swallow hard.

"You have to stop beating yourself up. You're doing the best you can with Dana. You're being a very good husband to her. You can't solve her problem, David. All you can do is be there for her. As for your career and your writing—I know how talented you are. The excerpts you've emailed me are fantastic. Even if you don't finish this book, there will be others, I know there will. You have to keep your eye on that no matter what. You can't give up. If the book isn't working for you, start another one. Don't be afraid to walk away from the first one. It doesn't mean you're a failure if you do."

"I know." I started doodling on the notebook I brought with me. "So, tell me about your promotion. What are you going to be doing?"

"I'll be working more with demographics and strategies, which is exactly what I want to do if I ever start my own consulting business."

We talked for what seemed like a long time, until I heard some creaking upstairs and quickly wrapped it up. After I hung up the phone my face felt hot and my elbow was stiff from cradling the phone.

Dana was still asleep. I went out onto the balcony and folded out the creaky aluminum lawn chair that was propped against the sliding glass door. The damp evening air was cool on my skin. The subtle signs of a San Diego winter were approaching: foggy nights, damper mornings, clearer days. I listened to the incessant hum of Interstate 5 just a few blocks away. I wondered where most of the people were headed at eleven o'clock at night. Home from work? Home from a date? From a night out with the guys, working off those last few beers on the dark stretch of freeway between Via De La Valle and Garnet?

I closed my eyes and imagined being on that freeway, driving farther and farther away from the hum, farther away from the lights, farther away from the ocean. I imagined what it would be like if I got into my car and just started driving. Gradually, the sky would become darker and clearer the more east I drove toward Arizona. The air would become drier, musky with the odor of desert vegetation. The sprinkling of houses would move out from the road and into the embrace of the surrounding hills, which would loom around me, mysterious and silent. I would glide alone toward an empty horizon, a dark point at the end of a long journey where my temporary life would end and my real life would begin.

Right before I opened my eyes again, I saw a blue-eyed, dark-haired woman looking up at me, her eyes half closed and her lips parted slightly as I leaned in to kiss her. It was Ellen.

***

A dusty blue, but freshly waxed old Chevelle pulled up in front of the "No Parking" sign on the side of the office. While the car idled, the driver carefully removed his sunglasses and placed them in a case. I watched through the dusty mini blinds as he got out of the car and turned the corner of the building and into the office. He was in his early forties, very tan, with closely cropped black hair.

He responded to my scowl with a friendly "Hey, how's it goin?"

"How can we help you today?" I was going to wait until I knew what he wanted before chastising him for his parking habits.

"I'm lookin' to store my car—I guess I need one of your garage-sized units." He retrieved his wallet out of his khaki shorts and unrolled it onto the counter between us. He smacked on a piece of gum as I retrieved a blank contract from a plastic bin.

"Those units are two hundred dollars a month."

"Fine."

From the corner of my eye, I saw Hans pulling up in the facility golf cart from a pre-auction inspection of delinquent units. He was with Tom McClelland, the auctioneer. I hoped he wouldn't notice the car parked on the side of the office, but as soon as I saw his bulky shape rushing through the front door, I knew it was too late to shut him up.

"Who in the hell parked over there?" he blurted, slightly out of breath. Dana's description of him in a similar panting state on his "crusty old couch" came to mind and I shuddered.

"It's the customer's, and it'll be in a ten by twenty soon, so don't worry about it."

He mumbled and left again after retrieving the bolt cutter. The customer looked after him.

"You guys cut locks?"

"It's standard procedure for delinquent accounts that are up for auction."

"What do you do when you go into the unit?"

"We don't go in, we just take a photo and then lock it back up with a temporary lock until the day of the auction."

"Would there be any other reason you'd go into a unit?"

"No." *Great*, I thought. *Another paranoid customer this week.* At least this guy wasn't asking me if we offered cryogenics or if there were scorpion nests under the stairwells.

He pointed to the application. "What do you use the credit card info for if you auction off delinquent accounts?"

I stuck my hand in the pocket of my jeans and shrugged. "Leave it blank if you want." I didn't have a clue as to why that was on the form. The contract was the same today as it was the day I started working here, but this was the first time anyone had asked about that.

After instructing him on the details of the security system, I gave him some coupons and mailing labels to use for making payments. He stuck his fingers into his wallet and shook his head. "No need for that. I'll pay for six months up front." He spread out twelve 100-dollar bills on the counter. I wondered how much the car he was storing was worth. Two thousand? Three? I didn't say anything as I issued his receipt. He stuck it into his pocket as he left, almost brushing shoulders with Hans near the front door.

"Check this out—that guy just paid cash for six months to store his car."

"No kidding? Guy must have money to throw around. He looks familiar. What's his name?"

I looked at the contract again, sitting down to input the data into the computer. "Richard Cutter." As I began typing, it dawned on me. "Hans?"

"Yeah?"

"The guy's name is Dick Cutter."

We both winced.

7

✧

He's Having an Affair

Driving south along the coast, I reached over and stuck my hand under the passenger seat, looking for a music cassette that had gotten lost in the car. I had agreed to meet Dana and her friend Alicia for drinks at a bar down on Highway 101 after I got off work. She had gone to a late-afternoon job interview and felt too keyed up to come straight home, because the interview went well and she liked the company. This had been her third job interview in three weeks; but the first one that she felt this good about.

I popped the old, scratched-up cassette into the tape deck and re-wound it. I was in the mood for something I could wail along with, and the old U2 tape was perfect. The past few weeks had been increasingly stressful between Dana and me. Lacking anything productive to do between job interviews, she had gone through all our closets and drawers and trashed half our clothes and knickknacks, declaring that if I hadn't worn or used the stuff in a year, I wasn't going to. I protested, feeling particularly violated when she threw out some of my favorite college drinking shirts and a ten-year old jacket that had been a gift from an ex-girlfriend. I had actually gone into the dumpster that night to retrieve my stuff and hung it back up in the closet. Her response to that had been to take the clothes back out of the closet the next day and drive them to the Goodwill truck behind the Ralphs Supermarket. We had screamed at each other so furiously that night that she ended up going over to her parents' house and spending the night there.

That was a week ago, and since then she has spent a lot of time hanging out with her parents or at the beach, working on her tan.

I had my fingers crossed that she would get the job she interviewed for today. We hadn't had any surplus in our checking account for a couple of years. My salary of $1350 a month wasn't enough to cover the car payments, insurance, groceries, and the hefty minimum payments on both of the credit cards, which had a balance of well over five thousand dollars each. I had even contemplated taking on a second job temporarily to get us through until Dana was working again. I hadn't done anything about it yet, it was just a thought at this point.

I turned into the lot of the Purple Oyster Bar & Grill and spotted Dana's red Honda Civic in the far corner of the lot. As I pulled in next to her car, I realized the U2 cassette was humming in the tape deck, stuck on rewind. I shut the engine off and hit the play button and sat in the car for a few minutes, tapping my fingers on the steering wheel, in tune to "Desire". I was parked facing the street and I watched the cars decelerate and stop in front of me as they made their way through the traffic signal.

Just as I was about to pull the keys out of the ignition and get out, I spotted Mrs. Vaughn sitting in the passenger seat of a rusty old sedan that was stopped at the light. She was sitting next to a man who looked to be in his sixties, with dark, thinning hair and wearing a brown, short-sleeved T-shirt. Even from this distance, I could see he had large sweat stains under his armpits. Mrs. Vaughn was sitting low in the front seat, staring straight ahead.

I was a little surprised to see her with someone. I had assumed she was single or widowed, since every time I saw her at the self-storage, she was alone. A few times in the past week she had asked Hans to help her carry large boxes up to her unit or had asked me to show her how to use the freight elevators. She was always very evasive and curt, at times even strangely demanding. She would ask to borrow screwdrivers and hammers, and I would ask her if she needed help with anything but she always shook her head, giving me no clue what she was going to do with the tools. Instead, she would stand in the office, staring me down until I relented and let her borrow them. I would send Hans or the maintenance man to check in on her occasionally to make sure she wasn't deconstructing the storage unit.

I got out of the car as I watched the sedan start to pull away. When I entered the dark bar, I heard Dana before I saw her. She was obviously way past her first drink, laughing loudly and making hooting noises. Dana and her friend Alicia were sitting side by side at a booth away from the bar, with a pitcher of Margarita mix between them. Alicia was lighting a cigarette as I sat down opposite them. Her hair was a lot longer than the last time I saw her, half of it scrunched up with a clamp on the top of her head.

"Hey stranger. It's about time you showed up." Alicia lowered her voice and smiled as she put her lighter back into her purse.

"Hi Alicia. How've you been?"

"Not bad. I was just telling Dana about my trip to Cancun last month. I went with Daryl." She rolled her eyes. "What a mistake. Never again."

"He got so sloshed at the cantina their first night there that he took the wrong woman to bed." Dana made a scissoring motion with her index and middle finger at Alicia, who then handed over her cigarette. "Alicia didn't see him again until he slithered back to get his suitcase out of their hotel room two days later."

"Are you kidding me?" I motioned to the waitress to bring another pitcher of Margaritas. "How does a guy go on a trip with a woman and then end up with someone else the first night there?"

"Apparently they knew each other. I don't know where from. I had never seen her before. She was there alone from what I could see. If I didn't think it was so bizarre, I would have said that she went there to meet him."

"You mean like she followed him?"

"Maybe."

"I don't know. Who cares? It's obviously over with us. Six months down the toilet. Fuck." Alicia kicked me under the table. "What about you, handsome? What bad things have you been doing since I saw you last?"

I watched Dana take a long drag from Alicia's cigarette again and contemplated what they would think if I told them about my almost daily phone calls to Ellen. I had started calling her at work a few minutes a day whenever I was alone in the office, and we continued to email each other. I beamed, remembering the laugh we had just that morning over some goofy thing that Hans had done, but then realized Dana and Alicia were both staring at me, their giddiness fading, still waiting for my answer.

"He's having an affair." Alicia nudged Dana's arm.

"What?!" I was suddenly very aware of my facial expression.

The waitress set down a full frosty pitcher and an empty glass, which I promptly filled. "So, tell me about your job interview, Dana."

"He's changing the subject." Alicia pressed her thumb under her front teeth, her eyebrows shooting upward. "He's fucking someone for sure!"

"If he is, he must be doing it in some dusty storage unit with a tenant because he never leaves the facility."

They both busted out laughing.

"I'm so very glad I came here tonight." I gulped down half the glass and waited for the buzz to start. The drink was good; plenty of Tequila. The bar was filling up—happy hour was well underway. A group of men pulled up some chairs and rearranged the tables next to our booth to watch a football game that was on the TV monitors throughout the bar.

"The interview went fantastic," Dana said. "I think she and I really hit it off. I was relaxed. I answered all the questions well. But the best part is that this company is great! They've got a gym on site, showers, all kinds of great benefits, flex time. She said she was going to contact my references tomorrow."

"What kind of company is it exactly?" I asked.

"They manufacture and distribute cellphones and pagers. You should see this place, David. It's more like some fancy hotel than an office building. Lots of natural light. Everyone is very friendly. I met some of the upper managers, too. She introduced me around."

"Sounds like you might get the job." I breathed a quiet sigh of relief.

"She told me to call her in a few days if I don't hear from her. What do you think that means?" Dana asked.

"That probably means that she's really busy and may not get around to calling you right away to let you know you have the job," Alicia said.

"You think?" I knitted my eyebrows. "That's a little weird. Maybe it means that she doesn't want to tell you to your face she doesn't want to hire you."

"Thanks, that's really encouraging," Dana said.

"You asked for an opinion; I'm giving it to you. I just think it's a strange thing to tell someone, as if you don't have two minutes to call and say, 'Welcome aboard, when can you start?'" I said.

Dana shot me a contemptuous look despite my explanation. She didn't try to smooth it out afterwards with a sneer this time, either. She turned and glanced at the TV. A touchdown sent the adjacent table into a momentary roar. "If she bothered asking if she can call my previous employers, I don't think she was blowing me off, is all."

"Let's just hope your references come through for you." I thought about Marilyn and my tension came back.

"They will. They'd better." She refilled her glass.

"Mmm."

"I gotta pee." Dana stumbled out of the booth. I felt Alicia's hand on the back of mine as soon as Dana disappeared around the corner of the bar.

"So, tell me," she leaned forward, whispering, "are you having an affair, David?"

I shifted in my seat. She moved her hand further up my arm and I felt her fingers curl around my wrist, caressing it. I braced myself to diplomatically brush her off, but the Margaritas were starting to kick in and I was suddenly in a playful mood. I leaned forward as well, so that our noses were an inch apart.

"Perhaps." I let the word out slowly, the last syllable leaving my lips like a slow air leak. "What if I was? Would that make you jealous?" I moved my face a little closer to hers. I could see a small bead of sweat form on her brow, her eyes suddenly wider.

A few months after Dana first introduced me to her, I realized that Alicia was becoming attracted to me. Her attention seemed to be split between where I was, how she could get to where I was, and whether or not Dana might be watching. She never missed an opportunity to brush up against me or stand closer or touch me in some way. I liked Alicia—she was fun—but I didn't feel comfortable responding to her insistent flirtations. I tried to ignore her, which seemed to motivate her more. This time, however, I could see that my sudden shift was throwing her off balance.

"It might. I wish it were me," she said wistfully.

She was so duplicitous. I wanted to tell her so but at that moment I realized that I was suffering from the same general malady. Certainly, I was in no position to be lecturing Alicia on the fundamentals of decency when just a few hours ago I had been asking Ellen what sort of under-garments she was wearing. Something clicked in my head, and I leaned back against the seat, watching Alicia's cheeks flush a deep pink as she tried to compose herself.

"I'm sorry." She looked down at her hand, which she curled back into her body. Her remark surprised me. She had never before apologized for her seductive outbursts. "I don't know why I keep doing that. I don't know why—I mean—it's stupid. I'm just asking for trouble."

"Don't worry about it." I noticed tears were welling up in her eyes and she was trying hard not to blink. "Nothing happened. Just forget it."

She wiped at her face. I saw her eyes had turned a deeper shade of green. "I don't know why it seems like everyone is so happy, except me. I'm starting to think there's something wrong with me. I feel so alone most of the time."

"You know, things aren't always what they seem. So quit beating yourself up about it. And you know what?" I reached over and took her hand, squeezing it.

"Hmm?"

"We all feel alone sometimes."

When Dana returned to the table, I let my mind wander. I tuned out their conversation as I looked around the bar, feeling very forlorn. I waited an hour for the drink to run its course through my head and then drove home with Alicia and Dana in the back seat, giggling drunkenly. I knew that Alicia would have to spend the night at our place, and I felt oddly relieved that she wouldn't be going home to an empty apartment.

8

∽

What Else Isn't She Wearing?

The time in the upper right corner of the computer monitor read 2:48 am. I couldn't sleep. I had quietly snuck out of the bed and turned on the computer and started a letter to Ellen. Dana was out cold, snoring in a drunken sleep. She would be hating life tomorrow morning for sure, I thought, as I clicked the keyboard.

There was a girl who haunted me from the moment I first laid eyes on her. Her name was Megan, and I met her during a fund-raising car wash my junior year in high school. To this day, I don't know what it was about Megan that drew me to her so much. She was pretty, but not knock-out, brain-numbing pretty. She wasn't very popular, she didn't play a lot of sports or hang out with the in-crowd at school. She wasn't especially funny. She didn't make me laugh. She was an average student, so when I was with her she didn't make me think. But I know how she made me feel. She was quiet and passionate and brooding most of the time. When I would talk to her on the phone, I wanted to turn off all the lights in the house, stand in front of the open window, and smoke cigarettes all night, listening to her voice. She was always so calm, but she always made me feel so alive.

We went out a few times before we graduated. We would make out on the beach, right before sunset, or sometimes in my dad's car in the front seat. And once I even laid next to her in my bed. I'll never forget the way her eyes would sink into mine right before I kissed her. She had an expression that was always a few countries, a few seasons away from where anyone else was. There was always this longing in her eyes. When I was with her I tried to convince myself that it was me she was longing for, and that by being with her I could make her happy.

Megan moved away after we graduated. She got accepted at some university in Washington state and I never heard from her again. For years afterwards, even though I had dated dozens of women and slept with at least half that many, even falling in love once—I had never forgotten her. I would dream about her. In my dreams, I would be deliriously happy because I had found her again and she loved me back. I would look for her face in the girls I'd see at school, in actresses I'd see in movies. They would have some of her features, but they were never her. She was unmatchable.

I don't know why Megan stayed on my mind for so many years. I think that maybe to this day, if I were to see her again, my love for her would pick up right where it left off. I often wondered if I was somehow destined to be with her; if she was in somehow my soulmate, and I had let her get away.

What do you think, Ellen? Are there people in this world who we are destined to be with? If so, would we know this right away, the moment we met the person? Or would it dawn on us much later? What if they don't love us back? What if we meet this person but we are not free? What happens then? What if we never meet them? Do we then spend our entire lives feeling like there's something missing?

I think I've married the wrong woman.

These are the issues clouding my brain at three o'clock in the morning as I lay awake in bed, thinking of you.

"Whatcha doing?"

Alicia was standing in the doorway to the office, wearing an oversized shirt Dana had lent her for the night. She was leaning against the doorframe, her hair softly framing her face, her legs bare and very tan.

"Hey you," I yawned. "I couldn't sleep. I'm doing a little writing."

"I couldn't sleep either. I was laying on the couch listening to you typing."

She must have taken her bra off to sleep because I could see the soft, low curve of her breasts and her nipples poking sharply through the fabric.

"What are you writing?" she asked.

I turned back to the monitor and accessed the Sign Off menu, forgetting too late that the program would say "Goodbye!" I turned on the desk lamp and flipped the monitor switch off.

"A little cybersex in the middle of the night, David?"

"You don't miss a beat, do you?"

"Not when it comes to you."

She was relaxed and clear, apparently sober. As she walked into the office toward me, I found myself wondering what else she wasn't wearing underneath the shirt. "How's the couch, anyway? Any good?"

"No. It sucks, actually. I was hoping I could get you to drive me to my car so I can go home. I need to get some sleep since I have to work tomorrow." She put her hand on the back of my chair and turned it so that she was standing directly in front of me, her knees against mine.

"Right now?"

"Is that okay? You're up anyway. It'll only take you twenty minutes there and back, tops."

When I stood up, she barely moved from where she was standing so that her belly was touching mine. "Who were you writing?"

"Excuse me?"

"Who were you e-mailing?"

"Nobody." My eyes began to sting. I ran my tongue over my teeth, tasting the stale sourness of that evening's Margarita. I pressed my chest into hers and pushed her back a little. "Are we going or not? C'mon."

She found her skirt in the dark of the living room and slipped it on under the borrowed shirt as I quietly walked back to the bedroom to find my shorts. I was wearing boxers, which would have been fine if I were driving anyone other than Alicia. I didn't want her to misinterpret anything. Dana hadn't moved. She slept with one arm draped over her head and the other holding a pillow up to her body.

There was very little traffic on the side streets that late at night. The ocean was a black void, not even a stray light from a boat illuminating the horizon. Alicia tuned the radio to a jazz station and let out a long, resigned sigh as I drove the short distance back to the Purple Oyster.

"You're a good man, you know that?"

"I am?"

"Yeah, you are."

"What makes you say that?"

"Fifteen minutes ago, you stood alone in a room in the middle of the night in front of an almost naked woman who wants you so bad she could taste it, and you didn't make a move." I could feel her eyes on me. "That's why."

I groaned. My stomach contracted tightly as I contemplated the best answer. "Alicia, you're my wife's best friend. I don't know if I would say that I'm a 'good man', but I'm most certainly not that big of an asshole."

"So, what are you saying?"

"What do you want me to say, that if you weren't Dana's friend I'd have been all over you in a heartbeat?" She opened the window and stuck her head out slightly, breathing in the damp air. When she didn't say anything, I added, "I think you've very attractive. Very sexy. But nothing can happen between us, and you know why. I just can't do that to her. I'm not made that way."

I was pulling up to her car now, and she flicked the radio off as I stopped the car and popped the clutch into neutral. I almost thought I could hear the faint chirping of crickets despite the low rumble of the idling engine, and then I realized my ears were ringing from the sudden silence. I found myself looking at her breasts again and when she spoke, I found it difficult to look her in the eye.

"I'll make you a deal." She put her hand on my thigh. "Kiss me. That's all I want. I promise. Just one kiss."

She was already looking at my lips. All at once I felt her breath on my mouth. Without thinking, I slid my palms over the soft curves of her chest, and my hand found a warm swell as her tongue explored my mouth. I started sucking hard on her tongue as I squeezed her with my hands. She smelled faintly of cigarette smoke and shampoo, and she tasted slightly salty. As she moved closer, I started yanking up her shirt, anxiously groping around for skin. When her hand pressed down into my crotch, I lost my footing on the brake pedal and the car started rolling forward.

"Shit!" I detached from her and put both hands on the steering wheel, taking long, deep breaths. "Goodnight, Alicia."

She pulled her shirt down and sat unmoving, still breathing heavily. I could almost hear her grinding her teeth.

"You know what? Fuck you," she hissed under her breath right before she slammed the door shut. She shook her purse around until she found her keys, which she fumbled and dropped before she finally managed to get the door unlocked. I waited until she was in her car before I pulled away.

She didn't look back at me, not even once.

9

◦◦◦

There Is No Enchanted Forest

The previous night's storm had washed the seaweed far up the beach, leaving the shore unlittered and free of gnats. I quickened my pace, trying to keep up with my friend Tom—who was also the auctioneer—whom I met with occasionally for a run. I was feeling sluggish and achy. My legs had fallen into a numb rhythm as I sucked in salty air in uneven breaths. It had been one day too many since my last run, and my body was not letting me off the hook.

"So, what'd you find up in LA this month? Anything good?" I managed to squeeze out between gulps.

"Not really. We bought out this unit up in Burbank the other day that seems to have a bunch of movie props or something; lots of stage makeup and whatnot." He swung his elbows out too far and jabbed me in the arm. "Whoops, sorry."

"Please keep your arms in the vehicle at all times," I chuckled.

"You're huffin' and puffin' more than usual, bud," Tom said.

"Tell me about it. Haven't been in the mood to run for a few days. I'm paying the price."

"Yeah, so anyway. We haven't had a chance to dig through the stuff yet to see if there is anything good."

"How old is this stuff? Like, from the sixties or what?"

"I dunno. Maybe a few years old. Can't tell. Probably not worth much on the pop culture market, although that's what we were hoping for."

"Maybe you'll find a pair of Boris Karloff's vampire dentures."

"I wish." He slowed a bit and I felt grateful. "So, what's with your wife? I saw her hanging around the office the other day."

"She's out of work. I think she's supposed to call today to find out about a good prospect, though. I guess I'll find out when I get home."

We had started our run a little south of Solana Beach and had now made it to Encinitas. The sound of traffic from the road above us was diminishing as the cliffs rose higher on our right. The shoreline was getting rockier, and we were approaching surfer alley. Soon we wouldn't be able to go any further because the beach would end. and the water would smash directly into the sandstone cliffs. There was a long wooden stairway leading up to the road that we usually sprinted, putting us back up on Highway 101, heaving for air. We'd walk it off for a while and jog downhill on the sidewalk the few miles back to where we had parked.

I watched a handful of surfers as they caught a big swell and jumped onto their boards. The sun was setting behind them, casting them in dark silhouettes as they hunched over the wave, some of them disappearing behind it. The waves were good today because of the storm, and I was surprised that there weren't more surfers in the water.

I felt the folded-up piece of paper I had stuck in my shorts pocket before I'd left the house. It was Ellen's email. Knowing I was already late and having to leave in a hurry since Tom was waiting for me, I had printed out a hard copy and taken it with me to read after the run. I wondered now as we approached the beach access stairs whether my sluggishness had less to do with the fact that my body was a little stale and more to do with wanting to read Ellen's letter.

"You gonna make it, buddy?" Tom was ahead by a couple of yards, and I saw him gearing up for the upward sprint.

"I don't think so. You go ahead. I'll just take the beach back." I stopped and put my hands on my waist as I stretched out the kink in my side. Tom bounded up the stairs, leaving me walking in small circles on the pebbly beach, catching my breath. When he was halfway up, I took the letter out of my pocket.

I've always had the impression that you were pretty happy with your marriage, even with its misgivings, so I was surprised to hear you admit boldly that you feel you married the wrong woman. This is a pretty difficult thing for anyone to have to admit to themselves, especially for someone who, I know, has no intentions to end said marriage.

It's a difficult thing for me to admit that sometimes I know that I will never be as happy with Jack as I had imagined. I suppose that if we can't get our needs met at home we can continue to try to fulfill our needs with long, lusty, passionate letters to our email penpals. And after all there's no harm in that, right? Right?

In regard to your unrequited love with Megan—perhaps the reason you obsessed about her so long was because you never fully possessed her. You were with her, but you didn't sleep with her. You're not really sure if she loved you back. What's worse is that she moved away, never giving you a chance to find out for sure. Perhaps what was killing you was not the not having, but instead the not knowing.

Perhaps the only difference in our attitudes is that I've become more of a cynic. A difficult thing to admit, too, but I guess I can't have it both ways. In high school and college, I was so filled with romantic visions. I wrote long, lusty love poems to Victor Storm. I spent evenings browsing through Shakespere sonnets.

My point here is that if college Ellen could read this letter, she might spit at me. Or at least shake her head in disdain. You see, if I'm going to be honest about it, I just don't believe in soul mates and true love or movies like Sleepless in Seattle anymore. I think marriage is, in fact, more about tolerance and friendship and levels of compatability than about true love and passion. Movies like Sleepless in Seattle are, in fact, dangerous adult fairy tales that poison reasonably working marriages like ours with this fantasy that somewhere out there, our soul mate walks about in similarly complacent misery. While I'm over here eating a humdrum plate of mediocrity with Bill Pullman, let's say, Tom Hanks might just be across the way at the most romantic place on earth, waiting to take my hand and walk me to the elevator of all that is beautiful. Then cartoon birds will start singing and use their beaks to tie a little wreath that will act as the canopy at my wedding in the Enchanted Forest.

Of course, if I sound patronizing here, feel free to slap me with your next email. The truth is I used to believe all that. But over the past year, I've given up tormenting myself. Marriage, with all its ups and downs, with all its arguments and make-ups, with all its struggles, its bad sex, its not-so-bad sex, its comfortable silences and its pet peeves, its diaper changing and toilet cleaning; with all its mediocrity and security and til-death-do-us-part, is, in the end, the reality that there is no Enchanted Forest. There's just us and the hope that we can find someone who won't irritate us into a divorce. Given that, perhaps the best we can do is lie to ourselves and our spouse in hopes of convincing ourselves and each other that we have, indeed, married our soul mate—one good lie that can only make our fated union at least a little bit more enchanted.

"Well, that's depressing," I said to myself. A surfer walking past me veered slightly away as I made eye contact with him.

I started stuffing the letter back into my shorts and began the long jog back to my car. Maybe there *is* an Enchanted Forest, Ellen. Maybe telling yourself there isn't is the lie, instead of the other way around. Maybe there is much more out there that we were meant to experience but we don't because we are afraid of making changes in our lives.

I thought about my relationship with Dana—mediocre at its best, venomous at its worst. There were days I would hear an angry refrain in my head: *the hell with this marriage*, it hissed. Get out, get out while you can. Don't waste another day with this woman. When I would hear that voice in my head, I would feel momentarily motivated and would begin to make a mental inventory of the things I had to do. I would have to tell her to move out, for one thing. The apartment was tied in with my job, so I would have to convince her to leave. I envisioned the scenario in my mind's eye—Dana looking up at me with that incredulous, hurt look that would slowly turn to a simmering indignation. She would scream and cuss. She would storm out and stay at her parents' house for a day or two. But would she leave? I didn't know.

What about the bills? What about that twelve-thousand-dollar debt we had racked up in the last four years? What is there to show for it? More importantly, would I be stuck trying to pay it all off after she was gone? Dana had thrown a big chunk of it away lately when she was in her closet-cleaning frenzy. We had charged the down payment on Dana's Honda on one of the cards (what a mistake that was). Dana took a trip to the Cayman Islands with Alicia during one of her unemployed periods, as well as several trips to see her sister in Missouri.

Then there were days when I would think about the future, about getting another job, perhaps as a columnist or an editor. Our debts would be paid off and together we could make enough to buy a nice starter home. I would drive through neighborhoods and window-shop houses, seeing myself someday mowing the lawn or trimming the shrubs or washing my car in the driveway of some stucco and Spanish-tiled subdivision. Those were the days when things didn't seem so bad, when I would convince myself, at least for a little while, that I was doing okay. I would let my mind anesthetize the resentment and disenchantment that got in the way of feeling optimistic about my life. I would tell myself that I was a chronic complainer, that my relationship with my wife wasn't all that bad, and that I needed to focus more on the positive. That was easy to do when there wasn't much better to compare it to.

The trouble was, there now was someone and something better to compare it to.

Not that it did me much good. She had her feet firmly planted in her life, in the rich soil of Having-Your-Shit-Together, on the other side of the country.

***

"I didn't get the job."

Dana's statement sunk in with the force of a falling brick in my stomach.

"Why?" I asked. "What happened? Did you call her?"

"Actually, she called me. She said that she was very excited about hiring me but that my references didn't all check out. She said, and I quote, 'I'm a little surprised that you put Marilyn Laclair on your reference list.'"

"Are you serious?" I asked. "Well? What did Marilyn say to her?"

Dana leaned back against the white tile of the kitchen counter with a glass of iced tea in one hand and a candy bar in the other. She chewed for a few seconds before continuing. "I don't know. Apparently, the issue was that I told her I left CSA Solutions under nothing but pleasant circumstances. Marilyn must have disputed that. You know what? I'm going to call her and remind her of her little photography collection."

"I'm still not sure that's a good idea. Instead of confronting Marilyn, why don't you just explain to the woman that you weren't happy at your job due to a conflict of styles, but that you felt confident about your former boss's recommendation, based on the fact that you were a good employee."

"What the hell is that mumbo jumbo?" Dana sneered.

"It's not mumbo jumbo, Dana. It's called being diplomatic and salvaging this job you want."

She wadded up the empty candy wrapper and threw it at me. "I'm not a brown-nose like you. I'm not buying into that corporate crap. I'm calling Marilyn first thing in the morning. Once she finds out I have her pictures she's going to be calling Quorumm herself to beg them to hire me."

As she left the kitchen, I found myself wondering if this sort of blackmail was punishable by law, and if so, could I possibly get away with anonymously turning her in.

***

I met Dana while I was working in the communications department at Siemens. It had been my first job out of college, and I had moved up through the ranks from an intern to one of the head writers. I cranked out mostly informational and sterile text for employee newsletters or regional marketing brochures.

Dana had been hired as an assistant for the department. Her first day on the job had almost been her last. She was in charge of collaborating the flow of projects between the designers and writers and various outside printing vendors. She wasn't too experienced with the process of design and printing, and consequently managed to make a mistake that had the potential of costing the company almost an additional ten thousand dollars in printing expenses. I had caught the mistake after I intercepted a fax she was sending, before it did any damage. I took the fax over to her desk, where she was reading the employee manual and eating a turkey sandwich. I started preparing a sensitive reprimand that wouldn't forever tarnish our co-worker relationship when she looked up at me with wide, brown eyes and smiled in a genuine, sweet way. Instead of spoiling the moment with a lecture on company policy, I had instead asked her out to lunch for the following day. I crumpled the fax behind my back and called the printer myself, making a mental note to instead give her some friendly pointers over our lunch date.

My impression of her sloped sharply downhill for a while after that first lunch date. I thought Dana was a little odd and almost too hyper. In the morning she'd come up to my desk, shove aside some papers and sit within inches of my keyboard, telling me stupid jokes or asking me about the television shows I had watched the previous night. I had very little tolerance for this because I was always behind on my workload and her desk visits always made me tense about the time I was wasting. After a few days I started avoiding her as much as possible. Sensing my irritability, she came back from a walk she had taken during her lunchbreak one day, carrying a bunch of droopy wildflowers.

"I picked these for you, Hemmingway." She kept changing my nickname daily. First it was Kafka, then it was Salinger. The day of the floral bouquet it was Hemmingway. She beamed at me.

"What are these for?"

"I'm sorry that I annoyed you. Friends?"

I don't know what happened after that. Either she changed or my view of her did. It wasn't more than a few weeks after the lunch date that I asked her on our first date outside the office. We packed some food and took it up to Balboa Park, where we ate cold chicken sandwiches, drank bad wine and then went museum hopping. She said she liked how cerebral and quiet I was. I listened to her stories and inflections and laughed so hard that I went home that night with a stomachache.

The next day I was laid off. That was the end of my professional writing career in San Diego.

I got the job as the property manager at the self-storage mostly because the owner was an old friend of my dad's from college. He wanted someone fresh and motivated at the helm. I started my new job and continued dating Dana.

After we had been seeing each other for eight months she called me at work and told me she was pregnant. I remember that at the exact moment she was saying this, a customer came into the office with a toddler who was having a meltdown in the office. In between the three-year-old's screaming and crying I could hear her explain how the diaphragm we had been using must have failed. I wasn't sure what to say to her. I knew I was in love with her. But at that moment it felt as if I was being rudely awakened from a long, warm sleep, the curtains thrown wide open and the covers ripped off my naked, shivering body.

Dana was a wreck. She was afraid of what her parents would think. She was scared about the pregnancy. She didn't want to be alone. Mostly, however, she didn't want to lose me. I reassured her in the only way I knew how. We drove that weekend to Vegas and got married.

Dana never told her parents why we had gotten married. As disappointed as they were that we had eloped, she said, they would be devastated if they found out that she got knocked up first.

"What are you going to tell them when you are as-big-as-a-house eight months pregnant?" I had asked her.

She didn't know. She didn't want to think about it.

When she was almost five months along, she went in for a routine ultrasound. I had gone with her, and I'll never forget the way the ultrasound technician's demeanor changed from routinely cordial to suddenly nervous and quiet. There was something wrong. Something very seriously wrong.

Two doctors performed two more ultrasounds on Dana that day. She was close to hysterical. The fetus had only two heart chambers. The stomach was missing. The spinal cord was malformed. There were various other abnormalities. It was just a matter of time, they told us, shaking their heads. The fetus would be a stillbirth.

After five months of being pregnant, after she had purchased a whole wardrobe of maternity and even some baby clothes, Dana would go home from the hospital that day without our baby inside her.

Dana never told her parents what happened. She spent almost six months in a deep depression, unable to work. That was four years ago, and since then we had never even broached the subject of another baby.

Not until the day Dana decided she wasn't going to go back to work—ever.

10

There Are No Dates on Polaroids

A large group had gathered in the parking lot outside the office, waiting for the auction to start. After verifying that all the units were still delinquent accounts, Tom and I went through, cut locks, and put on temporary wires with tags. He was now getting ready to lead the herd of potential buyers through the labyrinth of hallways and buildings to sell off the contents of the dozen or so units whose tenants had not paid rent in two or more months.

I recognized the tenant of one of the units. He stood outside the circle of the group, wearing torn jeans and a blue, wrinkled button-up dress shirt, smoking a cigarette with his thumb and forefinger. He owed about three hundred in back rent on one of the units that was going up for auction that day.

"Hans, what's that guy doing here? The one whose unit is being auctioned."

Hans wiped a glaze of doughnut sugar that had accumulated on his fingers on his shirt and looked out the window. "Who knows? Maybe he figures he'll buy the unit for less than he owes on it."

"Which unit is his?"

"I think it's the one in B building, isn't it?"

Tom walked in with a clipboard and signaled to me that he was ready. I grabbed a walkie talkie and approached the group. I noticed the cigarette-smoking tenant glaring at me while Tom gave the group a quick how-to speech followed by a list of disclaimers. I led everyone around to the first building. Most of the people in the group were familiar. I saw them practically every month. They made a living from speculating on storage auctions and picking through flea markets and garage sales.

As Tom cut the temporary wire on the first unit, I looked down the drive and spotted Mrs. Vaughn, sitting low to the ground in a beach chair. There were some green things all around her which I couldn't decipher. I walked away from the group toward her just as Tom rolled up the unit door and started the bidding.

She was wearing long white Bermuda shorts and a giant sombrero-style hat. The green things were houseplants, about a half dozen of them, placed around her in a circle. She was stretched out, quietly reading a book. The sun didn't seem to be affecting the pale, vein-laced skin of her short legs.

"Mrs. Vaughn?"

She held up a finger, signaling me to wait. I looked back at the auction, which appeared to be wrapping up at the first unit and going on to the next. Tom didn't need me to show him around; he knew his way. I took off my sunglasses and wiped my brow with the back of my hand.

"I think I mentioned before that you're not supposed to store perishable things such as food or plants," I said.

She adjusted the strap of her sandal. "Who says I'm storing any plants or perishables?"

"What about these houseplants?"

"What about them?"

"We don't allow houseplants in the storage units. They attract insects." I wanted to say "they attract rats" to gauge her reaction but thought better of it.

"I'm not storing these, young man. Do you see me storing these? I keep these in my car."

I noticed the title of the book she was reading. *Accessing the Power Within: A Guide for Every Woman.* She appeared to be halfway through it.

"In your car? Then what are they doing out here?"

"I just brought them out for company." She seemed to ponder her statement for a minute, then leaned forward a bit. "Listen, is there a reason you're badgering me? I really would like a little peace so I can get through this chapter." She nudged the book a little.

I sighed and put my sunglasses back on. "I mean it about the house-plants, Mrs. Vaughn." The ridiculousness of her reading a book as if she were on the Riviera instead of a storage facility didn't escape me.

She went back to her book, dismissing me. I heard a click from the walkie talkie and a low hiss before Hans's voiced buzzed from the speaker. "Dave, you copy?"

"Yeah, what?"

"Dana's here in the office," there was a pause, and then Dana's voice came blaring through the speaker.

"Can you come home for a sec? I need to talk to you NOW."

I casually walked back to the office, stopping a few times along the way to greet customers.

***

"David, you need to develop a sense of urgency. What took you so long?"

I looked at the time displayed in glowing green on the VCR behind her. It was 11:13 a.m. She was still in her robe. A half-eaten bowl of cereal sat on the coffee table, little brown flakes floating limply around a spoon. "What is it, Dana? I have work to do."

"I called Marilyn." She crossed her arms. "And I'm screwed. I'm so completely screwed."

I wasn't sure I wanted to hear this.

"She seemed very surprised to hear from me. 'I didn't appreciate the way you just up and left,' she said. At first I was very polite. I explained that her behavior was just stressing me out so much that I was becoming physically ill with migraines and stomach aches. I told her that on the day I quit, I had been feeling nauseous all day ever since she started in on me about the way I had organized the memos on the computer. I just couldn't bear to be there one more day, let alone to give two weeks' notice."

"So, what did she say to that?"

"She reacted in typical Marilyn fashion, acting like she didn't even hear me. She started in about responsibility and professionalism. I sat there on the phone listening to her drone on and on. It was like she was reading out loud a page-long block paragraph with no punctuation. 'You have to have a better attitude, Dana, otherwise you'll get nowhere in life.' As if I'd want to have an attitude like hers—making everyone around her crazy." She scratched her head. "Hang on, I'm gonna go make some coffee."

I followed her to the coffee maker and watched her dump the wet brown filter into the trash and replace it with a fresh one.

"So anyway, it was around that point that I started to think she had no clue that I had her pictures. I thought I should just blurt it out, but by then I was so irritated with her that I wanted to ease her into it. Make her squirm."

"Uh huh."

"But first, I told her, I said...Marilyn, all I want is to find another job and get on with my life. I would appreciate if you would at least give me a decent recommendation. So, she says, 'Tell me why I should do that, Dana? Why, exactly?'" She poured the coffee directly out of the bag and into the filter, slopping a little of it on the counter. She shoved the coffee pot under the filter and flicked the ON switch. "I asked her at that point if she had looked at the bottom of her filing cabinet lately. She says, 'Where?' Then it must have sunk in because she didn't say a word for a while. I just waited, let her simmer. Finally, she says to me, 'What do you know about the bottom of my filing cabinet?'"

I heard muffled shouts coming up from the office. I stopped Dana as she prepared her next sentence. "Shhhh—hold up for a sec." I moved closer to the stairway and waited. The shouting didn't resume.

"What?" Dana asked.

"Nothing," I said. "Thought I heard some shouting. Go on, what did she say next?"

"I told her that I knew what she did on those long lunch breaks with Chuck. She changed her tone a little. I could tell she had gotten up to close her office door. 'Tell me exactly what my lunch meetings with Chuck have to do with this conversation. And don't beat around the bush.' I said, okay, tell you what—you give me a good recommendation and in return I won't spring these photos on your husband."

"Ouch. What'd she say to that?"

"She laughed!"

"She laughed?"

"Yeah, she was overtaken with hilarity—that dumb bitch. She says, 'Well, my dear, now you can add blackmailer to the list of all the wonderful qualities you possess. I'm sure your future employers would like to hear about that.' I couldn't believe it. I thought, maybe she doesn't care that her husband finds out, right? Maybe she and her husband aren't getting along anyway. Okay, so then I got desperate and mentioned how upset Chuck's new wife would be if *she* got the photos."

"She would be—but you wouldn't do that, would you?"

"I won't have to, because get this—Marilyn says that she and Chuck had a year-long relationship before Chuck got married."

"You're kidding! So she admitted this to you? What about her husband?"

"Supposedly, her husband found out, but they worked it out."

"So why wasn't she worried about the photos? Sounds like she should be."

"I know. That's what I thought. I sort of hinted around about that. She got all snide, asking me if I saw any dates on those Polaroids."

"Oh, I see. There's no proof about *when* the photos were taken. They could have been taken back when they were having the affair. So she completely diffused the threat. It won't matter—"

"Exactly. It won't matter. Chuck's wife knows they were an item before they met, and Marilyn's husband has apparently forgiven her. So the pictures are worthless, as far as my situation is concerned anyway. She's right, there are no dates on the photos. She can just claim they were from before Chuck got married."

"Worse than that, they've become more of a liability to you than to her."

"Yeah." She filled her mug up with hot coffee and shook her head. "I'm going to have to do some fancy maneuvering at any future job interviews. You know, not mention her at all. It won't sound good when they ask me if they can contact my former employer and I say, 'no.'"

Once again, I heard muffled shouts downstairs. "I have to see what's going on. Let's talk later, okay honey?"

"You're not gonna tell me 'I told you so', are you?"

"I'm not gonna say squat. It's your thing. The ball's in your court."

"Whatever."

As I entered the office through the stairwell door, I wasn't surprised to see the former delinquent tenant in a tense posture leaning against the counter. Hans was sitting down, recoiling, as the man thrust his finger toward him. "That's fuckin' bullshit, man! I don't give a shit what your stupid explanation is, I still think it's a load of bull."

"Hey, calm down. What's the problem?" I was careful not to walk up behind him too abruptly. Somewhere in the back of my mind I heard a vague warning about spooking a tense horse and getting kicked in the balls, and I decided that might apply equally well in this situation. My instincts were right, because as soon as he heard my voice he spun around, teeth bared and fists clenched.

He and Hans spoke over each other.

"You guys took my stuff, man."

"He bought out his unit and says there's stuff missing."

"Hold on now, tell me what stuff is missing." I got behind the counter and stood next to Hans.

"Most all of it. I couldn't believe it when he rolled up the door. I had me a stereo in there, some speakers, a recliner. The only thing left was a few boxes of clothes and a fuckin' bike I had in there."

"Who else had access to your unit?"

"Nobody! Don't throw this back at me. You guys are the ones who went into my unit."

"We didn't go into your unit. We cut the lock, rolled up the door, took a picture and locked it back up. That was this morning. What's more, your lock was intact. There were no signs of forced entry."

He pounded the counter and turned his head, giving us a long side-long glare. "That stuff was worth at least a thousand dollars. I'm holding you two responsible. If I don't get my money for the stuff you took, I'm gonna call a lawyer."

Hans reached for the phone. "And I'm calling the police. There's nothing we can help you with at this point. You need to straighten this out with them."

"Fine! I'll be outside, waitin'." He stormed out, reaching into his jeans pocket for a cigarette. He paced around outside while Hans dialed the number to the police department.

***

He was *waitin'* quite a while, as it turned out. By the time the police showed up to take his statement, all the auction participants had either left or were exploring their purchases. He sat outside on one of the parking barriers, patiently smoking one cigarette after another.

I told Hans to take his lunch break a little early. He sniveled about not being hungry yet, so I gave him some cash and told him to waste a half hour getting me a sandwich from the deli down the road.

"What do you need me to take an early lunch for?" Hans asked.

"I need to make a personal call. Just go. Shoo." I waved him off.

He eyed me suspiciously as he stuffed his front pocket with the bills I gave him.

It was three hours ahead in Connecticut and as I dialed Ellen's work number, which I had memorized, I knew that she would probably be wrapping up her workday. I wasn't sure what I'd say to her. All I knew was that I needed to hear her voice. I needed to hear her warm, purring voice that afternoon.

Her phone rang too many times and I braced myself to leave a message. She had told me once to be careful about that, since she wasn't sure if it was possible for anyone else in the company to screen voice mail. I listened to her professional, and by now familiar recording and spoke quickly after the tone.

"Hi Ellen, it's me. I haven't heard from you in a couple of days and just wanted to talk for a bit. I hope you're doing well. Maybe we'll see each other later at our usual spot."

I hung up, feeling a wave of disappointment. A few minutes later I saw the police cruiser punch in the special code at the gate which I had provided to the department. As the gate rolled open, the tenant stood up from the parking barrier and sheepishly leaned against the fence behind him. I looked at the security printout Hans had prepared before he left. It was a dot matrix printout of data registering every security breach of a unit. If someone entered a unit without first punching in their passcode at the gate or in the office, an alarm would either blare outside or bleat in the office, depending on whether it was before or after office hours.

The police officer leisurely made his way into the office, the tenant following close behind. The process went quickly. The officer was efficient and unemotional as he took our statement. I offered him the security printout, and he noted that the tenant's unit had not shown up on the printout since the tenant had been in it last. That meant that no one had entered it without using the passcode.

"How in the hell am I supposed to believe this printout? You could've jimmied it somehow." The tenant, Jerry Wyler, had lost his edge a little from an hour and a half ago when he had been barking at Hans. His voice was now at least a couple of pitches lower, and his shoulders were hunched forward.

"There's no way to jimmy it. It is what it is."

"Yeah, but how do I know that?"

The officer concluded his paperwork and handed a copy of it to Jerry. Jerry growled one more complaint and left, leaving me alone in the office with the officer.

"Do you guys have a modem hooked up to your computer here?"

"We do. Why?" I folded my copy of the report and stuck it in a file.

"Well, we have this new software that we just tweaked at the station. It'll upload that security information to us daily via a phone line, so that we have a record at the station nice and handy for just such occasions."

"No kidding—huh! When did you guys start this? I've never heard of it."

"Not too long ago. But you should call this number," he handed me a business card with a number he'd scribbled on the back, "and have them set you up. We have a wide range of uses for this new software, including the monitoring of home security alarms."

"Ok, I'll give them a call." Or maybe I'd have Hans do it, I thought.

"As for this guy—Mr. Wyler? I'm thinking, since he insists he's the only one who knew his passcode, that he may be just setting you up for a lawsuit. My feeling is that he never had any of the items he claims to have stored in your facility."

"How can you know for sure, though?"

"His description of the stereo equipment is bogus. I know my way around stereos, and he was totally making stuff up. His makes, models, and components don't jive."

"Oh."

"Don't worry about it. But in the future, it would probably help alleviate some of the liability if you were on our system."

"Sounds like it."

I walked the officer outside. As I watched him return to his cruiser, I inhaled the strong odor of eucalyptus as the Santa Ana winds drove a gust through the surrounding trees. It had turned out to be a very warm day. I had the following day off, and as I stood there sniffing the air, I decided to spend it cruising up the coast with Dana. We both needed a change of scenery.

11

My Future, As Told by Madame Ptak

Dana announced that she wanted to drive up to Laguna Beach to check out some art galleries and antique shops, followed by an ice cream sundae lunch at the Ben and Jerry's. We left the house early, before Hans arrived to open the office at nine. Dana packed some cokes into a cooler and stuck it in the back seat of the Honda. We stopped by the seven eleven on the way to the freeway for some doughnuts for Dana and coffee for me. I was feeling sluggish about the excursion that morning for some reason, and I needed a quick attitude adjustment. I figured a super-concentrated cup of standard-grade convenience store coffee would do the trick.

The stuff was barely palatable. I slid the passenger seat back and got as comfortable as possible in the contours of stiff upholstered foam, careful not to spill the bitter hot liquid all over the car. Dana shot me a warning with her eyes as she made the turn onto the onramp to Interstate 5. She made it a rule when we bought the car that we wouldn't eat or drink in it. I had no such rules about my car, a fifteen-year-old Saab that I had bought one month after graduating from college. The old Swedish meatball, as

I sometimes called it, was parked in the garage that day. It needed a new muffler, which we couldn't afford.

Why is it that when money is tight, everything seems to start falling apart? I thought about what happened the other day, for example. One minute I was making a mental budget of how to save enough money to pay the telephone bill by eating peanut butter and jelly sandwiches for lunch all month, and the next minute I heard the back of the Saab slam into a crater in the bank's driveway, followed by a clanking and finally a distant "ping" as the muffler rolled into the gutter. So much for saving thirty dollars this month, I had groaned, as the car sputtered and roared down the street, mocking me.

Technically, we really shouldn't have taken the drive up the coast that day either, because we couldn't afford the twenty dollars or so in gas and snacks. But Dana had only been out of work about a month, and we had just gotten through paying the big round of bills a couple of weeks before with the help of her last paycheck. I was hopeful that by the time we had to pay those same bills again, she would have started a new position. The money situation wasn't that bad. Yet.

On the other hand, there had been a growing tension between us in the last few days that I wanted to shake. I had hoped that spending the day together without the distractions of the storage facility, Dana's parents, or the TV would help. I was getting worried about her increasing lack of motivation about looking for work and about her sliding mood. In the morning she would sleep in until ten thirty or so, get up and eat breakfast, and then watch TV until noon before she'd take a shower. Sometime later in the afternoon she would come down to the office to talk to me for a while or to use the phone to call her sisters in Missouri. She started out making follow-up calls to companies where she had mailed her resume, but quickly abandoned that step after getting rejections or the standard "don't call us, we'll call you." She had stopped going to the corner every morning to buy the paper. The weekday classifieds were a waste of time, she had said, because they were a repeat of the classifieds from the Sunday paper.

I was at least grateful that she hadn't been spending her days at the mall, buying expensive business suits and dresses like she used to when she had been between jobs. We had spent the last two years trying to whittle down the balance on both credit cards, and I knew that if she came home with bags full of charged purchases, I would have to either convince her to return everything or take it back myself. As it was, we were barely making progress on lowering the principle on the balance because we could barely afford to make more than the minimum payment of two hundred dollars on each card. This didn't cause Dana as much concern; mainly because I was the one who paid the bills and thus the one who had the monthly reminder of just how pathetically slow we were making progress on lowering our balance. Every time I made out the checks, I would hope that we could get through one more month where the car didn't explode or we wouldn't encounter any other major catastrophes that would set us back.

Dana and I had once discussed the possibility of buying a house or a condo but realized that in addition to needing a good down payment, our bills would have to be paid off. More importantly, however, I would have to find another job because my living on-site was tied into my job description.

It was frustrating for both of us that we would probably be in our mid-thirties before we could live in our own place. It would take at least five years to get in a position where we could start considering buying a house. By then, the average cost of a decent house in the San Diego area would be at least three hundred thousand dollars and the only thing we would be able to afford would be a one-bedroom condo with a view of a parking lot.

This was the price we paid for living here, I thought, looking out onto the blue of the Pacific on the left as we approached Camp Pendleton. The air was fragrant and clear after the previous day's Santa Ana winds had blown all the smog out to sea. I could even see the distant San Clemente Island, a military-owned chunk of rock some fifty miles off the coast, that was only discernable on the clearest of days. A few freightliners chugged along on the thin line of the horizon, heading north towards Long Beach or even further, towards Seattle.

I wondered what Ellen was doing right this minute. I hadn't gotten an email from her in a couple of days, and I speculated about the reason. Maybe she was out of town, or very busy, or perhaps she was sick. If she was sick, or if something ever did happen to her, how would I find out about it? Would I have to order back issues of the Hartford newspaper to try to research an obituary? Would her husband find a way to access her email and send notes to everyone on her email address list? Most likely I would probably have to call her work, posing as a customer, and speak to someone there to get information. It seemed odd to me that I could be such good friends with someone and be so cut off from their life.

"I talked to Alicia yesterday." Dana turned down the radio a bit and I ascended out of my daydream. I felt myself go involuntarily tense at the name. I hadn't seen or spoken to Alicia since the night we kissed in my car, and hadn't really thought about her that much, either. The first couple days after the incident I had felt a slight wave of apprehension every time the phone rang. I imagined it was Alicia calling Dana to tell her about what happened. When a week, then two passed and there was no word from her, I let myself relax and forget about it.

"Really? What did she say?" I felt the bitter, acidic taste of bad coffee at the back of my throat and swallowed hard.

"I called her to ask if she wanted to come over on Sunday so we could throw some steaks on the grill or something. She acted real funny at first, like she was looking for an excuse to bow out."

"Uh huh."

"It was really weird. I mean, she usually calls me at least once a week, but I haven't heard from her. And every time I call her house her machine would come on. But finally I figured out what the story is."

"You did?" My hand involuntarily reached for the door handle.

"Yeah, I think she's back with her old boyfriend and she's afraid to tell me."

"You mean the guy who dumped her in Cancun?"

"Yeah, him. I think she let him weasel back into her life and she's embarrassed to admit to me that she let him."

"How do you know that's why she hasn't called you?" I blurted, brainlessly. Why was I questioning Dana's speculation? I should just let her believe what she wanted to believe. I elevated my voice a little to cancel out the last statement. "Anyway, why should we care if she's back with him?"

"I don't know if that's it or not. I'll have to ask her when she's over on Sunday."

"So, she agreed to come over?"

"Yeah, I figured we could invite a few people, rent a couple of videos. Maybe make some Margaritas."

Great, I thought. That's all I need—Alicia over at our apartment getting sloshed on Margaritas. I wondered if I could get through a Sunday comprised of morning brunch at Dana's parents and an afternoon Fiesta of Avoidance with my wife's best friend who couldn't keep her hands off me.

"What's the matter? You're not saying anything." Dana looked over at me.

"Nothing. It's cool. Sunday barbeque. Gotcha." I opened the glove compartment and brought out an opened package of Juicy Fruit spearmint gum. I had to chase down this bad taste in my mouth. Laguna Beach was still at least half an hour away. I yanked the lever on the side of the seat and reclined all the way back, forcing my muscles to slowly ease back to a normal, relaxed state.

We were pleasantly surprised to find that there was a mini carnival going in downtown Laguna Beach as part of a week-long autumn festival. Booths were set up in the park adjacent to the beach and the stores on the main street had set out some of their merchandise on the sidewalk. We had a hard time finding a good parking space and ended up having to park quite a ways away from the main street in a residential area. We grabbed a couple of the cold sodas and walked down towards the waterfront, holding hands.

We ignored the shops selling souvenirs and T-shirts and instead browsed through some of the galleries on the main street. I became interested in looking at art back in college when I occasionally dated a girl named Joy who was finishing her master's in fine art. We used to go to show openings in galleries all over town, in La Jolla or downtown San Diego and sometimes even up in Los Angeles. She was very ambitious about networking the gallery circuit and made it clear to me that if I wanted to date her I'd have to tag along to these functions. I spent many evenings pacing the galleries, eating bad hors d'oeuvres and drinking boxed wine while Joy schmoozed it up with the owners or curators. I learned to look at art in a different way than I had in the past. I could tell the difference between a sofa painting and something worth investing in.

My eyes grazed a few of the paintings on display. This gallery featured very conservative ocean landscapes and watercolors. These were unlike the type of paintings Joy used to paint. Her work was somber and muddled with ambiguity. I remembered one painting in particular, a gray, shadowy image of an alley behind a row of old brick houses. A woman, barely discernable, stood leaning up against the streaked wall of her garage, her face in her hands. I had asked Joy what the painting was about.

"The woman is hiding from her husband, who's in the house. She ran out into the alley to cry."

"Why is she hiding from her husband?"

"Because the man she was having an affair with broke it off with her, and she doesn't want her husband to see her crying."

Her paintings always came with a big story.

She said that she would have visual flashes about moments in other people's lives, based on things she'd see on TV or hear from her friends. I loved her work. It certainly wasn't the sort of stuff you'd see hanging in some dentist's office, but it was the kind of mood piece you'd want to own just because it made you feel different. I wondered, as I looked at a wispy watercolor of a bougainvillea-laced porch, what Joy painted after she had broken up with me.

"Let's go check out the tent across the street."

"Okay." I followed Dana out of the gallery and toward a large, white tent under which were rows of long tables with stacks of books and crafts and antiques. We made our way through the labyrinth of chairs, tables and festival-goers into the center of the community yard sale. Dana stopped at a table that displayed hand-made, eighteen-inch-tall St. Nick dolls in a variety of outfits and themes. She picked up the one with the thick fur coat and hat, and I saw the price on the fluttering tag attached to the bottom.

"I'd love to have one of these," Dana gushed.

"Not for six hundred dollars, you're not," I said.

"Oh. Whoops." She placed the doll gingerly back onto the table and smiled apologetically at the proprietor.

Outside the tent were more booths with games where the prizes were cheap, stuffed animals mass produced in Taiwan. We watched as people paid money to throw darts at limp balloons or to toss dimes onto five-inch-wide flat plates. Next to a dunk tank was a small table with a poster board sign scotch-taped to the front: *Tarot Card Readings by Madame Ptak, $5.*

The woman sitting behind the table was in her forties and very attractive. She wore a long, red, crinkled skirt and blouse and her hair was pulled back in a tight braid which she had wrapped into a spiral on the top of her head. She smiled at me as we walked by. The sign caught Dana's attention.

"Oh, let's do this. This is fun." She sat down in the chair in front of the tarot card sign, slid a ten dollar bill out of her purse and put it on the table as the woman started shuffling the oversized deck of cards.

"Would you like change or are you getting two readings?" The woman looked up at me with a warm expression.

"I don't need a reading." I thought this was a waste of money, but I didn't want to say so.

"Oh, come on, David. Get a reading. It'll be fun." Dana looked up at me and clucked her tongue. "Please, Mr. Scrooge?"

"Who's stopping you?" I asked.

I watched as the woman let Dana cut the deck before she laid out a series of cards face down on the table. I crossed my arms and moved closer to the table and out of the way of the crowd. I noticed the woman had rings on almost all her fingers. Some of the rings were silver bands with intricate patterns and some were made of gold. She also had thin metal bracelets on both wrists, which dangled and shimmered as she began to flip the cards over.

"You are in a state of transition now, I see. This card represents change and an opportunity for new beginnings. You are on the cusp of something completely new in your life."

Aren't we all? I let my mind wander and looked around the park. There were a lot of people here even though it was a weekday morning. Most of the carnival goers were women and children, but very few families. A few couples had set up blankets on the ridge overlooking the beach and were eating sandwiches or just relaxing.

"What can you tell me about my marriage and having kids?" Dana asked.

"Let me see your hand and I'll tell you," Madame Ptak said.

Dana's hand was small and plain in the grasp of the fortune teller's jeweled fingers. "I see here you'll have two children. They will be very close together in age. I don't see a divorce."

Dana turned her head and winked up at me. Of course, I thought. What else is the gypsy going to say? She sees that Dana is wearing a wedding band and so she took a leap in assuming that she is too young to have been married before. I sighed and shifted my weight, growing slightly impatient.

"Ok, your turn now," Dana said as she stood up out of the folding chair, and I moved to sit down. I was apprehensive and didn't make an effort to hide that. I followed the woman's instructions about cutting the deck of cards and sat back as she began to flip them over one by one.

"I see there will be a transition for you, as well. But your transition involves a large body of water. I see that in the near future, perhaps within six months, you will be contemplating moving near a large body of water."

"I do live near a large body of water."

The woman looked up at me, puzzled for a second. "Of course, but this is different water, a different place."

"Ok." I bit my lip and stifled an exasperated sigh.

"You will have a lot to consider when making this move. You will be aware of the things you have to give up."

I pondered the statement she had made earlier. A different place, a different water. Did she mean the Atlantic? Would I be contemplating moving back east? And if so, would it have something to do with Ellen? Would I be giving up my marriage, my job? I leaned forward and focused my attention on what the fortuneteller was saying.

"I also see here that you have a talent that is in a dormant state right now. You are very distracted, perhaps by work or something else, and you are not paying attention to developing your talent."

That could be my writing. But then again, this statement could be applicable to anyone, about anything. I always considered Tarot Card readings and horoscopes to be similarly ambiguous and deceivingly universal in their messages, and so I tempered my sudden interest.

She continued, "There is someone who is deceiving you at your work. I can't tell whether it's a man or a woman, but this person is doing something behind your back that could jeopardize your future. It would be wise for you to watch your step with this person."

"Could you be more specific?"

"Well...I don't know. But you are distracted by a lot of other things. You should be more alert at work."

Right. The fortuneteller told me someone's gonna fuck me over, guys, so I have to go around like a paranoid asshole, I thought.

"Ok, well thank you very much." I looked at the ten-dollar bill that Dana had placed on the table. I didn't see her making a move to put it away and I wondered if she was waiting for a tip.

"There's one more thing. It's not in the cards, though." She smirked. I got a weird feeling that she had been reading my mind about the tip.

"What's that?"

"I sense that even though your mind is here, your heart is already far away, and soon your body will follow."

"Uh huh." I turned away, feeling exposed and nervous.

Dana looked at me quizzically. "You ready for that ice cream yet?"

"You betcha."

***

I dove into the chocolatey goop with pleasure as we sat on a bench with our decadent lunch. The sun was melting everything quickly, and I scooped out the melted cream from the sides of the container.

"Sounds like we have similar futures. What do you think?" Dana looked at me and smiled.

"What do you mean?"

"Well," Dana licked a spot of whipped cream off the handle of her spoon, "she told me that I'm about to have some big change come my way, and she told you that you'd be making a move."

"I can't imagine why we would move. Unless you got some fantastic job offer in New York or Florida or something."

Dana's smile faded and she looked off at the ocean. "I don't think that's going to happen."

"Hey, listen, don't start moping. You'll find a great job soon. I know you will."

"I don't think I want to anymore."

"You don't want to what?"

"I don't want to do the same thing. I want to do something else. I don't want to be someone's secretary anymore," Dana uttered.

"What do you want to do?" I ran through the list of Dana's qualifications and skills in my head and tried to guess what sort of change she wanted to make.

She took a deep breath and answered softly. "I want to be a mother."

I bit into a bad chunk of pecan and cringed at the bitter tinge, spitting it out onto the sidewalk. Dana's proclamation began to make connections in my brain.

"What does that mean, you want to stay home and have a baby?"

"What's with the attitude?"

"There's no attitude."

"Yeah, there is. You're acting like I'm a freak for wanting to do something a little more meaningful than answering the fucking phone for people."

"Hey—whoa!—that's not what I said and that's not what I was thinking."

"Then what?" She slammed her ice cream container on the bench next to her and glared at me.

"I don't know what you want me to think, Dana. This is so out of the blue, for one thing. And for another, I can't see how we could afford a baby if you weren't working."

"I'm not waiting until I'm forty years old to have a kid."

"No one said you had to wait that long. Don't exaggerate."

"Yeah, right. It's never going to be a good time, is it?"

"You sound like your mother."

"Fuck you."

I felt the conversation getting away from me and quickly began to formulate a plan to get the animosity under control. I scooted closer to her on the bench and put my arm around her. She stiffened.

"You know that I love you and I want to have a bunch of kids with you someday," I whispered and caressed her shoulder. "You know that, don't you?"

"I dunno."

"We just have to wait for the right time, or else it's not going to work for either one of us. We'll both be so stressed out. Trust me, I know from what my parents went through. It was hard on them to have two children and have to scrape and scratch to make ends meet. It was hard on all of us. I just don't want to repeat that."

Dana was silent as I continued to rub her arm and shoulder. Her expression was bordering explosive, her jaw clenched and her lips pursed.

"Dana, talk to me."

"I'm just not happy. I hate my job. I hate being a secretary. It's not what I want to do with my life."

"But you don't—"

"My mom says she'd help us pay off our bills, if that's what you're worried about."

"What?!" I slid away from her. "No way, Dana. There's no way I'm letting your parents give us money." I can just imagine the condescension that would result from such a situation. I shook my head. "That would be the kiss of death for our marriage. It really would."

"Why?"

"Why? Because your parents hate me already, I can only imagine how they'd feel if they had to bail out their loser son-in-law."

"They don't think you're a loser." She kicked at a pebble with the tip of her sandal.

"Gimme a break, Dana. Every time we go over there I have to—" I stopped abruptly and contemplated how to best phrase what I had to say.

"Fine, then. You don't have to go there anymore." She got up and started walking away. I followed her, tossing the remains of the melted swirl of ice cream into the trash.

We wandered aimlessly around the shops along the adjacent street, not saying a word to each other. I was still slightly in shock, trying to understand what had developed in the last few weeks to convince my wife that the next reasonable step to take was to quit working and have a baby. What did this mean? For one thing, she wasn't pregnant yet. Or was she?

I thought back frantically to the last few times we had sex. She was on the pill, so there was no way for me to gauge whether I had unknowingly impregnated her if she had stopped taking it. I glanced at her as she picked up a small porcelain figurine and pinched the tiny price tag that swayed from it. Would she have stopped taking the pill without telling me? She usually took it at night, before turning in. I broke out in a cold sweat of relief as I remembered seeing her press a tablet through the foil and slip it into her mouth a few nights ago.

I understood her disdain for her work as a secretary. She was certainly not well suited for taking direction and being diplomatic. Dana was at her best when she was in charge, on the move, and autonomous. I would sometimes make suggestions to her about getting into some sort of professional or corporate sales position, where she would be responsible for her own time and productivity. She scoffed at the suggestion, saying sales was a fancier term for professional ass-kissing. If there was one thing Dana didn't subscribe to, it was ass-kissing.

In light of that day's revelation, I was worried. When she wanted something, she was capable of displaying a lot of strength, almost bordering on selfishness. She almost always took the direct approach ("I want to have a baby") rather than dilly-dallying around. If I were to predict her next course of action, I would venture to say that she would wait a few days for her news to flavor my palette and then she'd begin a brazen campaign to get pregnant. But it wasn't going to happen. I had at that moment decided to take birth control matters into my own hands until we resolved this issue. I didn't trust her suddenly.

Meanwhile, however, her objection to her line of work spelled imminent trouble for our financial situation. I hoped that the intent of her proclamation was to bring my attention to how miserable she had been feeling about her life and did not literally mean that she wasn't going back to work. If we didn't get more money in the bank soon, we would start defaulting on some of our loans and credit cards.

I spoke to the back of her head. "You ready to head back?"

She didn't turn around right away. Instead, she continued to absentmindedly thumb through the pages of an old hardbound book by James Joyce. I slowly made my way out of the store.

Dana almost didn't want to get into the car for the drive home. She balked at me as I stood at the car door, holding it open for her. Finally, she conceded and slumped into the passenger seat. I started the car and headed back toward I-5. I looked forward to a long run to work out the tension that had reached a nauseating peak in my throat. My plan to spend a restful day with Dana had bombed. I didn't feel rested, we weren't any closer, and I hadn't managed to cheer her up.

As the traffic thickened around me, I sank deeper into the numbed silence of the air-conditioned car, feeling more alone than I had in a long, long time.

12

You'll Remember Next Time

A couple hours after we returned to our apartment Dana sulked out, grumbling something about having dinner at her parents' house. I put on my running shoes and went for a long run, looping from the self-storage and down along the beach a few miles.

That night after a late dinner of canned soup and toast, I went downstairs to the office to see if there had been any pressing messages or problems left for me for the next day. I stifled a yawn as I flipped the light switch and walked behind the counter. The office always felt a little creepy after dark. The blackness of night outside the windows made it feel oddly smaller and my ears protested the normally-unnoticed high-pitched hum of the fluorescent lights. There were a couple messages, written in Hans's tight, fussy handwriting on pink slips of paper. *Call the accountant. He has a question about last month's reports.* Not again. Is that guy a moron? *FYI: Mr. Wyler called, and he wants to know if we have any sort of insurance so that he can file a claim on his stolen property.* Nope, tough luck, Ted. You should have thought your scam through a little better. Done your homework.

Next to the messages lay a letter addressed to me, in care of the self-storage. It was marked "personal" along the bottom. The envelope was almost square, and the address had been handwritten in blue ink. I picked it up and flipped it around, finding no return address on either side. The postmark was slightly smeared but I could still make it out. The letter was from Connecticut. I felt my heart stumble in my chest.

I began to open it up, mindful that I was now touching what Ellen had touched only a few days before. I carefully slid out the enclosed card. It was a distorted view of a golden retriever with his nose stuck up into the camera lens, tongue hanging out, eyes eager. Inside, the greeting stated, "I'd give anything to lick your earlobes."

Groaning, I put the card aside and unfolded the letter that was inside. A dried, red maple leaf fell out of it and onto the floor. I picked it up gingerly by its stem and placed it on the counter as I began to read.

> *Hi.*
>
> *We've had some problems with our computer and I won't be able to write you for a few days. I am hoping it's okay that I mailed this to your work address. See, I told you I don't forget a thing! I remember you told me where you worked. The address was easy to find on the Internet.*
>
> *I can't write from work, either—yet. I got a new office along with my promotion and the computer in my office hasn't been set up yet for email. So, I decided to just write you the old fashioned way. Plus, this way you can see what my handwriting looks like and if you're so inclined, you can even analyze my loops.*
>
> *I was doing a little autumn clean-up in my garden the other day. We have an unfenced, large piece of property that is situated on a ridge overlooking a valley. I wish you could have seen the view that day. The trees were overripe with color, creating an effect like cascading fire down the hillsides. I stood there, looking out at the low clouds and breathing in the brisk air, which was tingeda little with the smell of burning wood. It was such a delicious smell. It reminded me of cozy Saturday afternoons by the fireplace, reading a good book while waiting for the oven timer to go off when the cookies were done.*
>
> *Are you puking yet from the sugar-coated taste of suburban living?*
>
> *I really wish you could have been there that day, David. That*

day I realized that there is such a quiet, gentle power in the steadiness of nature. In all the things that change in our lives, in all the ways we change, I can always count on autumn in New England; on smoky evenings in November, on shorter days and colder nights. In my whole life, this will never change.

I also felt painfully lonely that day, and my only comfort was thinking of your warm letters and the sound of your voice. Jack has been home only four days this month. Can you believe that? Pete misses him. I thought I was finally getting used to feeling like a single parent, until that moment. At that moment, I didn't like that he wasn't there, that he wasn't at home. As hard as I tried to tell myself I was in his heart, I knew that he was probably too busy with work and clients to be thinking of me.

But when I thought of you, the loneliness subsided just a little. I took a deep breath and closed my eyes, trying to picture your face. When you finally appeared before me, I saw you look at me with those beautiful eyes of yours and it made me feel so good. At that very moment, something brushed against my nose. It was this leaf that I am sending you. It kissed me, just as if you had, on my nose.

Take care, love.

Ellen

I wanted to kiss her on the nose. As a matter of fact, I wanted to do a lot more than that. I ached to hold her in my arms, but instead I held the thin paper of her note between my thumb and forefinger. I looked at the round plastic clock that was mounted on the wall. It was 9:18 pm, which meant that it was past midnight in Connecticut. Was she asleep already, or was she tossing and turning in bed thinking of me, as I had been doing lately? I wanted to pick up the phone and call her, but I knew I couldn't. I didn't know if she was still alone or if Jack had come back home. Even if she were alone and awake, I would feel like a complete psycho for calling at such a late hour.

She had sent the letter at least three days ago and I still hadn't received an email from her, which meant that her computers were still offline. As I folded the letter back up and replaced the card in the envelope, I decided to call her at work the next morning. I shut the lights off in the office and tucked the card into my back pocket as I made my way back up to the apartment.

I turned on the computer and re-read the letter as I waited for the system to boot up.

I saw you look at me with those beautiful eyes of yours...

So she liked my looks. I had found three decent photos of myself in one of my photo albums a couple weeks ago and had gone to Kinkos to have them scanned to disk. One was from a weekend trip to San Felipe with a couple of college buddies. I was very tan, smiling ear to ear after one too many Coronas. Another was a photo of me in a black tux at a wedding where I was the best man. The third one was more of a close-up—a photo Dana took one day when we were goofing around at home on a rainy Saturday afternoon. My hair was a little ruffled and I had a five o'clock shadow. I looked a little like Alec Baldwin in that photo. In real life, though, I look nothing like Alec Baldwin.

As I signed on, I looked around the office for a good hiding place to put her card. I didn't want to throw it away yet. Looking at the stack of papers and books that were crammed into a cheap oak bookcase, I spotted the pocket folder notebook where I kept the outlines and notes for the book I was writing. I put the card inside one of the pockets, behind some papers, and replaced it on the shelf. Dana would never look there. She wasn't the least bit interested in my writing.

I didn't have any email. I sat staring at the empty mailbox icon for a few minutes, hoping that Ellen would pop online at precisely that moment. When she didn't, I shut the computer back down and retreated into the bedroom. Hoping for a better start the next day, I sprawled out across the cold, empty bed and fell fast asleep.

***

"Hans, do you have a computer at home?" I asked.

"No, why?" Hans was at his desk, inputting customer information into the database. He continued typing with two fingers, his expression pinched.

"You should get one."

"Why? Is there some work you want me to take home?"

"No, I was just thinking that you might enjoy chatting online, meeting new people. You know, maybe a nice lady." I gave him a half smile even though he was still focused on his monitor and not me.

"No way." Hans shook his head violently.

"Why no way?"

"That sort of thing is for geeks and retards."

"What is? The Internet?"

"Yeah, that whole online dating thing. Yuck."

"How do you know if you've never tried it?" I eyed the purple suspenders Hans was wearing over his dirty T-shirt and wondered about what kind of person Hans would consider a "geek".

"No way," he reiterated.

"How else you gonna find yourself a lady?"

"What's that supposed to mean?" he asked, and finally turned his head to look at me.

An electronic ping began chiming from the computer. It was a unit alarm. I rolled up to the keyboard, reading off the number to Hans. "Whose unit is that?"

"I can find a lady without the benefit of some computer, thank you very much."

"Hans, whose unit is F-29?"

"I dunno."

Hans refused to budge toward the computer that displayed the alarm information. I rolled my chair toward it clicked through a few menus. The alarm was on Richard Cutter's unit.

"You're not going to be mad at me all day now, are you?" I was trying hard not to sound as if I were making fun of him.

"I'm fine. You want me to check that alarm out?"

"No, I'll get it." I hit the enter key and the pinging stopped. Grabbing the walkie talkie, I left the office, the bright sun slamming me in the face as I stepped outside.

I rounded the corner of the building where Cutter's unit was located. A new Chevy Suburban was parked in front of it. I could see a dark-complexioned man wearing sunglasses, sitting in the passenger seat, his attention focused on me as I walked past.

Cutter was in the unit. The car he was storing was parked facing out, and he was at the back of the unit closing the trunk. When he saw me standing at the entrance he froze momentarily, his hand still on the trunk lid.

"Hey, what's up?" His face contorted into a grin.

"Did you not punch in your code when you drove in?"

"Mmm...maybe I didn't. I don't know. Why?"

"The alarm went off on this unit. You have to punch in your code each time to prevent that."

"Oh, sorry buddy. I think I just followed some car in."

"That's alright. You'll know for next time."

He didn't take his eyes off me as he came around the side of the Chevelle, his hands in the pockets of his dark denim jeans. As before, he was busy chomping open-mouthed on a piece of gum. He stood in front of me, shoulders relaxed, chest out. "You guys are pretty diligent about the security system around here, aren't ya?"

"We try." I took a step backwards away from him. He was a little too close and it was making me uncomfortable.

Hearing a door slam I turned to see the guy who was sitting in the passenger seat of the Suburban make his way toward us. He looked from me to Cutter and stopped at the back of the truck, leaning against it. "Everything okay?"

"It's cool. This guy's the manager." Cutter pulled down the door to the storage unit and replaced the combination lock on the latch.

"Oh." The Hispanic man nodded toward me, unsmiling.

I unclipped the walkie talkie from my belt and pressed the button on the side. "Hey, Hans? Unit F-29 checks out. Over."

There was a brief crackle of static and then I heard Hans drawl a response. "Dick Cutter forget to punch in his code?"

I started walking away, turning around to make sure Cutter and the other guy were out of earshot. They still stood at the front of the Chevy, staring at me.

"Yeah, that's what happened. Over," I said.

"Jeez. What's with people?" Hans complained. "Idiots. Like we have nothing better to do than run around all day, babysitting."

"Hans?"

"What?"

"Shut up. Okay?"

The radio remained silent until I returned to the office.

"What's up with you?" I asked Hans as soon as I stepped inside.

Hans knitted his eyebrows, making his narrow-set eyes comically chimp-like. Then he shrugged.

"First of all, how many times do I have to explain to you that we have to use the proper protocol on the radios?" I asked.

He scratched his nose and looked away. The phone rang but he made no move toward it.

"Second of all, you don't sit there and say 'idiots' when you know damn well that the customer might still be right there, listening." I shook my head and picked up the phone.

"They're still idiots," he mumbled. He shuffled around some papers and scooted his chair closer to the desk until the edge of it pressed into his belly.

"Coastal Storage, may I help you?"

"David? This is Alicia."

I froze for a minute, thinking *Alicia who,* still in work mode. When it registered a second later, I replied, "Oh hi, Alicia. What's up?"

"Dana invited me over on Sunday."

I waited through her pause, not knowing what to say.

"I just wanted to talk to you first, to make sure everything is okay," she continued.

"Everything is okay. What do you mean?"

"I mean between us and stuff."

"It's fine. Don't worry about it." I hoped my tone wasn't too flippant. I didn't want her to think that I was planning a continuation of the kiss from the other night.

"You sure? Dana was in a weird mood today when I called her. She wouldn't tell me why."

"It has nothing to do with you, trust me."

"Okay." She let out a long sigh. "How about you? How are you?"

Shitty. Like you really care. "Fine. Just a little busy. We'll talk on Sunday, okay?" I noticed that I was forcing my voice into a friendlier tone than I was in the mood for. Was I afraid of pissing her off again? Probably. I still felt a little queasy with guilt when I thought about the way I had squeezed her braless breasts through her shirt.

"Yes. I can't wait." She murmured before hanging up.

Oh no.

Looking out the window, I saw Cutter's Suburban exiting the facility.

"You know, there's something not right with that guy," I said.

"Who?" Hans said. He was still mad at me, I could tell.

"Cutter. I see him driving that Chevelle in and out of that unit all the time, and then today I saw him putting something in the trunk."

"Like what?" Hans scratched his nose.

"I don't know. It's just all really suspicious. The guy who was with him today looked like he was ready to pull a gun on me," I said. "You gotta wonder why he's paying close to two hundred bucks a month to store a car that's worth maybe three grand, at the most. Maybe he's keeping it for sentimental reasons—has a lot of money, but doesn't have room for it where he lives."

"You think?"

"Fuck, I dunno." I rubbed my temples. "I've got bigger problems to worry about right now."

13

∾

Drink Like a Real Man

As the weekend approached, I anticipated it with the enthusiasm of a languid coastal fog. I was going through the motions at work, not really caring about how many units we rented out or how our profits compared to last year. The only finances I cared about were my own.

Dana spent a lot of time at her parents' house or in front of the television, watching a lot of programs with a live audience. She made a good effort at ignoring me ever since our standoff about having a baby. She spoke to me as little as possible and at night she rolled tightly into a ball on her side of the bed without so much as a kiss. It was fine by me, since I still didn't know how we would go about returning to our normal sex life in the middle of a war on conception.

At work, Hans was wearing on my nerves. He would engage customers in long-winded conversations, which slowed what should have been a simple fifteen-minute transaction to an hour-long study in pointless banter, leaving me to answer phones and perform most of the data entry and daily record-keeping functions. I had moments in the past where I would wonder if I should find new office help. And lately I was re-visiting the idea. But I knew my desire for a perfect employee was going to forever go unfulfilled. I couldn't offer any prospect more than a dollar over minimum wage, so I couldn't expect to find anyone too on the ball—

certainly not much more than Hans was. At least he was honest. I didn't have to worry about leaving him alone with the cash register. He showed up for work and on time. Most days he arrived ten or fifteen minutes before the office opened at nine o'clock, rarin' to go—twitching and jumpy from too much coffee, donuts, and nicotine.

So I put up with the boring office chat and the lack of professionalism. I put up with his prying questions about Dana and our marriage. *How is she doing?* he would ask. *Maybe she should sign up with one of those employment agencies,* he would offer. *You should buy her some flowers,* he would suggest. *A woman like that,* he once blurted, blushing, *certainly deserves to be pampered and shown the finer things in life.*

I would sit there, silently staring at him, wondering if he was aware that he was wearing the same shirt two days in a row.

I had emailed a couple of notes to Ellen that remained unsurprisingly unanswered. I didn't forget her telling me that her computer wouldn't be up and running until the weekend. I wrote anyway and gazed at least a dozen times at the handful of photos of herself she had emailed to me over the last several weeks. I couldn't get over how beautiful she was. I loved the way her black hair contrasted with her creamy white skin. I imagined running my fingers along her sculptured jawline and back through the hair along the nape of her neck.

It all seemed so disconnected—the photos, the voice, and the eloquently written letters. It was at once too much and yet never quite enough.

***

Dana and I stood in the center of the beer and wine aisle at the Ralphs Supermarket, contemplating what we wanted to drink that night at the barbeque we were throwing. Besides Alicia, we had invited Tom, who was going to come with his live-in girlfriend Lynda, and bring a case of beer and a half dozen steaks. We had a couple of pounds of chicken marinating in the refrigerator, and Dana had brought home a German chocolate cake her mother had made.

I was in a good mood that day, partly because Dana had decided to end her five-day grudge against me, and partly because I had gotten a good amount of writing done on my book the night before. After a dry spell that had lasted at least a couple of months, I sat down and cranked out three hours of solid writing. The main character in my story, a third-generation farmer in the Midwest, was facing the threat of foreclosure after a record heatwave wiped out most of his soybean crop. I had gotten stuck at that juncture and had trouble bringing my story out of the rut of predictability. Last night, however, I had devised a new leg to the plot—about a mysterious, out-of-town investor who made my protagonist an offer he couldn't refuse.

Dana picked up two six-packs of Corona and placed them in the cart while I estimated the total price of the few items stacked in there. We were down to our last fifty dollars that had to last until I got paid at the end of the month. I was grateful that Tom had offered to bring a lot of food and beer, even though I had made it clear that he didn't have to bring anything. I looked at the pint of expensive ice cream that I had thrown into the shopping cart on impulse and reached back in for it as Dana made her way back to the produce section for a couple of limes to garnish the Coronas. I wheeled back to the glass doors of the frozen food aisle and put the carton of Haagen Daaz back in, misplacing it among the Ben and Jerry Sorbets.

I tried to look at the bright side—at least I was going to be forced to eat a little better. No more bowls of ice cream while watching television. Instead of buying cases of soda, I started brewing quarts of iced tea. Until recently we had been very lazy about cooking, often eating sandwiches, frozen dinners, or fast food. There were no convenience foods in the cart today. Dana and I had planned out a few stews and soups that would last us the few days until Thanksgiving, and had purchased precisely what we needed to make it all.

"Think we have everything we need for tonight?" I rolled the cart toward one of the lit checkout signs.

"I think for fun we should buy a bag of those deep-fried pork skins," Dana said. "What do you think?"

I picked up a package of two pink, coconut sprinkled cake balls and tossed them at her. "I think for fun you should stuff both of these in your mouth at the same time."

"Oh yeah, I bet you'd like that. I bet you miss seeing me with my mouth full of creamy goo." She flung the package back at me.

"It hasn't been that long." I glanced back over my shoulder at her, smiling. "Has it?"

"Not long enough, apparently."

"Hey, if I didn't know any better, I'd say you're missin' something yourself."

"You wish."

Dana's final throw of the pink cake balls missed my head by an inch and hit the cashier square in the nose.

We laughed so hard on the way home I had to pull the car over twice to catch my breath.

***

We set out a Styrofoam cooler in the corner of the balcony filled with ice, sodas, and beers. The charcoal was emitting waves of heat from the grill and was almost ready for the citrus-soaked chicken that was filling up a large bowl next to the cooler. I sat in one of the plastic chairs we had cleaned of its glaze of outdoor grime, watching a piece of lime float around the foam in the cold bottle of beer I was nursing. Not having eaten since early that morning, I was quickly developing a buzz only halfway into the second beer. I propped my feet up on the railing and relaxed as the late afternoon sun warmed my legs.

I looked at my watch. "You think we have time for a quickie before anyone shows up?" I shouted loud enough so that Dana could hear me from the kitchen, where I heard the clinking of dishes.

"You getting drunk already?" she asked.

"Do I have to be drunk to want a blow job?" I said.

"No, but I may have to be drunk to want to give you one," Dana grumbled.

"Then you'd better start slamming down some booze now, woman." I leapt from my chair and tiptoed into the kitchen, watching as Dana reached up to put some plates away in the cabinet. Her jeans seemed unusually tight around her hips and the crotch seam rode high up her butt. She didn't seem to hear me as I stealthily came up behind her and put my hands around her torso and on her breasts. I felt her lean into me as her arms dropped down to her sides.

I instinctively put my lips on her neck through her hair. Her nipples hardened almost instantly between my fingers. I cupped the swell of her breasts, and my tongue found the soft skin of her earlobe. She began to slide out of my grasp as she squatted and turned. My tongue was still halfway out of my mouth as she stood facing me, her body pressed between me and the kitchen counter.

"I don't want to do this now," She whispered, pushing at my chest with her hands.

"Why?" My hands found their way back to her breasts. My eyes were closed and I could taste the saltiness of her tanned skin as I kissed her temples.

"David, stop. I'm not kidding."

There was a loud knock on the side door and Dana looked at me with an I-told-you-so expression. She went to answer, and I went to retrieve my half empty bottle of Corona off the porch, afterwards retreating to the couch with it.

Alicia's conspiratorial laughter echoed from the bottom of the stairwell. I reached into a large, plastic bowl of tortilla chips that were on the coffee table and sat back with a handful. At the top of the stairs Dana took a couple grocery bags from her and disappeared into the kitchen.

"Beer's on the balcony in the cooler if you want some." I tried to appear nonchalant as Alicia made a beeline for the couch toward me.

"In a bit." She sat down close to me with one leg folded underneath her and her arm extended out over the cushions. As I shifted up to face her, I realized my erection from the encounter with Dana was still pressing hard into the seam of my khakis. I grasped the bottle that was perched on my knee, and with both hands rested it over my crotch in hopes of camouflaging the temporary problem.

"Looks like *you* need another one, though."

Alicia's hand wrapped around the neck of the almost empty Corona. I held on firmly.

"David, let go. I'll get you another one."

"It's fine, I'll get it myself."

"No big deal. C'mon, let go."

I let her take the empty bottle. She didn't get up. I stared straight ahead, willing her to go away for a little while. When she didn't budge, I braved a glance her way. Her eyes fluttered, shifting quickly from my pants to my eyes and back down again.

"Something wrong?"

Her tongue slid out of her mouth and curled around her upper lip as she raised her eyebrow at me. "I'll get you that beer."

"Good idea."

Great, I thought. Now she's going to think that sitting so close to me on the couch had given me a woody. I took a deep breath and felt the warmth of the alcohol trickle into my muscles. My mouth was already dry. I needed another drink, fast. I moved over to the stereo and put in a stack of CDs I had picked out earlier.

"I think the grill is ready, David. You want me to put the chicken on?" Alicia was still bent over the cooler when I looked up to answer. Her short skirt splayed out in the back, revealing the black fabric of her panties. She made no attempt to be modest. In fact, she bent down lower as I croaked out an answer.

Tom arrived with his girlfriend Lynda a little later, much to my relief. I finished my third Corona and took charge of the grill. The women gathered in the living room while Tom and I stood on the balcony watching the flames lick at the meat. The sun trickled in through the top of the surrounding eucalyptus trees and the breeze began to have a slightly cold, damp bite.

"What are you and Dana doing for Thanksgiving?" Tom asked.

"Going over to her parents' house."

Tom dragged the plastic chair closer to the railing and sat down. "What about your parents? Do they live in San Diego?"

"Both my parents are dead," I said.

"Sorry, man. So you don't have any family here in town? I know your brother Greg lives in Phoenix."

"A couple of aunts and a few cousins. Most of them live up in LA, but I don't know where exactly. My family wasn't very close knit when I was growing up."

"What does your brother do in Phoenix?"

"Last I heard he was a sales manager at a dealership and doing quite well. He's married. Wonderful wife, great kids." I poked and flipped the steaks. "He moved out to Arizona after our mom died. Quit his job, got in his car and drove east."

The twang of guitar music wafted from the stereo. Dana had put in some Chris Isaak.

"It's too bad you don't have any close family here. I know how much you love spending time with the in-laws." Tom smirked.

"Tell me about it." I nodded toward the living room and Dana. "I feel lately like they're all three ganging up against me. Dana wants to have a baby and there is just no way we can afford it right now. Especially since she wants to stay home and not work."

"Ouch. That's a tough spot."

"Her mother thinks I'm the world's biggest loser because I'm working a job that can't support a family."

"That might have been true in the sixties when your mother-in-law was raising her kids. But not in this day and age, pal. And certainly not in Southern California. Not unless you have some PhD in computer programming or something. Hell, I'm barely eking by. I've got child support and alimony along with the mortgage on the shack."

I thought about the house he referred to as a "shack." It was actually a nice three-bedroom house in a well-groomed neighborhood a few miles away. Tom had invited Dana and me over for dinner a few times in the past.

I stifled a yawn. I was either going to have to drink more or go lay down to nap. "So how do you do it, Tom? You got something going on that you can't tell me about?"

He opened his mouth to say something but paused. Before he spoke again, I noted the way his eyes squinted slightly, as if he was debating what to say next. "Those steaks ready yet? I'm starved."

"As ready as they're gonna be."

***

As the evening wore on and I continued drinking, things became increasingly murky. At one point I remember telling an old college story about an incident regarding a squirrel, a plunger, and an old hollow television. I must have completely botched the story because even though I ended up laughing hysterically, flat on my back on the floor with my head near a leg of the coffee table, everyone else was looking down at me, dumbfounded. I spent what seemed like the next half hour staring at the rough, unfinished underside of the oak tabletop. I contemplated going into the spare bedroom and getting online to try to find Ellen, but was still semi-rational enough to realize that I could barely walk a straight line, let alone type coherently.

I felt warm hands on my bare ankles and glanced sideways to see Alicia sitting cross-legged on the floor next to me.

"Get up, David. I'm gonna teach you how to drink like a real man."

She was well on her way to being completely blasted herself, as evidenced by her soupy eyes and slumped posture. She had a shot glass in one hand and a bottle of brandy in the other and was holding both too close to my face.

"What the fu—?"

"C'mon, get UP!" She reached over and tugged on my forearm until it felt like she was going to dislocate my shoulder. "It's not bedtime yet. The night is still young!"

The room bounced and jiggled around me as I got up to a sitting position. It felt like I had cotton in my head.

"Where's Dana?" I looked around the room, which had turned dim. "Who turned the lights off?"

Alicia filled the shot glass with brandy and then produced a lighter out of the pocket of her jeans. She flicked it a few times and when the flame flickered up she held it close to the glass.

"Whaddya you doin'?"

"You'll see." A languid blue flame appeared on the surface of the liquid, swirling and undulating. Without hesitation, she brought the glass up to her mouth and swung her head back, emptying its contents down her throat. She swallowed and licked a trail of wetness off the edge of her bottom lip. "Now you."

"No fuckin' way."

"C'mon, don't be a chickenshit." She put her hand behind my head and pulled me toward her as she rolled backwards. I pivoted forward on my knees and lost my balance, landing on her torso with my arms up around either side of her head. As my face rolled off one of her breasts, I started laughing uncontrollably.

When I finally composed myself enough, I moaned, "I can't drink anymore. Leave me alone."

"Lightweight."

We lay next to each other, looking up at the ceiling. I heard voices outside on the balcony. Dana was telling Tom and Lynda about the compromising Polaroids she found in Marilyn's office. From the sound of it, she was putting on a show and tell. Lynda was gasping and there were brief silences followed by grunts of disbelief.

Alicia rolled over and put her face between my shoulder and neck. Her lips grazed my ear as she whispered, "Do you know how gorgeous you are? Do you have any idea?"

I didn't answer. I lay still and closed my eyes, feeling the room turning a slow clockwise circle with me as the center axis. Her face remained in position against my neck, and I felt her breath come faster a few seconds before she began kissing me. Her wet lips worked their way up my jawline and to the corner of my mouth before I registered what was happening and sat bolt upright.

"What are you doing!? Are you insane?" I grabbed my head in both hands to keep it from snapping off and rolling down to the dining room. I felt my stomach tighten and fought back a wave of nausea. "Christ, Alicia. Dana's only around the corner." I wasn't sure if my words were coming out that well. My tongue felt swollen and limp.

"Then let's go outside for a little while." She wrapped her arms around my waist and kissed the back of my neck.

"No."

"Yes, c'mon."

I stood up and held on to the edge of the nearby wall unit for balance. Alicia was on her knees in front of me, her head inches away from my groin. She coiled a hand around my thigh and looked up at me with drunken eyes.

"Stop this right now, goddamn it. I don't want to do anything with you. Do you understand me or not?" I stepped out of her grasp. "Jesus! Get a grip, Alicia. I'm not interested in you."

I stumbled toward the bathroom, already feeling the bile coming up fast. I vomited over and over until I didn't feel sick anymore. My head rested on my arm as I straddled the toilet, trying hard not to think about how close I was to the urine spattered porcelain bowl. When I finally managed to move away from the toilet without feeling faint, everyone had gone, and Dana was crashed out in bed.

14

∽

Thanksgiving

The electronic buzz of the alarm clock felt like shards of glass in my brain. I felt around the nightstand for the top of the clock radio and pushed the snooze button. It was 7:30 am. I was slightly confused the first few seconds, unsure of what day it was. Normally I wouldn't have been jolted by the alarm. I was awake much earlier than most mornings, and even spent an hour or so tossing around on the soft mattress before I finally clicked the alarm off and headed for the shower.

I stretched out and sank my face back into the pillow. My lower back felt a little sore. It was then that I remembered I had spent most of the previous day ruining it, slouched in the deep cushions of the couch in Dana's parents' living room, watching football and eating nonstop. It was the day after Thanksgiving, and I had set the alarm by mistake the night before. The office was closed that day and I didn't have to work.

We didn't have any plans so there was no reason for which I had to get out of bed so early. Already awake, however, I lay around listening to the drone of the interstate through the open windows and decided I wasn't going to doze back off. I got dressed and went into the kitchen to make coffee. Dana was still asleep and I didn't expect she would be stirring much before ten o'clock anyway. I opened the kitchen window and breathed in the fresh, salt-tinged air as I waited for the coffee to fill up the pot.

We had mounted a black plastic bin on the wall next to the refrigerator to hold all our receipts and bills. It was stuffed with old slips of paper, various business cards and coupons, and a half dozen unopened envelopes. I took the envelopes out and began separating the remittance slips from the advertising, laying them out on the counter one by one.

Two credit card payments were due on December fifteenth. Each had a minimum payment due of two hundred dollars. The car payment was due December first. That was $265. A third credit card had a minimum payment of $110 due on December tenth. The phone bill came to seventy-five dollars and twelve cents. Cable was around twenty-five dollars.

I would be getting my $650 paycheck in a few days. That had to last until the fifteenth and would cover at least the car payment and one of the credit cards, leaving us just enough for groceries and gas. The other two credit card payments would have to wait a couple of weeks until after my last paycheck in December. That didn't leave much for Christmas spending money, but at that point I didn't care. I wasn't much in the holiday mood anyway.

I scanned the details of the month's transactions on one of the credit card bills. Nothing but the payment that was made last month. The next two, however, showed a couple of charges that Dana had made since last month. The first charge was for sixty-seven dollars at the Chart House Restaurant. The other one was for over a hundred dollars at a department store. Because our balance was so high, our finance charges combined with the purchases had cancelled out last month's payment.

I resisted the urge to crush the invoices in my hand and barge into the bedroom to bounce them off Dana's forehead to wake her up. After a few gulps of hot coffee, I deployed a better strategy instead. I scanned the bills for a phone number and congratulated myself for what I was about to do next.

"Yes, hi. I would like to cancel my charge account, please." My hands were shaking with the sudden influx of adrenalin. What the hell was wrong with her? Did she not care that we were going to go down in flames? She had to fan the fire on her way down? I listened to the soft clicks of fingers on a computer keyboard as the credit card rep processed my request. "Also, could you tell me if there is a way I could negotiate a payment smaller than the minimum for a few months?"

"That could be arranged, sir. Please tell me what sort of payment you would like to make and how many months you need this grace period."

"Drop it down to a hundred dollars for say the next six months?"

After I repeated the process with the other two credit card companies, I dug around in the junk drawer for a pair of scissors. I found Dana's purse on top of the speaker in the living room and retracted the three cards out of her wallet. After cutting the cards in half and dumping them in the trash, I put on my sneakers and left the apartment to go on a long run. I was still seething and needed to work the tension out of my head as well as the knots out of my back.

As I jogged through the quiet residential streets between the self-storage and the beach I thought about the previous day. Dana's sister Kelley had flown into town with her husband and baby to spend the holiday with my in-laws. Kelley's husband, Scott, a vice president at a large investment firm in St. Louis, never seemed to have any problem finding a common topic of discussion with Frank, who used to head a large bank before he retired. They spent most of the day talking about the stock market and IPOs and investment strategies. At first, Scott had been polite and tried to include me in the conversation, but after a while it occurred to him that I was more interested in watching the game on tv than pondering the market fluctuations of the technology index. So he and Frank moved their discussion to the patio.

I spent a little time playing with Kelley's baby, who was definitely very cute, as he attempted to crawl around the living room with his pudgy limbs. I caught Dana beaming at me as I handed my nephew a rattle, darting a look back that implied, "Don't get any ideas."

I had never been comfortable spending time with Dana's family. For the most part they did their best to be polite and friendly, but something never quite clicked between us. I know that Frank and Susan expected a lot more from a son-in-law. They would have preferred that I had been an Ivy League graduate, an up-and-coming businessman who pulled in a starting salary of at least six figures. When Dana and I were first married, my in-laws were slightly hostile towards me. But since then they had seemed to grudgingly accept me. "Grudgingly" was the key word.

Dana wasn't used to financial responsibility. Her parents had paid for her college tuition and all her expenses, including rent, when she attended San Diego University for a year. When she dropped out, she moved back home to her parents' house in Missouri and attended a few classes at junior college. That lasted a couple years before she decided she wanted to live in San Diego after all, college or no college. That's when she landed the job at the company where I worked and where we had met. She had been living with a couple of roommates for a short time before we got married and moved in together.

In essence, it was hard for me to blame Dana for her sloppy spending habits and her lack of focus about her career. Her parents always paid for everything. Her mother stayed at home and took care of the house and children while her dad put in long hours at work. That was what she grew up with. That was what her friends grew up with. That's what she was used to.

If I expected her to change, I was going to have a long fight ahead of me. My choices were limited, however—either she and I would work this out or we would have to split up. I was tired of struggling with her.

I quickened my step and closed the five-mile loop I had started, seeing the beige stucco of the office/apartment half a block away. It was almost 9:30. If Dana was still asleep, she wouldn't be for long.

***

"Get up. We need to talk." I nudged Dana's legs on my way to the shower. She stirred a little but remained in bed as I began running the water and stripped off my sweaty clothes.

"Why? What's up?" Her voice was groggy and hoarse. I didn't answer her. I stepped into the stream of hot water and began soaping up a washcloth. As I lathered my face and neck, I heard her voice echo in the bathroom. "What's going on? You sound pissed." She leaned over the sink and looked in the mirror, wiping at the inner corners of her eye.

I squeezed a glob of shampoo onto my palm. "I looked at the bills that came in the mail this week. We've got a problem, Dana. We can't pay them."

She filled up the red plastic cup with water and stuck her toothbrush into her mouth.

"My paycheck is $650 dollars. The bills come to over seven hundred. That would leave us nothing for food or gas or whatever else. So I had to do a few things."

"Like what?" she spit into the sink.

"I cancelled the credit cards."

"You cancelled the cards? What for?" She turned around and leaned her hip against the sink.

"Because we're trying to pay them off and you keep using them. I saw a charge on there for the Chart House. What's that about?"

"I took my parents out to dinner."

"We can't afford that sort of thing, Dana."

"Whatever." She resumed brushing her teeth.

"How do you think we're going to get through if you're not working? Especially if you keep making these charges? If we don't make at least the minimum payment on these credit cards, our balance is going to be bigger every month, not smaller. They're raping us with finance charges." I maneuvered my head under the showerhead and rinsed the last of the shampoo out of my hair. "Dana? Do you hear me?"

"I heard you." She moved toward the toilet and pushed on the handle. "I heard you loud and clear." The flushing toilet shifted the water pressure and sent streams of scalding water down my back.

***

Weekends can be the doldrums when you don't have the money to go out to eat or to see a movie or even fill up the gas tank in the car and go for a long drive. They can be even worse when there's an underlying tension between you and the person you live with. Dana opted to hang out with Kelley and Scott before their flight back out and I opted to spend my weekend reading, writing, and catching up on some emails. She avoided any discussion about our financial status and I pretty much concluded that my point was made and that she just needed some time to let it sink in.

Before Thanksgiving, Ellen had written that she and Jack decided to go away for an extended weekend to visit his brother in Chicago. The idea that I wouldn't have an opportunity to chat with her or even get a note for at least four or five days made me that much more forlorn. I willed the weekend to end. I almost wished that I could simply fall asleep until Monday.

I called my brother Greg over the weekend and left a message on his answering machine. I had no idea where they were or what they were doing, but he never returned my call. Perhaps they had left town, too.

I was not looking forward to Christmas.

15

Real Jobs

I was showing a new tenant his unit Wednesday afternoon when I spotted Dana walking towards me, dressed in a powder blue suit. Her hair was neatly pinned in swirling strands on the top of her head. I felt hopeful that she had some good news about a job because she had a relaxed grin on her face.

"Hi honey. You look nice. I didn't see you earlier when you left." I leaned down to kiss her temple.

"I got a job," she stated matter-of-factly as she backed away from me.

I wasn't sure how to proceed. She seemed to challenge me with her expression.

"You did? Oh good. Tell me about it."

"I went to one of those employment agencies. They found me a position where I would be taking over after this woman goes on her extended maternity leave."

"What kind of job is it?"

"Admin assistant. Seems tame, but it's close by and the hours are good."

"So when do you start?

"When the woman goes into labor. Probably not for another couple of months."

"So it's a temporary job that doesn't start for two months?" I wondered for a second if this was Dana's way of telling me to get screwed.

"That's right. Maybe you'll find a better paying job in the next six months or so and it won't matter anyway."

That was the first time Dana had brought up the notion of me finding a new job. The thought had also occurred to me in the last couple of weeks, although another problem arose if I landed a new job that wasn't on-site property management. We would have to move out of our office apartment immediately and find a regular place to live. This meant we would have to have enough money for first and last month's rent and a security deposit. As of that day, we had maybe a couple hundred dollars to our name and all our credit cards had been cancelled.

"We'll figure something out." As I watched her walk away I marveled at her ability to so quickly land exactly the sort of job she wanted: one that both appeased and irritated me at the same time.

I wanted to complete my weekly inspection of all the hallways for burned out lightbulbs, trash, or vandalism. I entered the blue metal doors of F Building with a clipboard to make notes for the part-time maintenance man. The hallways were stuffy, due to the lack of regular ventilation. My footsteps echoed in the labyrinth of particle board flooring, thin drywall and metal roll-up doors. I spotted a few old spiderwebs hanging in wispy strands in the corners and scribbled a note on the clipboard.

I bounded up the stairs to the second level, noticing that my stamina seemed to have improved recently. Probably because I had been running more than usual, and for longer distances. My breath was regular and steady as I finished the climb in one long stride. I rounded the corner and began to make note of a flickering lightbulb when I heard a rustling sound, followed by soft humming. I was approaching the open cavern of Mrs. Vaughn's unit, suddenly aware that I had slowed my gait and rounded out my stride so my approach would be quieter.

She was humming a familiar tune. Was it a Tom Jones song? I couldn't quite place it. From my vantage point ten feet away, I saw the corner edge of a small cherry wood end table, a lamp, and the curled-up edge of a dark-colored carpet on the floor of the unit. I walked closer, at first confused because I didn't see Mrs. Vaughn. As I stopped in front of the open door, I saw her facing away from me in the shadowy corner of the unit in front of a stack of boxes, naked except for a bra, which she was trying to hook together.

I jerked back a few inches, looking back in the direction from which I had just come. Besides piles of books and boxes in the unit, there was also a portable closet, now unzipped. A navy blue dress hung facing forward as if on display. Some clothes lay in a small pile behind her. She was busy looking through the contents of a medium-sized cardboard box as I tried to stealthily turn around.

The humming stopped abruptly.

"Excuse me! May I help you, sir?" Alarmed, she now had the blue dress, still on the hanger, wrapped tightly around her bosom with her arms. It was bunched up and hanging slightly below her upper thighs.

"I'm sorry, I was just going through the building—I mean—I was making my rounds."

"May I have my privacy please?" Mrs. Vaughn had stepped forward into the light that beamed in from the sixty-watt bulb in the hallway, her forehead creased in deep lines and her lips carved into a tight, round pucker.

I cleared my throat and walked backwards a few steps. I wanted to ask her what she was doing getting dressed in her unit, but after I caught a glimpse of the gray-white folds of her naked waistline, I turned around and headed back down the stairs silently.

I finished the walk through of the rest of the facility an hour later and retreated back into the office, where Hans was engrossed in the newspaper and picking at a blemish on the side of his face with his index finger. Even though it was well past the time I would be going upstairs to make myself a sandwich, I realized I wasn't the least bit hungry.

"This office is a pig sty," I declared.

"Huh?" Hans looked up from an article he was reading in the entertainment section and relocated the mining project to his nose.

"I said, this place is a pig sty. Let's get out the Windex and paper towels and clean the desks and stuff. The floor needs a good sweep and mop, too."

He looked around the office slowly, his eyes not seeming to register anything. "Oh, okay." He went back to the newspaper.

"Hans?" I raised my eyebrows at him.

"Oh. You mean now?"

I got the cleaning supplies out of the storage closet and started by sifting through the day's stack of mail. I separated the payments and bills from the junk mail, flinging the unread advertising into the trash can that I pulled out from under the desk. I scanned a small postcard and as I positioned to chuck it, something caught my eye.

Earn up to an extra $1000 a month delivering newspapers in your neighborhood. Work your current job while earning extra cash. Routes are available in your area.

I put the postcard by the phone. Earn extra money while working your current job. I could do this! I could do it at least until Dana started her new job. I felt a little better as I resumed spraying and wiping the sticky film off the desks and counters. I felt my mind let loose its tight grip of worry about our money problems.

"You'll never believe who I saw naked earlier," I announced.

"Naked?" Hans stopped sweeping and straightened his shoulders out.

"Mrs. Vaughn."

"Are you kidding? What was Mrs. Vaughn doing naked?"

"The old bat was getting dressed in her unit. I accidentally barged in on that while I was inspecting F building."

"That must have been quite a sight," Hans snorted. "What'd she say?"

"Not much. I got out of there as fast as I could."

"What was she doing undressing in her unit?"

"It looks like she stores a lot of clothes in there. I don't know. Maybe she was going somewhere fancy and needed her fancy dress out of storage."

"That woman's really wacky. Just the other day, she came in here to ask if we ever go back behind C Building."

"What did she want with the area behind C Building?"

"That's what I asked her, and she said something like, 'It gets a good southern sun. Would it be okay if I plant some flowers back there?'" Hans tried unsuccessfully to imitate Mrs. Vaughn's voice. It made him sound like a sissy.

"Why would she want to plant flowers on our property?"

"I asked her, and she said that she lives in a place without a yard and doesn't get to do any gardening."

"Yeah, but that's stupid. Behind C Building? Who the hell would see the flowers, besides the occasional possum or maybe one of the migrant workers that sometimes spends the night in the eucalyptus grove?"

Hans shrugged his shoulders and resumed his slow, deliberate sweeping.

"I hope you told her to stay out from there," I said. "That's all we need is loony Mrs. Vaughn taking a dive into the ravine behind C Building."

***

When I called the newspaper later that day to ask about the part-time paper delivery job, they faxed me an application and a list of routes. I could choose the size of my route according to the hours I could put in every day. After asking some questions and making my own calculations, I figured out that I could probably bring in five hundred dollars a month by delivering 150 papers a day. The woman on the phone said it would probably take me around three to four hours to deliver that many papers by myself on foot. It might take me longer the first few days before I got a system worked out, though.

The routes they had available were all within a few miles of the self-storage. I would have to drive to a pickup point first, where papers were distributed to the couriers out of a large truck. After that, I would have to roll each paper with a rubber band before depositing it on driveways.

On rainy days I had to slip the paper into a plastic bag as well. The paper would provide the supplies.

I could begin the route within a week. I faxed back my application, and after a short telephone interview I received a carrier number, start date, and a map with a list of addresses.

Since I had to be at work in the self-storage office when it opened at nine a.m., I figured I would have to hustle out the door by three a.m. my first day, just in case it took a lot longer than I expected to deliver all the papers. I looked at the map they faxed me and wondered if it would help if I jogged the route a few times before my start date.

The idea that Dana might even offer to help make the deliveries crossed my mind for a split second. If this were the case, I could take on even more papers and make twice the money. But when I came up to the apartment after work and saw her burrowed into the couch, the flicker of the *Jerry Springer* show illuminating the dark living room, I dismissed the idea of even telling her that I had gotten a second job. She was such a sound sleeper; I would bet that she wouldn't even know I had been gone half the night, working. I watched her stare unwaveringly at the television even though I was standing not two feet away. Even if she did know, she probably wouldn't care.

She didn't seem to care much about anything these days.

***

Ellen,

Tomorrow I start a second job delivering newspapers. I am going to be doing this everyday before work and on weekends. Dana got a job finally, but the job doesn't start until the woman she's replacing goes into labor. I figured that I could at least bring in another five hundred a month until then to help us from going further into debt. I'm not really thrilled about the prospect of having to get up in the middle of the night every day, but I can swing it for a month or two.

I am done fighting with Dana. I swear to God, I am so tired of her moods and her stubborn attitude and her unrealistic view of life.

She still thinks that we should start a family fairly soon. This has caused a rift in the bedroom. She's harboring resentment towards me for wanting to hold off having a baby just a little while longer. Just another year, I tell her. Meanwhile, I am still going to use birth control. We were in the bedroom as this was being discussed. She rolls over and sighs. "Forget it, then. I'm not in the fucking mood anymore." Literally.

I have decided that after she starts working again I am going to make a tremendous effort to get out of this property management gig and return to a writing job. We need to save up enough money to move to an apartment first, though, and so I need to take this paper route so that we aren't spending the next year trying to pull ourselves out of a debt that only took three months to incur.

I need to make a lot more money and I don't forsee that being a possibility here at the self-storage. Raises are few and far between, and there is no other position for me to move up into—I am already the manager here. I can't be the owner. I am hoping perhaps I can find another corporate writing job or even land a few columns in some local papers or e-zines. I am going to start inquiring now about getting a column. If I get one, I can write it on my days off. That's not a problem.

There is no challenge left here at the self storage. This job is sucking the creativity out of me. My only source of creative inspiration these days seems to be you. Having you in my life seems to spark a glimmer of hope and motivation. I am noticing things around me that I never noticed before. I am paying attention to things that I never paid attention to before. I don't know why this is, exactly. Maybe it's because I want so desperately to show you my world. I want so desperately for you to know all about me.

I want so desperately for you to be in my life, even in this small way.

***

A half dozen cars and pickups were parked around the newspaper truck as I pulled up in my Saab. I cringed at the rumble my car made as I accelerated up to where I would load up with newspapers. Several people turned around as my broken muffler spit and popped.

I pulled in next to an old Ford pickup. A middle-aged man was standing in the bed of the truck, arranging a dozen stacks of bundled papers while another man threw in a few more from the semi. I leaned over to unlock the passenger side door, then got out of the car, holding my paperwork like a permission slip.

"Your first day?" The man unloading the semi-truck stretched out his hand to take my papers. After a quick scan, he handed the stack back to me and produced a pen from the back pocket of his faded Levis, making a notation on a clipboard that hung nearby.

"Yeah, first day," I mumbled as I watched a moth have a spasm in front of the lit headlights of the Ford pickup.

He started handing me the heavy bundles and I rushed back and forth from the open passenger side door of my car to the truck. I filled up the backseat first, then slid the last two stacks in the front.

"Rubber bands and plastic bags are over there," he pointed to a cardboard box to the left of the truck. "You got anything to cut the cord with?"

I felt my brain struggle through the sluggishness of being awake in the middle of the night, pondering if I had anything sharp in the car. I must have looked confused because he asked me again, slower this time.

"The cord that bundles the papers. You have anything to cut it with?"

"Shit, no."

"No problem," he disappeared into the back of the truck and returned with a small plastic utility knife. "I'll let you borrow this for today."

"Thanks." I put the knife in my pocket and drove out of the lot. It was 3:2 a.m. I was making good time so far.

I made a few turns until I was on San Miguel Way, the starting point that I had planned out for my route. I parked in front of a small house with big red clay pots on the porch steps. There were no garages in this neighborhood, so I had to throw the papers near the front door somewhere, according to the newspaper's rules. I cut the cord on three bundles and began to roll the papers, sticking them into the large canvas bag I had brought to carry them.

I worked quickly by the dim yellow glow of the dome light, feeling a little agitated. I was able to fit about twenty-five papers into my sack, which meant that I would have to walk back to my car six times to get more. I would have to get a larger bag or maybe a second one so that I wouldn't waste so much time walking back and forth after today.

Because it was still dark, it was hard to aim the papers with any degree of accuracy at the shadowy facades of the houses. It was cool and quiet, the air pungent with the fishy smell of the ocean. A cat scurried out from behind a shrub and darted under a parked car, his eyes gleaming white as he watched me walk by. This wasn't so bad, I told myself as I took a deep breath and flung the fifth paper at a dark porch. I was starting to feel a little more alert now, the exercise of the walk warming my legs.

I congratulated myself on the fact that I was able to read the addresses I'd transcribed in large block letters onto some notebook paper. I tried to remember something about each house on my list, so that I wouldn't have to rely on the notes for more than a few days. Lace curtains. Bird bath in the front yard. A juniper tree in the shape of a claw. A nice flower garden.

I emptied my bag and looked at my watch. I rotated my wrist around the light of the streetlamps until I was able to see the digital display. 4:19. Not bad. At this rate I could get done around eight a.m., hurry home for a quick shower and maybe even have time for a bowl of cereal before work. I jogged back to the car and stuffed the bag full again.

When I was in college, I had a series of about a half dozen part time jobs. I made pizza deliveries, I bussed tables at the commons in school, I cashiered during the start and end of the school semester at the college bookstore. But by far my favorite of the short-term, low-paying stints was going door to door stuffing flyers into people's front doors. A real estate firm had hired me, and every week would give me hundreds of magnetic calendars, flyers, postcards, and other promotional materials to distribute. My hours were flexible, and I liked the freedom of working outdoors after being stuck inside stuffy classrooms all day. I didn't have to work when the weather was bad, and no one sat around looking over my shoulder. It was the ideal job for a college kid needing to make a few bucks for books, gas, and living expenses.

My flyer route was near the school in an upper-middle-class area. I would admire the meticulously landscaped yards and the sprawling houses and occasionally even allowed myself to imagine being a wealthy novelist living in one of the villas on my route. I imagined my office, which would be in the upstairs loft; a large open space with vaulted ceilings and lots of windows. I would have a custom-made desk with the fastest, most impressive computer. The walls opposite the large windows would be lined with paintings, preferably all of nudes.

I snickered as I recalled my fantasy and threw a newspaper toward a white stucco house with bars on the front windows. Those were the days. I had some lofty ideas about what I wanted to do and who I wanted to be. Whatever job I was doing during college, it was always my "shit" job until I got a "real" job.

So what was I doing now? Was this a "shit" job, too? Where was my "real" job? I never felt like the property management job was my ultimate job. I was almost thirty years old. When was I going to feel like I was finally doing what I was meant to do?

By the time I finished dropping off the last newspaper it was 7:40 a.m. I congratulated myself on my timing and drove home, feeling my stomach churning with hunger and my head again yearning for sleep.

16

Spare Some Change?

David,

A day is such a short little hiccup these days. It seems that it was only a few minutes ago that I was sitting here in the same exact spot bringing a warm cup of coffee to my lips and reading your letter.

Where does the time go? That's such a sad cliché, isn't it?

We do the things we have to do every day from the moment our eyes squint through the new light of early morning to the moment our bodies retreat back to the warm folds of blankets and pillows at night. We do what we have to do; we get through the moment, we get through the hour, we get through the day. Before we know it, a month has gone by, a season, a year. We feel like we are never caught up with everything that we have to do and yet we are shocked to discover that we have let half our lives pass in this state of anesthetized drudgery.

It's so easy to let things get away from you if you aren't paying attention at every turn. Before you know it, you've put back the ten pounds it took you months to lose. You let a mathematical error in your checkbook snowball and everything is bouncing. You can't believe you've been married seven years to a man you hardly know anymore. You've put yourself two jobs away from what you really want to do.

Is that what happened to you, my dear? Has the momentum of everyday details blinded you to the big picture?

Ellen,

I don't know. What is the big picture? Are we driving ourselves crazy trying to live up to some ideal future we've envisioned for ourselves?

What if there is no ideal future? What if, in the words of Jack Nicholson—this is as good as it gets?

P.S. Ten pounds? You're not getting fat on me, are you?

David,

Stop that right now. "This is as good as it gets?" C'mon. I think I might have heard that mantra blurted by a transient from under the eighth Street bridge this morning on my way to work.

Don't tell me you're going to lay down and let life wash over you.

P.S. I don't think I'm getting fat on you. It's hard to tell. You'll just have to come over here and feel for yourself.

Ellen,

This is ridiculous. I want so badly to hear your voice and talk to you but I haven't had a private or free moment in days. Are you going to be home alone tonight? Screw it. I might just sneak off to a payphone.

P.S. "You'll have to come over here and feel for yourself." Is that an official invitation?

The change in my pocket equaled about four dollars, roughly. Earlier that day I had busted into a coin jar that was collecting dust on a bookshelf in my office and picked out the dimes and quarters. I wasn't sure how much time four dollars would get me on a phone call to Connecticut, but I didn't care. I just needed to hear her voice, if only for a minute.

"I'm going to go pick up some milk."

"You are? Wait, I'll come with you." Dana got up off the couch where she had been watching a sitcom rerun and shuffled over to the top of the stairs where I was standing.

"I'm just going to be five minutes. I'm going down to the seven eleven."

"I don't care. I need to get out of the house. I've been sitting here all day."

"Alright, whatever." How was I going to sneak my phone call if she was coming along? My mind went through a list of possibilities, none of which made any sense.

"I'll drive," she said. "But let's go to Ralphs instead of the seven eleven. I need to get a few other things."

When we were in the car I was surprised at Dana's unkempt appearance and wondered if she had showered that day. Her hair was greasy and pulled back in a short, stringy ponytail. She wasn't wearing any makeup or jewelry. On the way out the door she had slipped on her summer flip flops. She was always very conscientious about her appearance, even when she was just relaxing around the apartment. How many days had she been like this?

Since my paper route job, my free time after work in the evenings had been cut drastically short. I ate dinner, watched a little tv, occasionally did some writing and hit the sack about nine o'clock. Deeply absorbed in my own exhausting schedule, I hadn't been paying much attention to her whereabouts or activities.

I felt a pang of guilt about my original plan to sneak off to call Ellen. I put my hand on the nape of Dana's neck, rubbing it.

"I know things seem a little grim right now, sweetie. It'll get better, I promise."

"What are you talking about?" she asked.

"You know. You seem a little depressed."

She kept her eyes on the road and both hands on the steering wheel. A strand of her hair freed itself from the rubber band and rested against her ear. "I'm not depressed. What makes you think I'm depressed?" Her voice pitched higher with every word. "Because my life is a big disaster area right now? Because I don't want to end up being an old crusty secretary when I'm fifty, childless and bitter?"

I shook my head, "Childless, probably not. Crusty? I hope not. Bitter? Mmmm..." I bobbed my head up and down and laughed.

"Shut up."

I could tell she was trying hard not to smile.

"I don't understand why suddenly you want everything all at once. You have to just chill for a bit until we get over this hump," I said.

"Why are you in such a good mood all of a sudden?" She threw me a suspicious glance as she downshifted.

"Why? Why not? Do I have to be morose all the time?"

We pulled into the parking lot of the Ralphs and Dana found a spot near the entrance of the store.

"Then let me ask you something," she said.

"Shoot."

"Why have you been going to bed so early lately? Are you avoiding me?"

"No, I'm not."

"Then what's up with you? Plus, you seem to be up early too. When I woke up the last few nights you weren't in bed. I figured that you were either up really early or crashed out on the couch or something."

I had my hand on the door handle as I tried to think of a way to change the subject. I hadn't told Dana about my paper route job, and now I felt stupid.

"Well?" she asked.

"Can we talk about this later?"

"Later? Is there a reason you don't want to tell me now?"

She started getting out of the car and I pulled her back in.

"Fine, I'll tell you," I sighed. "I have a second job. I've been going to bed early because I wake up every day at three to go deliver newspapers."

Her expression didn't change. She looked at me like she was still waiting for an answer. When I didn't say anything else, she frowned. "Is that supposed to be a joke?"

"No. I'm serious."

She stared at a point just above my shoulder while she absorbed the information. "You started a fucking paper route, and you didn't tell me?"

I shrugged.

"What is THAT?"

I shrugged again, meeker this time.

"What is that, David? Huh? Since when did you start deciding you didn't have to talk to me?"

"Since when? Since you quit your job and put us in the hole."

"Oh! So now it's all my fault. I guess it doesn't matter that you've been swimming in circles the past few years working a job that you don't really like and that doesn't pay squat. I guess that doesn't count, does it? You can't figure out what it is you want but when I tell you what I want, I am being unreasonable."

"You *are* unreasonable."

Before she slammed the car door shut, she leaned down and looked me squarely in the eye. "Grow up, David."

I sat in the car until I saw her disappear inside the grocery store. The fact that Dana seemed uninterested that I had been working a job in the early morning hours didn't escape me. The conversation went almost exactly as I had predicted.

I contemplated my next move. I could just wait in the car until she got back, I could go inside the store to find her, or I could walk over to the payphone that was twenty yards away and call Ellen. I opened the car door and let some fresh air into my lungs.

After a few minutes I got out of the Honda and went looking for Dana. The last thing I needed was her walking out of the store and spotting me, then asking me who the hell I was calling from a payphone at night.

***

When I woke up, it felt as if I had been sleeping for hours. I felt the tail end of some troubled dream trail off into the dark corners of my memory as my eyes blinked open. I leaned over to the nightstand to look at the red glowing numbers on the clock radio. 10:15.

Ugh! I had only been asleep for an hour. My body felt clammy, and I struggled to untangle the top sheet from my legs. The television was droning in the living room. What had I been dreaming about? I had been driving somewhere. That's right. My brother was in the car with me at one point, then Dana. I was lost, the roads were unfamiliar, and I wasn't quite sure how to get to where I was going. I saw Ellen at the side of the road, but I couldn't stop the car to talk to her. The brake pedal hit the floor, unresponsive. That's when I woke up, I think, my foot pressing against the mattress.

I shifted my body around and fluffed up the sheet and covers with my arms and legs. Why was it suddenly so hot in the room? I got up and opened the window a little bit.

I resumed the sexual fantasy about Ellen that I had started before I dozed off an hour earlier. We were in a large hotel room with a view of the beach. Ceiling fans made slow lazy circles above our heads as she swayed back and forth above me, riding me. Her breasts were as white as vanilla soft serve ice cream and just as pointy. I reached out to press my thumbs into her pink-red nipples as she squeezed my hips between her thighs, nearing orgasm.

My mind made a loop from her hard nipples to the way her hair stuck in sticky strands on her sweaty shoulders to the way her fingers dug into the flesh of my belly as she pressed her body lower onto my groin. I wanted to know what sounds she made when she closed her eyes and braced for an orgasm. Did she breathe in shallow spurts, alternating with soft moans, or did she shudder and hold her breath as she tensed her body to bring on her pleasure? I wanted to know.

We had spoken on the phone so many times. Usually while we were both at work, so we always had to be on alert. I loved the way her voice would soften and purr when she whispered something flirtatious. Once,

I told her how much I loved looking at one of the photos she had emailed me, how absolutely intense her eyes were.

"You have no idea how much I want you, David," she had replied, making me harden instantly.

I lay very still, willing my muscles to relax and get comfortable. Just as I began to feel the buzz of slumber take hold, the bedroom door flew open, jolting me back. I groaned as I looked at the clock again. 11:26. Dana flushed the toilet in the adjacent bathroom and then rolled into bed, making it bounce and jiggle.

I couldn't stay comfortable on my side, so I rolled over onto my belly. That felt good for about a minute before I felt the need to shift back onto my back. I felt my boxer shorts twist around my waist and bite into my skin. I yanked the fabric out of my crack and looked at the time again. 11:41. I knew that feeling irritated would only keep me awake, so I tried once again to focus on the sexual fantasy.

This time, she was sprawled out on the bed, exhausted from our long afternoon of lovemaking. The sheet draped softly over the small of her back, hiding the top half of her buttocks. She was sleeping, relaxed and beautiful, her arms outstretched over the pillows. I slid into bed beside her and nuzzled my face into her black hair. She stirred briefly and murmured something. I kissed the arc of her shoulder, then let my lips glide down her back until my face was pressed against the swell of her—

"Why is the window open? It's freezing in here!" Dana threw back the covers and walked across the room to shut the window I had opened earlier.

"No, leave it open. It's stuffy in here."

"It is not. It's freezing."

I stared up at the shadows on the ceiling for a while, alternately feeling too hot or too cold. In almost two hours I would have to get up. I contemplated taking some Nyquil that we had in the medicine cabinet to get drowsy, but I knew that I would have at least eight hours ahead of me until the effect wore off.

Would I ever meet Ellen? Setting aside the fact that I didn't have the money for a plane ticket anyway, I couldn't think of how I could fly to

Connecticut by myself without rousing a great deal of suspicion from Dana. Ellen never travelled for her job, but she was alone a lot. Maybe she could take a few days off and come out here? Would she do that?

My mind clamped on to this puzzle, and for the next two hours I tossed and turned, envisioning hotel rooms and airports and secret afternoons in the arms of a woman whom I had never really laid eyes on before.

Finally, at 2:45, I gave up any notion of sleep and started getting dressed for work.

***

Right around the middle of my route, my thoughts started getting ridiculous. I was going on a sort of auto pilot, unsure if I was even throwing papers at the right houses.

An old memory of a grainy driving school film filtered through my thoughts. A man was sitting behind the wheel of his Torino. It was dark outside, and he was driving alone. He was very tired. He kept trying to focus on the passing billboards to keep alert but wasn't having any luck. His eyelids began to droop, his posture got soft. Suddenly brilliant head-lights flared in his face and he was alert again, frightened that he'd barely averted a head-on collision.

The narrator's voice was clear in my memory. *Pull over*, he said. *Pull over in a safe place and get some sleep. Sometimes just a twenty-minute nap is enough to restore you for the rest of the drive.*

Pull over, I thought as I returned to the Saab to re-fill my bags. Just twenty minutes is all you need to restore. I looked at my watch. Since I had started so early today, it was only four thirty and I was already half done. I could spare a short nap, no problem. I got in the car and reclined the seat all the way back and closed my eyes. Twenty minutes. Just a little nap.

***

It was hot and stuffy again, and when I opened my mouth I tasted the thick, unpleasant film that coated my tongue. I was momentarily disoriented, wondering why it was so bright in the bedroom.

"Oh, shit!" I sat up, feeling my body protesting. It was 8:15 and I still had to do the rest of the route. I threw open the car door and wobbled out of the car with the canvas bags in tow, the adrenalin pumping me awake.

The problem wasn't so much that I was going to be late for work. My bigger worry was that most of the newspaper customers expected their paper to be on their doorstep early in the morning, before they left for work. I sprinted down the street, chastising myself for sleeping so long in the car. What was I thinking? The last thing I needed was to have someone lodge a complaint about not getting their paper on time that morning, and I would be fired.

"Oh please, oh please." I willed the faceless customers to be nice, to give me a break. It was only a week before Christmas, after all.

When I finished I felt tired again, and instead of driving back home I pulled up next to the payphone at a nearby gas station. The smell of freshly baked dough from the Dunkin Donuts next door permeated the air and I felt a pang of hunger as I dialed the number to the storage office.

"Coastal Storage, how can I help you today?" Hans answered.

"Hans, it's me."

"You upstairs?"

"No. Listen, I'm not going to be in today. Something has come up. Can you handle it on your own?"

"Sure, no problem. It's probably going to be dead around here any-way. So—why aren't you going to be in?"

"I'll catch you tomorrow, then. Thanks." I hung the receiver back on the hook with a loud click.

I started my way toward the donut shop when I thought about the lump of change that was still in my pocket. I could call Ellen now. It was late morning over there and I was still dying to talk to her.

The automated operator voice instructed me to deposit three dollars and seventy-five cents, please. I fed almost all the change into the box and waited impatiently through the clicks and beeps for the phone to start ringing.

It rang four times and I listened to Ellen's voicemail greeting, disappointed.

"Hi, it's me," I sighed. "I'm sorry I missed you. Maybe I'll try again later. Have a great afternoon."

I put the receiver back on the hook and waited for my change from the $3.75. Nothing happened. I slammed the receiver up and down again. Still nothing. I took an inventory of the money I had left in my pocket. Twelve cents. Certainly not enough for a donut.

When I got home Dana was still in bed. I crawled in next to her and slept a long, dreamless sleep.

17

∾

Holiday Cheer

Dana was getting dressed to see a movie that evening with Alicia, who offered to pay for the ticket and the popcorn after Dana complained about not having any money to do anything. I wasn't invited, but that didn't surprise me.

Much to my relief, Alicia hadn't come over to the apartment since the barbeque, either. I had the hazy recollection of us kissing on the living room floor that night and every time it flashed into my forethoughts, I recoiled from it. What had Alicia been thinking? Had I said something to her that I didn't remember? Was it just that she had been so drunk that all her inhibitions and restraint flew out the window?

I had slept until about two in the afternoon that day. At seven p.m., only a couple hours before I was supposed to get to bed again, I was wide awake and antsy.

"What movie are you guys going to see?"

"I'm meeting her in Hillcrest to go see a movie there. It's some foreign movie. It's supposed to be pretty good."

"Foreign movie? That doesn't sound like something you're into."

"It doesn't? Oh well, she's paying. And I haven't been out with her in weeks." Dana came out of the bathroom, trailing a cloud of hairspray. "Something is up with that girl and I'm going to get to the bottom of it."

"What do you mean, something is up with her?"

"I mean, I've invited her over to watch a video or come over for dinner, but she always has an excuse. It's almost like she doesn't want to come over here." Dana smoothed the front of her white silk blouse and smiled at me. "How do I look?"

"You look nice." She did look nice. I was glad that she was getting out of the house for many reasons, not the least of which was that I had a whole evening alone with the phone. But it worried me that she was questioning Alicia's motives. I contemplated diffusing her suspicions.

"I think Alicia is mad at me." I admitted.

"She's mad at you? Why is she mad at you?"

"I don't know. Last time she was over here I was really hammered and maybe I said something I don't remember saying that pissed her off."

"That's funny. I think she would have told me if something like that had happened. I'll have to ask her."

I clucked my tongue and shook my head. "No, don't ask her."

"Why? Don't you want to know what's up?"

"It'll blow over, whatever it is. I say just leave it alone."

"You're good at that David."

"What?"

"Avoiding your problems. Not facing reality."

I couldn't believe I was hearing those words out of her mouth. I watched as she put on her brown suede coat and dug around the pockets.

"Oh hey, look." She opened her fist and showed me a crumpled bill that she found in there. "Five bucks. And some change. Cool."

"I should start going through my winter jackets. Or the couch cushions," I chided sarcastically. "You know, do something useful while you're gone. Maybe I'll find enough money to pay some bills so I won't have to do the paper route anymore."

"Why are you being an asshole? Don't suddenly start coming down on me because you're doing a second job. I told you my parents could help us out."

"And I told you that I'm a big boy and don't need anyone's parents bailing me out."

"Ok, big boy," she draped her purse over her shoulder and started her way down the stairs, "suit yourself."

Our holiday decorations were limited to a long string of Christmas cards that Dana had draped from one corner of the entertainment center to the other. I hadn't bothered to read any of them yet, so I got up and flipped open each one to see who they were from.

There were cards from Dana's sisters and cousins, a couple from some old college friends of mine who had moved away, and one from my aunt in Los Angeles. She didn't write anything other than to sign her name. I think I was just a name on her Christmas card list. I actually wasn't even sure she still lived in L.A., since I wasn't able to see the envelope the card came in.

The face of the next card had a cartoon of a Santa wearing shorts and a tank top, sweating in front of a sign surrounded by large cactuses. There was a note handwritten on the inside in tight longhand.

> *Hey bro,*
>
> *We got your message over the Thanksgiving weekend. Sorry we weren't home. We were out of town visiting Vicky's family. How are you? How is Dana? Have you published that book yet?*
>
> *We just closed on a new house in Scottsdale. It's a little bigger than our old place in that it has four bedrooms and three full baths. We needed the extra room since Vicky is expecting again. The yard needs a little work but overall this place is a gem. We're planning on expanding the deck in the back and also eventually putting in a pool. It'll be a while, definitely, before we move out of this place.*
>
> *Work is going well. The dealership is expanding and sales are up every quarter. I am investing heavily in the stock market and pumping a lot of money into mutuals so that I can retire early.*
>
> *So when are you and Dana going to come visit? We're going to be here for Christmas if you two would like to join us. Let us know. I'm giving you my email address too if you want to get in touch that way.*
>
> *Greg*

A vivid memory of a past Christmas gripped me. Greg and I were at my mother's house, helping her cook and set the table. She had invited her friend Cynthia and her husband to join us for dinner. She was beaming because she loved the holidays and she loved to entertain. No matter the occasion, my mother had always put out her best china and linens any time she had someone over for a meal. That night she also lit three dozen candles around the house to give it an extra glow.

Greg's girlfriend, whose name I couldn't even remember now, had been sitting on the couch, nibbling on the homemade cookies she had brought over. She was very pretty, and she was very much in love with my brother. Her eyes seemed never to lose sight of him.

"So, what did you get her for Christmas?" I whispered, nudging him in the ribs as I laid out the silverware in parallel strips around the plates.

"The most incredible piece of lingerie you have ever seen in your life." Greg smiled slyly and winked at me.

"For Christmas?" I gasped, feigning shock. "You're such a pagan."

"That girl is a viper in bed, bro." He nodded towards her across the room. She smiled at him uncertainly, perhaps aware that we were talking about her. "She'll do anything I ask her."

Her expression softened and her eyes glowed when she saw Greg blowing her a kiss. I remember feeling a little sorry for her at that moment, knowing that it was just a matter of time before Greg got bored with her and went on to his next conquest. As it turned out, however, they remained together on and off for a lot longer than I expected.

The following Christmas my mother found out she was in an incurable phase of breast cancer. Her condition deteriorated quickly and by spring we were scattering her ashes in the same place we scattered our father's ashes only five years earlier. Greg had completely broken down after that. He quit his job and drove out of town, leaving everything and everyone behind, including the sweet girl that loved him so much.

That was a long time ago. Now he was living in another state, working a new job, and raising a family with a woman who was almost an exact duplicate of his former girlfriend. Time had healed him. He was living the life he'd always wanted.

I was still gripping the card. When I let go, it fell back into place among the other cards, the whole arch swaying from the fishing line they were strung on. The apartment was quiet, the hum of the refrigerator the only sound keeping me company. I went into my office and turned on the computer.

There was a letter from Ellen.

On Christmas Eve morning we are taking a flight out to spend a few days in Miami with Jack's parents who live there. I took the day off today to pack and get some last minute presents. I will try to find a few minutes later on to call you and wish you a Merry Christmas, in case we don't connect before the holidays for some reason.

I can't stop thinking about how exhausted you must be from working so many hours almost every day. It's awful that you have to deliver papers on Christmas, too. It makes me realize that there are people who have to work while the rest of the world seems to be taking for granted the time off they're spending with their families or friends or whatever. There are people who work so that we can do those things with our families—like the pilots and airport crew and taxi drivers. Like the gas station attendants. Like the power station workers. Like you.

Except you aren't doing this for some noble cause, I know. You're doing it because you have to, because you've been forced into this tight spot by someone who is going through their life in denial. I'm sorry if I am crossing a line by telling you this, but I can't help but feel incredulous! While you are dragging yourself out of bed every day in the middle of the night (because you have to) I wonder—what is she doing? What is she thinking? How is it that she is able to sleep in oblivious apathy while you are wearing yourself out?

I don't understand Dana. I know that all I know of her is what you tell me, so perhaps I'm not being fair here. But David, this woman isn't your partner. You are such a good man. You need a partner. You deserve one.

Ah, but look who's talking. I should practice what I preach. After we return from Miami, Jack has announced he is going to be 'very busy' the next few months, and will be mostly living out of a suit-case until spring. I feel like I have nothing to talk about with him anymore, even though there are volumes of things to discuss since he's hardly ever home.

I keep asking myself every damn day what I want to do. Should I leave him? Where would I go? I know I could afford to find an apartment for Pete and me—that's not an issue. But every time I try that idea out, I keep returning to the same place. What's the difference between my life now and how my life would be if I lived alone? Not much difference, after all. Maybe I'm just lazy. Maybe I'm just a coward. I don't know.

If you read this tonight, call me. I'm here alone.

I picked up the handset of the cordless phone and lay on the couch with it while I waited for it to ring.

"Hello?" Her voice was soft and sexy, as if she had been expecting my call.

"Finally! God, it's good to hear your voice," I said.

"I know. I've missed you." her voice was barely above a whisper.

"Is it still okay to talk?"

"Perfectly. As a matter of fact—"

"Mmm?"

"I was just sitting here wondering—what do you want for Christmas, David?" Her voice was as soft as a kitten.

I let out a long sigh, trying to curl my body around the pleasant knot that was forming in my stomach. "Right now, all I can think of is that I want to hold you."

She let out a purr. "How do you think we could possibly arrange that?"

"I don't know." I closed my eyes and pictured her face as I listened to her breathing. I willed my body to be transported next to her.

"I've been thinking about this, about us meeting someday," she said.

I sat up a little. "So have I. But I can't see how it can happen any-time soon."

"I know what you mean. It's just that I have this feeling we'll see each other soon."

"You do, do you? Is there something you're not telling me? First, you ask what I want for Christmas, and then you say that you have a feeling we'll see each other soon?"

"Hah! Don't get the wrong idea," she said. "Stop analyzing."

"Me? Analytical? Never."

"Anyway, the two statements aren't related. I'm just going off on tangents."

"Here's a tangent for you: so, what are you wearing tonight?"

"Are you kidding me?" We laughed together. She paused a bit and continued, whispering, "Do you really want to know what I'm wearing?"

"Sure. Tell me. But please—be kind. I haven't had any sex for weeks."

"You haven't? Then I'd better be honest and tell you that I'm sitting here on my big leather couch in nothing but a big fuzzy robe."

"Ooompf! Woman, you torture me." I shifted around so that I was laying on my stomach. I ground my body into the cushions.

"Why haven't you had sex in weeks?"

"You remember—because Dana and I are in disagreement about contraception."

"Ohhhh, that's right. Because she wants to get pregnant, and you don't?"

"Exactly. It's become a test of wills to see who blinks first."

"Who blinks first? Hmmm. Unless you're doing a lot of—er—blinking on your own, I would put my money on you. Men always cave when it comes to sex." I thought I heard her stifle a laugh.

"They do not!" I protested.

"They do! Such weak creatures." She was giggling now.

"I guess it all depends on what it is you're missing. If you had me around, you couldn't go five hours without it."

"Oh really? Hah!"

"Seriously, though. It has been getting pretty bad between me and Dana lately. I keep thinking that we just need to make it through the next few months until I find another job and we move out of here."

"Are you sure that's all that's wrong? How is moving to a new job and apartment going to solve your marital problems? It seems to me that your troubles have deeper roots than that."

"Maybe. Maybe you're right." I picked up a throw pillow and started squeezing it with my free hand. "How did my life get so screwed up? At what exact point did it all start going to shit?"

We remained in silence a few minutes, letting my statement sink in.

"Promise me something," she murmured.

"Anything."

"If you still feel this way in six months, promise me you'll do something about it, okay? Don't spend another year letting this drag you down."

"What? You mean, like leave? Leave her?"

"Yes."

"Truthfully? I don't think I can last another six months. Right this minute I don't feel like I can last another day." I threw the pillow across the room. It bounced off the edge of the recliner and landed against the wall. I rolled over onto my back and looked up at the popcorn-textured ceiling.

"It does feel like that sometimes, doesn't it? But you *will* last another day, and so will I. We get a little crazy every now and then and start believing that we can change our lives, just like that. But every morning when I wake up I feel my resolve has gotten lost in the night. And every night when I realize nothing has changed, I feel a little more numb." She paused. "Before you know it, you've spent years with someone you're not happy with, and it's changed you. Usually, it doesn't change you for the better."

"Sounds like you have a plan, too."

"I always have a plan. I just don't know exactly how to implement it," she sniffed.

"But then you know what they say? The best laid plans..."

"Of mice and men? Yes, David. I know. I know."

18

At the Cusp of Something Wonderful

The radio alarm brought me out of my dream slowly. I kept my eyes closed and felt around for the kill switch on the clock radio.

"You were right about Alicia."

Startled by Dana's voice, I nearly dove off the bed. "What are you doing awake?"

"I dunno. I couldn't sleep. I'm worried about you."

"What are you worried about?"

"You've been acting funny lately."

"Of course I've been acting funny. You'd act funny too if you had to start getting up in the middle of the night." I put my feet down on the floor and stretched in the dark.

"There's something else besides that, David. I don't know what it is. You've been very distracted."

"You're imagining things, Dana. So, what was that about Alicia? What was I right about?"

"The reason she is uncomfortable about coming over has something to do with you. She said so."

"Did she? Was she specific?"

"Not really. She just said that you were a jerk to her at the party. I told her she should forget about it—that you were drunk."

"What did she say to that?"

"Nothing. But she seemed very hurt. I think you should talk to her. Maybe when she comes over for New Year's Eve."

"Why? What's happening on New Year's Eve?"

"I thought we'd have some people over, you know— "

I pulled on some sweatpants and dug around the sock drawer while I listened to Dana. I didn't want to talk to Alicia. As a matter of fact, I would be more than happy if I didn't have to see her again, ever. But I couldn't tell Dana that. Not without telling her everything.

"So will you talk to her?"

"Yeah, we'll see. I don't know if it'll do any good."

I made a pit stop in the bathroom and grabbed my wallet off the dresser before heading out. I could feel Dana watching me the whole time in the dark.

I squinted to see if she was looking my way. "I'll see you later, Dana," I whispered.

"David?"

"What?"

"You're a nutcase."

"I know. But hopefully not for much longer."

David,

Our phone conversation sure took a strange turn the other night. I am not quite sure if you were serious about all the things you said, and I don't know if I was, either.

I have been thinking about you nonstop ever since I hung up the phone. We are leaving in an hour to go to the airport and even though I won't be any further away from you than I am now, it still feels awful because I won't be able to talk to you for a few days.

I ache for you, David. I ache to hear your voice. I miss you all the time. I read your letters over and over to feel closer to you. I don't know what's happening to me or why I feel this way. It scares me. I'm beginning to think I'm falling in love with you.

Ellen,

It's December twenty-fifth. Merry Christmas. I can't stop thinking of you, either.

I printed out your incredible letter to take with me today on my paper route. I don't know why—I barely have enough time to rush through the neighborhood, delivering the mound of papers that fills up my car every morning. I thought maybe I could take a five-minute break and re-read some paragraphs, some sentences, some words. On most days, your words soothe me. This morning, they electrified me.

It was cold and rainy before the sun rose this Christmas morning. It wasn't a deliberate rain. It was a quiet, trickling rain that almost turned into a mist before it covered the sidewalks and lawns. In my groggy state at 3:30 a.m., I had forgotten to bring the umbrella that I had propped up against the side door. I remembered your letter but I forgot the umbrella. By the time I was half done with the route, I was soaked to the bone and shivering from the cold. I picked up the pace to warm up and took a longer break in the car with the heater cranked up full blast.

Because of the rain, the sky was cloudy and there was no light from the moon or stars to illuminate my trek. In the dark, I kept tripping and stumbling as I sprinted the second half of my route, trying to finish. I was getting nauseous from the way the rain condensed on my eyebrows and dripped down the side of my face. I finished half an hour earlier than usual, thank God. But instead of going back home right away, I drove down Highway 101 and parked at the beach access.

I turned on the dome light and squinted at the printout of your email with shivering hands.

'It scares me. I'm beginning to think I'm falling in love with you.'
When I huddled over your words in the half light of dawn,

watching the clouds suddenly break and the sun reflect thin slivers of gold over the steel blue of the Pacific, I knew with an unabridged certainty that I was on the cusp of something wonderful. But it wasn't the sunrise or the vastness of the horizon over the ocean. It was what's happening between us.

So thank you for your letter, for your words, for your love. It was the best gift I could have hoped for today.

19

Dream Jobs

That Christmas was one of those that one wants to get through as quickly as possible. We had no budget for gifts, so I felt like a charity case at my in-laws. When you're five years old you're expected to be penniless and to give handmade gifts at Christmas. It's cute when you're five. But when you're thirty it doesn't quite cut it to bring homemade tree ornaments and hand decorated sugar cookies when your in-laws are buying gifts at Neiman Marcus.

I got paid from the paper route the week between Christmas and New Year's, which helped pay some of the lingering bills from the previous month. The check wasn't much—a little over five hundred dollars, which came out to around $5.50 an hour for the time I spent on the job. Much to my relief, I hadn't heard of anyone at the self-storage complaining about the day I had been a few hours late delivering the morning edition.

Business at the storage facility was predictably slow because of the holidays, which gave us a chance to catch up on some maintenance and repairs. Mrs. Vaughn was coming almost every day, bringing various knick-knacks and more clothes, and then spending most of the day in her unit arranging everything. One evening I ran into her at the grocery store, and when she recognized me she threw me a wild glance, as if I had caught her shoplifting. When I opened my mouth to say hello she scurried off like a frightened cat.

Dana didn't mention Alicia anymore that week except to say that the three of us would be staying in on New Year's Eve. I secretly hoped that she would find a date for that night and bow out of coming over so I wouldn't have to confront her. I had no thoughts on what to say to her that wouldn't further piss her off or insult her.

The night before New Year's Eve, I drove up Highway 101 to a dive called The Breaking Point to meet up with Tom and shoot some pool. I hadn't been joining him for runs in the evenings because of all the walking I had been doing delivering papers. So I hadn't talked to him much all month.

The bar had no street-side windows and just a small dusty wooden sign above the door. I followed a short-clad surfer who appeared to be in his late thirties as he made his way through the thick, stale air to the back of the place.

I spotted Tom at one of the pool tables, setting up to break.

"Hey bud, grab a stick. We're just about to start a new game."

Two men flanked the pool table next to Tom. One of them nodded at me as I approached. I selected a pool cue from the rack on the wall and waited for Tom to break. I looked around as the sharp crack of the balls colliding echoed against my eardrums. A small color television was mounted above the bar, and the flickering images reflected a dozen times in the mirrored tiles behind the stacks of liquor.

"You want anything to drink?" Tom circled the table.

"Not really."

"Actually," he said, "from the way your pants are hanging off your ass, I should order a couple of cheeseburgers for you."

"Is that what you were doing as I walked in here? Checking out my ass?"

"No, but I can't help noticing you're looking pretty haggard." He gestured towards the bartender, who raised his hand in acknowledgement. "I'm going to buy you something to eat just so I can feel better."

"C'mon, I don't want anything. I'm fine."

The bartender took Tom's order for some cheeseburgers against my protests. As he went towards the kitchen to call in the order, Tom called after him, "And throw some chili on those fries, too."

"You didn't have to, but thanks."

"David, this is Jerry, who's a regular here at the pool tables. And this is Miguel, a long-time friend of mine. He's in town from LA for a while."

I shook hands with Miguel, who stood next to me, and nodded across the table at Jerry. Jerry was the only person in the bar smoking. Weather beaten with sun-bleached hair, I guessed him to be in his mid-forties. He flicked his cigarette ash into an empty beer bottle and leaned over the table to take his shot. The cigarette dangled from the corner of his mouth as he squinted against the smoke.

"You still working that paper route, right?" asked Tom.

"Every day," I said.

"How's that going?"

"Eh, you know. It's alright. Although, I can't seem to shake feeling tired all the time. I guess I still haven't adjusted to getting up in the middle of the night."

"That's because you're a prima donna who needs her ten hours of sleep." Tom teased.

"Fuck you."

Tom stifled a laugh as he chalked his pool cue.

"How much longer are you going to have to do that?" he asked.

"Hopefully not much longer. Another month or two at the most." I felt my throat burn from Jerry's cigarette smoke. I stepped away from the table, but it didn't help because Jerry followed.

He pointed a crooked yellow finger at me and drawled out "Y'know, I did a paper route for three years. Mornin' and afternoon edition, both. I surfed between shifts. Wuz the perfect job." He coughed into his fist and continued. "Problem came when my van broke down. By the time I got the damn thing fixed they gave the route to someone else and that was the end a that." He swayed slightly before taking another drag off his cigarette and hissing out the smoke. "Fuckers."

I saw Miguel glance at Jerry and then lock eyes with Tom, who rolled his eyes and then cleared his throat. "I guess there's always something getting between us and our dream job. Right, Jerry?"

"Damn straight."

When the food arrived, I felt surprisingly ravenous. The burger was salty and greasy, and I found myself mopping up the pools of grease and ketchup with the French fries. Skimpy dinners at home made me appreciate it that much more.

"What about you? What's your dream job, Tom?" I said in between fries.

"What's my dream job? Hmm. The auctioneering isn't bad. I've got autonomy. The money is okay. It's not the career I wanted to have when I was younger, but still."

"What did you want to do?"

"I wanted to be a federal agent."

I busted out laughing. "Oh, you're shittin' me."

"No, man, I'm serious." He joined in my laughter. "I had some lofty notions, didn't I?"

"Didn't we all? So, what stopped you?"

He took a sip of his beer. "Life stopped me. My own stupidity stopped me. You know, the usual."

"Like what?"

He came around and patronizingly put his hand on my shoulder. "Someday, son, when you're older, I'll tell you all about it."

"Screw you."

"Hey, you're one to talk. You graduated with a degree in English. How come you're not a writer? How come you've been dinkin' around that self-storage for the past few years?"

I remembered what Ellen had written to me once in response to my whining about that very issue and replied, "I *am* a writer. I don't have to do it exclusive of everything else to be a writer."

"Is that what you've been telling yourself?" He cocked his eyebrows at me.

"No, actually, I've been telling myself that I'm a loser; but that's what someone else who believes in me told me."

"Oh, really? Who, Dana?" He paused. "No, wait. Can't be Dana. She doesn't believe in you any more than you do."

"Thanks." I was starting to tire of the verbal roughhousing.

Tom walked up next to me and lowered his voice. "What's up with you? You got something going on you want to get off your chest?"

"Maybe. Maybe one of these days." I shoved him off me and grinned. "Maybe I'll tell you all about it when you tell me what it was that stopped you from becoming FBI."

We were both suddenly distracted by Jerry, who had apparently been listening to our conversation. Suddenly he belted out a loud belly laugh, attracting the attention of everyone in the bar. "You? An agent? Hoooo! That's a good one!"

Tom shook his head and grumbled to me, "I've gotta stop coming here."

20

It's Not What You're Thinking

The last day of that year was the last full day I spent with Dana.

She'd gone to the video store and rented a couple classic comedies to watch that night. A small turkey was roasting in the oven for dinner when I came upstairs from work, and Dana was in the kitchen spooning chocolate cake batter into a round pan. It was below fifty degrees outside, and the rain had been coming down hard since noon. I was glad that we were staying home that night for New Year's Eve.

I was in front of the computer in my office editing a chapter of my book when I heard Dana talking on the phone with Alicia.

"Why don't you want to come over?" she was asking her.

I stared at the keyboard, listening, my right index finger poised on the "J" key.

"You know, I don't buy that excuse. I just got done making dinner and baking a cake and I've got the table all set and now you're going to tell me you're bowing out because it's raining? No, that's not right."

I heard Dana pacing the apartment.

"Look, I know that you're probably mad at David, and he doesn't know why, so I suggest you come over and you two straighten this out." She stopped at the door to the office and I swiveled my chair around to face her. "Yes, I did tell him." She put her hand on her hip and looked at me, nodding. "What do you mean, why? Because you guys need to talk about this. He obviously was completely drunk off his ass that night." She listened and shook her head at me, then frowned.

"No, Alicia. Stop. Why are you crying?"

I was starting to feel clammy.

"What the fuck is going on? I want you to tell me, now. I *did* ask him. You want to know what his response was?"

I bit my lip.

"He said he doesn't remember what he could have said to piss you off."

"Let me talk to her." I reached for the phone.

Dana turned her shoulder away from me. "What? Why? Right now? Fine, I'll be there in a few."

"What happened?"

"I don't know, but I'm going to find out." Dana started for the closet to get her jacket.

"What did she say?"

"She said she wants to talk to me in private. She was crying on the phone, David."

"Uh huh?"

"Why do you suppose that is?"

"Maybe you should sit down, and we'll talk about this. Before you go over there."

Dana slipped on her sneakers and shook her head. "No, I'm going over there right now."

"Dana?"

"What?!"

"Sit down, we need to talk about this."

Her mouth hung open and she eyed me suspiciously. "Waaait a minute. You're hiding something."

"No, it's not that. It's not what you're thinking."

"Like hell it's not. Suddenly you're as pale as the wall. You're sweating bullets, knowing that I'm going to debrief Alicia."

"I'm not sweating bullets. I just need to tell you something."

"Fine, go ahead—talk." She stood in front of me, arms crossed, waiting.

I gathered my thoughts and tried out a few introductory sentences in my head before I opened my mouth to speak.

"Time's up." She began tromping down the stairs. "You're standing there formulating some lie in your head and I'm not going to listen to it."

"Dana, dammit, come back here!"

She slammed the door on her way out. I picked the phone up off the banister where Dana left it. I hit the redial button. Alicia answered.

"Yes?"

"It's David. Listen, Dana's coming over to your place right now and I want to know what you're going to tell her."

I listened to her sniffling on the other end. "I don't know."

"You better start knowing, right now."

"God, you are such a jerk. I can't believe I thought otherwise."

"I don't know why you're so upset. Huh? Why? Because you want to have a fling with your best friend's husband? Is that it? I don't know what you expected me to do, in all honesty."

"You're right, I may have crossed the line a little. I may have misunderstood. But you turned so nasty on me." She blubbered out a sob. "I thought you wanted me."

"I don't believe this. Alicia, I don't know how to make you understand the difference," I sucked in my breath angrily, "between wanting something and acting on it. Do YOU understand the difference?"

"What's that supposed to mean?"

"If you don't know, then I don't even know how to begin explaining it to you."

"You know what? I don't need this shit from you. I really don't." She hung up the phone.

I hit the redial button and listened to it ring ten times before I squeezed the TALK button to disconnect. I thought about driving over there, but instead walked to the coffee table and kicked it over.

After an hour when Dana hadn't returned yet, I decided to carve up the turkey and eat some dinner. I sat at the dining table between two empty place settings and chewed my food in silence. I considered my state of mind. I shouldn't worry, I told myself. I didn't do anything wrong. Yes, but I *did* kiss her in the car that one night. And I did touch her breasts. So if Dana comes home mad, I'll have to deal with it. Besides, I'm not happy with Dana anymore anyway, so maybe this is just as well. But then again, I wasn't ready to end things quite yet. There were still all those bills to pay, still a lot of loose ends.

So, what had I been doing the last couple of months? Biding my time, waiting for Dana's new paycheck to get me into a position where I could tell her to get lost? Is that what I had been doing? That didn't seem right. I pondered this, asking myself what my true feelings were for my wife.

I couldn't muster an answer. I felt numb. I felt tired and numb and just a little resigned. My thoughts kept rattling around like a loose nut inside my head. I wanted to get in my car and go for a long drive somewhere and not come back. I visualized the various destinations in my head. Nothing seemed appealing. No place seemed to make sense. Least of all the one place where I really wanted to go—Connecticut. Going there didn't make any sense either. Besides, I didn't have the money to go anywhere, even if I knew where I wanted to go.

I heard a car pull up outside and braced myself. When I heard Dana open the door downstairs and make her way up, I felt a wave of panic hit me, and my throat constricted. I walked to the kitchen and rinsed off my plate. Dana didn't come into the kitchen. Instead, I heard her in the bedroom yanking opening the dresser drawers. When I craned my head from across the kitchen to see into the bedroom, I saw her piling clothes on top of the bed.

"What are you doing?" I asked.

"I'm moving out," she said, matter-of-factly.

"You're doing what?!"

"Alicia told me the whole story, you sonofabitch."

"Wait, wait, wait, wait. Just a damn minute. What in the hell did she tell you?"

Dana threw a rolled-up sock at me. "She told me how you practically raped her in your car that night after the Blue Oyster."

"What?! I did no such thing!"

"And how you made out with her right there on the living room floor with me just around the corner." She shook her head. "And when she tried to pry your grimy hands off her you told—ugh!!"

"I what? What did I do? Tell me, because this is all news to me, Dana. I have no idea why she twisted things around like this—"

"How you told her never to show her slutty ass around here again." Dana growled, her face red.

"Dana, she totally twisted everything around. I never said any such thing. She's the one who came on to me. I had to practically peel her off me at the barbeque."

"That's right, David. You're always so damn innocent."

"In this case, I am! I'm going to go over there right now and straighten this out. This is ridiculous."

"You go over there and she's calling the police."

"The police? Are you kidding me?"

"She's terrified of you. And I don't blame her." Dana stuffed all her T-shirts and jeans into my big suitcase. "Now I understand why you've been so spacy lately."

"I haven't been spacy. I've been tired!"

"Tired, my ass. You've been worried about me finding out, haven't you? Maybe you've been trying to figure out a way to talk her into fucking you. I don't know. All I know is, I'm done. I am SO done with you."

"So now you're just going to leave without even getting my side of this? Without even trying to believe me?"

"Why should I believe you?" Dana slammed a bottle of cologne into the trash can and it shattered. "You've been lying to me about everything lately. Your stupid second job. That you've been writing. You haven't been writing. I've been keeping track and YOU HAVEN'T BEEN WRITING."

"You've been keeping track?" I made an instant mental inventory of my writing files and anything else I may have saved in the same drive. Fortunately, all my emails to Ellen were composed directly in Outlook, which I had figured out how to password-protect.

"I don't know what the hell you do in that office every night, but it hasn't been writing. You've probably been online, jacking off to porn, as far as I know."

I gripped the edge of the dresser and shook my head in disbelief.

"You're a total fuck up, David. Tonight I found out just how much of a fuck up you really are."

"How have you been keeping track?"

"I've been reading your story." She arranged all the makeup and toiletries in a small bag and zipped it shut. She threw it on the bed and stood in front of me, smirking. "And you know what? It *sucks.*"

I took a deep breath and pressed my lips together. The next couple of sentences rolled off my tongue with venom. I was pissed now. I was so pissed that I didn't care what I said or how I said it. "So, what are you going to do now, run home to mommy and daddy? Go ahead, Dana. Go ahead and run away again like you always do from everything in your life that requires a little effort."

"You're not worth the effort anymore."

Struggling to control my breathing, I knew I had to get out of there. I got up, ran down the stairs, and bolted outside into the rain. Somewhere in the distance someone had lit off a series of firecrackers in celebration of the New Year. I walked blindly between the buildings in the dark and the rain until I reached the ravine behind the property. There, I sat down in the muddy ice plant and rocked back and forth, clenching and unclenching my jaw. How did everything go to hell so quickly? Dana was leaving, and from the sound of it, she had been contemplating this for a while. She was just looking for an excuse and tonight she found one.

The rain drenched my jeans and sweatshirt, and I shivered uncontrollably. The pain of the cold felt good in a way; it kept me from sinking into panic mode. I remained as still as possible, watching the way the eucalyptus trees swayed and shook in the dark. The sound of rushing water echoed below me.

I didn't know how much time had elapsed. Perhaps only a few minutes, perhaps an hour. I willed myself to get up and move. A glimmer of unreasonable hope welled up inside me—a vision that Dana would still be in the apartment. I imagined that the events of the past few hours were all a dream, that none of it had happened. I would walk into the living room, and she would greet me with a big, warm towel and a slice of that dark brown cake. I would eat it all. I would devour it and wash it down with a tall glass of milk and then collapse on the couch in blessed relief.

Something caught my eye before I turned around to go back—a large rectangular patch of upturned soil with patches of darker shapes inside. When I stepped closer my legs buckled and I began laughing hysterically. Mrs. Vaughn, ignoring our protests, had planted herself a happy little flower garden on the crest of the ravine.

***

Hey beautiful,

I just got home from my paper route. It's New Year's Day, and I am home alone. I wish I could call you.

Dana left last night. It's a long story, but suffice it to say that she didn't even bother listening to my side of things or get the truth. Her best friend has been hitting on me for years, and recently made some bold advances on me. When I tried to ward her off, I inadvertently insulted her and she lashed back by twisting everything around to Dana. It was all my fault, she said. I am practically a rapist, according to her.

Dana believed her and used that as a perfect excuse to leave me. And all this time, I thought I was the one looking for an excuse. I guess I wasn't paying attention.

The closet is half empty. It looks like she took just about all her clothes. I know that she went to her parents' house (where else?) and later on after lunch, when she's had a chance to cool down, I might go over there. I feel somewhat obliged to at least do that. But you know, she pissed me off so bad last night that I really don't want to talk to her anymore.

The problem is that I know for a fact Dana's going to stick me with all the bills. There's just not a chance in hell that I could get her to pay her share. So I'm thinking of going over to the in-laws to try to get them to see the situation for what it is. Maybe they'll talk some sense into her. Maybe, (and I say this now against the force of my principles) I can convince them to bail her out financially.

I'm sitting at my computer, looking out the window while I write you. There is a gray mist settling over everything outside. It's been raining for a few days but it looks like it's finally stopped, at least for now.

I hope you're doing well. Thinking of you and missing you.

After I sent the email I went back to bed and slept most of the day. I didn't call Dana or drive to her parents' house like I'd originally planned. As a matter of fact, I didn't talk to or see anyone that day.

21

✣

One of These Days You'll Understand

"That old bat went ahead and planted that flower garden out back," I said.

Hans took a loud slurp of his coffee and shook his head. "I told her not to."

"Yeah, I know you told her not to but obviously she is doing whatever the hell she wants regardless." I was stretching a beige rubber band between my index fingers. I aimed it toward Hans's head and let it fly across the office. "What I want to know is when she did this. When could she have possibly done this without us seeing?"

The rubber band landed short of Hans's chair. He didn't see it. "It wouldn't take that much time to sneak a few plants back there. What did she plant, anyway? Does it look nice?"

I found another band and squinted an aim. "What do you mean, does it look nice? I don't care. It don't matter if she planted fucking roses or Venus fly traps; I don't want customers back behind C Building."

The rubber band hit its mark. Hans swiped at his hair in slow motion and then looked up at the ceiling, as if looking for a fly or a bat.

"Have you seen her lately? I'm going to have a word with her."

"I saw her earlier this morning, I think."

"You *think*?"

"Well, it looked like her. Back over by F Building. Say, where's Dana's car? Did she have an appointment this morning?"

"Nope. Dana's gone."

"I know she's gone. It's just she is usually not up so—"

"Dana left, Hans. She's not coming back anytime soon," I sighed, "if I were to guess."

"What do you mean? What happened?"

"Oh, it's a long story. One I'm sure you'll find very fascinating. But right now I'm going to go track down Mrs. Vaughn."

"Are you going to tell me about it when you get back?"

"Maybe."

I went directly to her unit but didn't see her there. I hadn't seen her car parked in the street when I left the office, but that didn't matter. Apparently she didn't live too far away and sometimes she walked here to get things out of her unit or rearrange it. On a whim, I decided to check the back of C Building to see if she was there tending to her new botanical venture.

I ran into her on the stairwell as I was leaving. She didn't look up or acknowledge me as she passed me on the stairs, so I followed her down the hallway.

"Mrs. Vaughn, can I have a word with you?"

She took a few more steps before she stopped and turned around. "What do you want?"

"Mrs. Vaughn, do you remember asking my assistant manager about permission to, ah, plant flowers on our property?"

She furrowed her eyebrows, looking perplexed. "Yes."

"And do you remember what his response was?"

"What is this? Twenty questions? You got something to say to me, say it."

"Ok, fine. I saw that you had gone ahead and planted back behind one of the buildings anyway. Unfortunately I'm going to have to ask you NOT to go back behind there again."

"Uh huh."

"It's dangerous back there. When it's muddy, you could slip and fall. And we would have a tough time explaining to our insurance company why a customer was hurt while gardening on our property."

"I didn't plant anything on your property." She was unamused. She turned around and started walking away.

"Mrs. Vaughn, please don't leave while I'm talking to you."

"I've got nothing to say. You're babbling on about something I didn't do."

"Now come on. I wasn't born yesterday." She wasn't stopping, so I talked as I followed her. "First, you ask permission to do something, and then you do it anyway. I don't care if you deny it or not. I'm just telling you right now I don't want to see you back there for any reason whatsoever. Am I making myself clear?"

She stuck a key into the padlock on her unit and then turned around to face me. "You know, I don't understand what this world has come to these days. I really don't. We are supposed to live in a DEMOCRACY, but it seems to me that we've governed ourselves into having to ask permission to do the most basic, innocent things, for Pete's sake. We practically have to get a license to use the toilet!"

I waited for her to say something relevant. She rolled up her door and negotiated her way around a maze of boxes. The way she had stacked the items, it looked as if she had walled off the second half of the unit.

"I mean, I was thinking how nice it would be to plant some petunias and some pansies and just sort of add a little nature to this god-forsaken piece of corporate land, and this is the thanks I get for it."

"So you admit you did it, after all."

"I tell you what, Mr. Two-Bit Manager," she stood only inches away from me, her breath smelling of onions, "one of these days you'll know what it's like to be squeezed out of everything you hold dear, everything that is familiar to you. One of these days you'll understand where I'm coming from."

"Mrs. Vaughn, I'm not telling you this to punish you. I'm telling you this for your own good."

"Don't lecture me about what's for my own good!" she yelled. "I hardly think you are qualified, young man."

"Ok, whatever." I headed back to the stairwell. "Just consider this a warning. I see you back there, and I'm evicting you."

Before I reached the stairs, I could have sworn I heard her hiss at me.

***

Hi sweetheart,

We just got back into town last night from Miami. On the flight back all I could think of was rushing home to check my email.

I can't believe what I'm reading. Dana left you! This news has hit me like a truck. I can't imagine what you must be going through right now. I know you two have had problems recently but for her to pack up and not look back—I am reeling here. Surely there is—there must be—more going on than you've told me. More than you yourself know. I believe you about the fiasco with Alicia. Perhaps you've forgotten that you once mentioned to me how consistently she pursued your attention? Yes. I remember Alicia.

When I say that there is more going on than you've told me, I mean that I suspect there are issues here that you aren't even aware of. It is hard for me to imagine a person giving up so quickly on a marriage. So quickly and so abruptly. It's even more difficult to imagine that she didn't trust you enough to allow you to straighten things out, to explain things.

I certainly don't want to make things worse by seeming suspicious of Dana's motives. I just hate that you're alone and feeling so torn apart.

You should make every effort to talk to her, David. I admit that a part of me wants you to move forward with your life without her, but another part of me (the logical part) knows that despite what has happened, you must find a way to reconcile the situation. Ultimately you may end up alone, but you need to establish your ground with her. You need to make her understand what happened. If you don't, you'll be forever haunted by a sense that you've left something un-finished, unforgiven. If anything, you'll need to know exactly what her underlying motives were. There's just no way it's as cut and dry as you think. If you don't find out, you may spend years blaming yourself for something that wasn't even your fault.

Whatever you decide to do, know that I'm here for you. Always.

XO

***

The call I had been dreading came a few days after the New Year. I saw the number on a pink message slip where Hans had written:

San Diego Chronicle - please call ASAP. Ask for Heidi Williams.

I waited until the office cleared of customers and then dialed the number, drumming my fingers nervously on the desk.

"Hi, Heidi. This is David Bailey. I'm returning your call."

"Yes, hi David. The reason I called you is because we've gotten a couple of complaints from the customers on your route."

Uh oh, I thought. Here it comes. I was late delivering the paper a couple weeks ago. Whoop de doo.

"About?"

"Apparently they're upset that your car is very loud, and that it's waking them up at night."

"My car?" At first her statement seemed ridiculous, until I remembered my broken muffler. I had gotten used to the rumble and it hadn't even crossed my mind that I was making a racket. "Oh, right."

"They say it sounds like a broken muffler, and the couple of people who called gave a description of the car. What kind do you drive?"

I thought about lying for a second but instead blurted, "A 1984 black Saab."

"That does match the description they gave us."

"I've been meaning to get my muffler fixed," I lied easily this time, "I'm sorry."

"We're going to have to insist that you do it before your next shift."

"You mean today?"

"Yes. I'm sorry. We've already gotten cancellations from these customers who called, and we don't want any more."

"But it's already past noon. What if I can't find a garage that'll do it on such short notice?"

"Can you borrow someone else's car until you can get yours fixed?"

"I'll see what I can do."

I rubbed my temples and jammed the phone back on the receiver. Crap! I had gotten an estimate over the phone for the repair two months ago but blew off getting it done because there had been more causing noise than just the muffler. The estimate came to three hundred fifty dollars.

I went up to the apartment and checked the balance in the checking account. Assuming that Dana hadn't gone to the ATM and made any withdrawals, I had about $412 left. I didn't get paid again until mid-month.

What choice did I have? I had to get the car fixed or lose the job. Postponing the expenditure wasn't going to help. I waited until Hans returned from lunch and then took the Saab to San Diego Muffler to spend the last of the money I would ever spend from my self-storage paycheck.

22

January 5

It had taken me about three weeks to get the paper route down to a solid three hours, so on the morning of January fifth it was barely seven a.m. when I punched in my access code at the self-storage gate on my return. The glow of the sunrise reflected in long orange strips on the stucco of the office apartment. I pulled into one of the four spaces allocated for customer parking inside the facility, too lazy that morning to go unlock my garage and park there.

The apartment was starting to look neglected. I threw my car keys on the kitchen counter next to a pile of unopened mail and a mug half full of two-day old coffee. I made a mental to-do list as I looked around the small apartment on my way to the shower. The dishwasher had to be emptied of clean dishes and re-loaded with the stack that was towering in the stainless-steel sink. The kitchen counters needed a good wiping and degreasing; toast crumbs and grease spatter from the stove glazed the tiles. In the living room, a thin layer of dust had settled over the television screen and the top of the black stereo and VCR casing. CDs were scattered like playing cards on the coffee table from the previous night when I lay in a half daze in the dark, listening to Peter Gabriel.

The bathroom sink was crusty with soap scum and small, dried globs of Crest. I turned on the faucet and splashed water on the side of the basin where a long brown strand of Dana's hair clung in the shape of a question mark. As I watched it struggle against the current of tepid water and finally disappear down the drain, I looked up and surveyed my own disheveled appearance in the mirror.

I hadn't even bothered putting a comb through my hair that morning before I left. Long overdue for a haircut, the shagginess began at the nape of my neck and ended in straight spikey clumps at the top of my head. I needed a shave, too. The bags under my eyes were the worst I had seen in days. In weeks.

I turned on the shower faucet and let the water cycle into warmth while I scraped out the last blob of toothpaste onto my brush. As I brought it up to my mouth, I heard the alarm buzz downstairs.

I was momentarily confused. It had been at least a year since an alarm had gone off this early in the morning, and at first I almost lunged into the bedroom, thinking I was hearing the alarm clock. I looked at my watch. 7:05.

I turned off the water for the shower and went downstairs into the office. The first thing I had to do was check which unit it was. I walked up to the computer keyboard and tapped one of the keys, bringing up a menu. The alarm was F-29. Cutter's unit. Had he followed someone into the facility *again* without putting in his code? I found it infuriating that he would repeat his blunder after the last reprimand I gave him. I tapped a few more keys and looked at another list, this time showing me all the access codes that had been entered that morning. My code was the only one on the list.

Great, so you followed me in, I thought.

I knew the delay between when the gate opened and began to close was at least thirty seconds. I didn't remember a car following me in, but then again I was up inside the apartment fairly quickly. It was possible someone may have pulled in just as the gate was almost closed, tripping the sensor.

Irritated, and not in a big hurry to investigate, I went out through the side door and made my way toward the back of the facility. I shuffled closer to the building as I was about to round the corner, suddenly in earshot of a car approaching. A silver Volkswagen buzzed past me, the driver a blonde-haired blur. Even though I didn't get a very good look, I knew immediately that whoever had been driving wasn't Cutter. I watched as the car pulled up to the gate. It was a Jetta, perhaps only a couple years old. This must have been the person who entered Cutter's unit, and the situation shifted from an irritation to an actual problem. Realizing a theft may have occurred, I began to backtrack a few steps to get a look at the license plate. There hadn't been enough time. The car was up on the incline of the driveway and speeding away before I had gotten ten feet closer.

The unit door was rolled down, but there was no lock on the latch. I stood staring at the door for a few seconds, listening. I looked down both ways of the drive. It was quiet and desolate. I walked a few steps to the center of the door and wedged my sneaker under the door handle, opening it as I lifted my leg. The door glided open with a loud click-click-click and I stepped inside.

There was nothing in the unit besides the car. I put my face close to the passenger window and looked inside. The interior was tidy—no scraps of paper from gas receipts, no empty fast food containers, no empty soda cans. Nothing but a bright red and blue Mexican blanket tucked tightly over the backseat.

I walked toward the back of the car and stood in the narrow gap between the trunk and the back wall. If someone indeed had broken into the unit, what had they taken? What were they looking for? I thought back to the last time I saw Cutter in the unit. He had just put something into the trunk.

I strained to see better in the low light. The trunk lid didn't quite line up with the body of the car, indicating that it wasn't shut all the way. I took a few breaths and wondered what to do next. Normally I wouldn't have even come this far. Normally I would have been back in the office, contacting either the customer or the police. I knew I would have to do that, but first I wanted to know what the story was with the car. My curiosity was clouding my judgement. I had been wondering for months what Cutter had been doing paying two hundred dollars a month to park an old car.

I carefully slid my finger under the edge of the trunk lid and pulled it open. It creaked a little, the hinges rusty from old age. Surprisingly, a trunk light came on. It wasn't part of the original makeup of the car. It was just a small bulb crudely wired and mounted under the rear console.

The trunk was empty. Whatever had been in it was gone. A black rubber mat lined the bottom of the trunk, covering the spare tire compartment. I peeled back a corner and checked. Just a tire and some tools. Just as I was about to reach up to shut the lid something odd caught my eye. I wouldn't have noticed it except that I had followed the path of the bulb wire into the rear of the trunk. The wire wasn't tucked in through a drilled hole, it was caught in what looked like a slit in the metal.

I crouched lower and saw a tiny knob, almost out of view, up and to the very rear of the trunk. I pulled on it, and a thin metal flap lowered to reveal bulky dark green fabric. I pulled it out onto the rubber mat. It was a small nylon duffel bag, and it was full of something heavy.

I ran my fingers along the sides for the zipper. I felt a tingling in my chest. I knew instantly that whoever had broken into the unit had been looking for this. That's why the trunk had been ajar. Perhaps they had jimmied the lock. It was too dark to tell. Or they had jimmied their way inside the car and pulled the trunk latch. However they had gotten in, they had not found what was laying in front of me.

The sound of the zipper opening was almost too loud in the claustrophobic space. I let it glide slower, cringing at the sound. Before I looked at the contents, I checked the driveway one more time to make sure it was still deserted.

At first I thought I was looking at a bag full of paperback books, but when I reached in it became apparent the bundles of paper were money. I pulled out one of the bundles. The top bill was a fifty, and when I flicked the bundle with my thumb I saw a few dozen more.

My heart pounded at the base of my throat in fear and excitement. Whoever had broken into the unit had driven away without the prize. They must have known somehow that Cutter was stashing money in his car. It was as I had vaguely suspected all along—Cutter was involved in something illegal, and the car was his bank vault.

I replaced the wad of fifties back into the bag and zipped it shut. I felt my mouth water with the secret glee one gets when finding a twenty-dollar bill lying on the sidewalk. But this was more than twenty dollars. I couldn't even guess how much more. Perhaps a few thousand, at least?

I ran through my options. I could put everything back the way I found it and call the police. The police would show up, Cutter would probably take his money and his car after he found out about the break-in and that would be the end of that. Or maybe the police would be suspicious and do a deeper investigation and Cutter would get arrested for whatever crimes he's been committing. If I went that route, I could just go back to my two jobs and my mound of debt and misery.

My other option was to take the money, go back and call the police, and let them pull the assumption that whatever was taken out of the unit was taken by the blonde man in the silver VW. But if I took the money, I would have to be careful about giving them too many clues. What if they ran fingerprints on the car and found mine? Thinking this, I took the edge of my T-shirt and ran it along the bottom edge of the trunk lid. I then took my knuckle and rubbed it on the corner of the rubber mat where I had grabbed it to pull it back. If I took the money there would be no proof one way or the other who took it, and even if they somehow caught the guy in the silver VW, why would they believe that he wasn't simply lying about not having the money?

They'd never catch the silver VW guy. Why would they? What information did they have? I had no way of knowing where he had touched the car, so I started buffing out the entire edge of the trunk lid. I figured that cleaning up any fingerprints was key—as long as they didn't catch the guy, I was okay with taking the money. No one would know. I could spend a few bucks here and there at first, for groceries and gas and car repairs. I would hold off spending large chunks of it for a while, until I was sure that the situation had remained unsolved. And why would the police even investigate the crime? After all, Cutter was not about to admit that he had a chunk of cash hidden in a secret compartment in his car.

Why would Cutter suspect that I had the money and not the person who broke into the unit? He wouldn't. I was beginning to think the plan was foolproof, and I began to go through the list of things I could do in the next few months with the money. I could find a new job and use it to get an apartment. I could pay off the credit cards faster. Not all at once. Just a little at a time. But certainly much faster than I could on my own. I could travel. I could do a lot of things with the money without attracting too much attention. No more Hamburger Helper. No more canned soup. My hands were starting to shake from the possibilities.

I grabbed the bag and replaced the scene just as I had found it before I exited the unit, rolling the door down. I looked at my watch. It was 7:32. Any time now cars would begin rolling into the facility. I practically ran back to the apartment, my heart pounding every time I heard the hum of a car engine approaching. When I got to the side door of the apartment, I leaped inside, slamming the door shut behind and letting out a long raspy breath.

"Oh shit oh shit oh shit." My knees felt rubbery as I bounded up the stairs. I considered a good hiding place for the bag. My hand was getting raw from carrying the heavy thing, the nylon handle biting into the skin on my palm. I decided to put it in the spare bedroom closet, behind a cardboard box full of old magazines. Then I went back downstairs to the self-storage office. If I was going to call the police, I had to do it soon so they wouldn't wonder why I had dilly dallied around so long after the alarm. I dialed the non-emergency number for the local precinct.

"Yeah, hi. This is David Bailey, the property manager over here at Coastal Storage. I had a break in at a unit this morning and was wondering if I could have someone come out to take a look? Sure, I'll hold."

I walked over to the filing cabinet to pull Cutter's file, stretching the phone cord to its limit while I waited for the dispatcher to come back on the line. I had to get a hold of him next, which worried me for some reason. I could handle the cops, but Cutter was another story altogether. He was intimidating, to say the least. I scanned the application for his phone number, stopping instead to look at the address he had given. 5413 San Miguel Way. Something wasn't right about that address. I had been parking on that street for over a month, and I knew that the numbers didn't run higher than three hundred. It was a short street.

"Mr. Bailey?"

"Yes?"

"What's the address and phone number there?"

I gave them the information.

"What leads you to believe that a unit had been burglarized?"

"Oh, the unit alarm went off. You guys have a duplicate printout of this, I think. I signed up for that service. Uh, anyway, the unit alarm went off and when I went to investigate, I found the unit unsecured."

"Did you see anyone exiting the unit or your facility?"

The silver Jetta began to change make, model and color in my mind, but instead of committing myself to a lie, I answered, "Not really."

"Did you go into the unit yourself at all?"

"No."

"We'll send someone over shortly, Mr. Bailey."

"Thanks."

It made sense that Cutter wouldn't want to provide truthful information about his address and phone number if he was leading a criminal existence. When I dialed the number on the form, I relaxed a little, knowing that I probably wouldn't reach him.

"This is Candy and Bill's. We're not available to take your call right now..."

I didn't bother listening to the end of the greeting. It wasn't Cutter's number. Hell, Dick Cutter was most certainly not his real name, either. Hans and I had laughed at that, making fun of his name. The joke had been on us the whole time.

I wanted to go upstairs and shower or at least change into some decent clothes, and not the sweatpants and T-shirt I had worn under my jacket to deliver papers. I wanted to make a pot of hot coffee and eat a bagel. I was starving. But mostly I wanted to go upstairs and count the money. I ran my fingers through my greasy hair and looked out the office window. No, I shouldn't start showering until after the police showed up. I was anxious to get that part over with and didn't want to miss them because I was shampooing and conditioning.

I shouldn't get too immersed in the duffel bag or the money, either. At least not until later when I had a lot of time and privacy. I would hate to have it all spread out on the floor for counting and then get interrupted. I wanted to be careful to not let my curiosity and anxiety ruin things.

I opted to make some coffee and eat breakfast while waiting for the police to show up. The apartment seemed brighter since only an hour or so ago. I shoveled a few scoops of Maxwell House into the coffee filter and toasted a big onion bagel. My hunger was searing a hole in my stomach, and I happily spread out the last of the cream cheese in generous layers onto the crispy surface of the toasted bagel. From now on, I could stop skimping on things. It all depended on how much money was in the bag, of course. I might not be completely out of the woods yet.

The police cruiser arrived about forty-five minutes later, just as Hans was arriving for work. I walked outside to meet it and nodded at Hans, who walked past me holding a lunch bag and his usual pink paper box full of donuts.

"Door's open," I said.

"What are the cops doing here?" He clutched the box of donuts closer to his chest and it buckled slightly.

"I'll tell you later."

I greeted the officer as he got out of the cruiser. It was the same one who had come a couple months ago. I waited as he produced a pen and a metal clipboard out of the car and began writing on it.

"Do you have the tenant file on the unit?" he asked.

"Yeah, right here." I had brought Cutter's file with me, knowing he would probably ask for it. I handed the folder to him.

"Have you contacted the customer yet?"

"No, I haven't. I think the phone number on the contract is wrong."

"Alright. You want to take me over to the unit, then?"

"Sure." He followed me as I was still formulating what story I was going to give him for the record.

"What time did you get an alarm?"

"It was right after seven. I was about to take a shower when it went off. I came down to the office, checked the report, then—" I stopped talking abruptly, realizing I was blurting out information nervously. I knew that he would let me talk as much as I wanted to. That was the trick—say as little as possible and pretty soon you'll have the criminal spilling the beans because he didn't like uncomfortable silence.

"When you went to check out the unit, did you see anyone in the facility?" he looked up at me from his notebook.

"No, but..."

"But?"

"I saw the gate closing so I knew someone must have just driven out."

"You didn't see the car?"

"No." I swallowed hard.

When we arrived at the unit, he paused to write a little more on his report and then squatted down by the lock.

"Where's the padlock for this?" he asked.

"It was missing when I showed up," I said.

"You didn't see it laying anywhere?"

"No." I looked around the driveway, realizing that I hadn't thought to look for a cut lock.

"Did you enter the unit?"

"No."

"Do you know what the customer is storing?"

"A car."

"A car?"

"Yeah."

"What kind of car?"

"An old Chevy. Late sixties model or something."

"A classic?"

"I don't think so."

"What else is he storing?"

"That's it, I think. I've never seen anything else in there besides that."

"Does he drive the car or is it just stored?"

"No, he drives it. He drives it in and out of the facility."

The officer frowned and reached into his pocket, producing a pair of latex gloves. He slipped them on and grabbed the door handle, opening the unit. I waited on the drive as he made his way methodically around the car, trying both door handles, which turned out to be locked. He stopped at the back and made a few more notes before he opened the trunk.

A pickup truck drove past and parked a few feet away. Two men got out and began unloading boxes into their unit.

"Did you enter the unit?"

I paused before I answered. I couldn't see him from behind the open trunk lid. Why was he asking me that again? "No, I didn't. Why?"

He didn't answer. He was looking through the front windshield at the driver's side. He unclipped his radio and began to relay instructions. "Could you run a plate number for me? Yeah, it's California, CSZ321. No, no VIN number. Right."

He walked up to me and replaced the radio. "I'm going to secure this unit closed for the time being." He rolled the door shut and slid a plastic zip-tie through the latch. His radio crackled to life again.

"Yes?"

I could barely make out the tinny voice. "Vehicle last registered to a Mandy Binkowsky. Last valid registration 1994. Vehicle not reported stolen."

"Ten four. Could you also run an I.D. on a Richard Cutter? Address on 5413 San Miguel Way in Encinitas?" He looked up from the file. "What did you say about the phone number?"

Was this guy really forgetting what I was saying or was this some police tactic to ask the same question over and over to see if the answer is consistent? "I called it, but I don't think it was the right number. Some answering machine message about it being Candy and Bill's place or something."

"What makes you think it's not the right number?"

"His name is Richard."

"So? He might be staying there." He let out a quick breath and shifted his stance.

I didn't like feeling chastised. I shrugged and looked away. The officer's radio came back on. There was a string of indecipherable words and then, "No listing, no such street number on San Miguel Way."

He acknowledged the information and clipped the radio back onto his shoulder strap. "Let's try that phone number again anyway. In the meantime, I'm going to call for an investigative unit to come out and print the car."

"You're going to take fingerprints?" I asked.

"Yeah," he answered, then paused as he thought of something. "Tell me, have you ever noticed any suspicious activity around the unit?"

"Like what?"

"Different people coming and going?"

"No, not really. I've only seen the tenant a couple times. Once I saw him inside the unit. That's about it. Why?"

"I think this tenant might be involved in drug running. I'm going to bring a dog out here, too. To sniff it out."

"Oh, okay." I didn't like the sound of that. I didn't think the cops would get so involved in the investigation. I had thought he would come out, take a report and leave, maintaining a bored apathy from start to finish. I was starting to realize I had underestimated the situation.

Hans appeared more confused than usual when we walked into the office. Holding an envelope in one hand and a letter opener in another, he looked up at me quizzically.

I anticipated his question and answered it as I picked up the phone. "Cutter's unit was broken into."

"No kidding? Is the car gone?"

"No, it's still there."

"So, what'd they take?"

The officer went back to his cruiser while I left a message on Candy and Bill's answering machine.

"This is a message for Richard Cutter. Please call Coastal Storage or come by as soon as possible. This is David, the property manager. If there is no Richard Cutter at this number, please let me know. My number is 494-8030. Thanks."

"What happened?" Hans asked as I hung up the phone.

"I told you. Cutter's unit was broken into."

"The alarm go off?"

"Yeah, this morning around seven. When I got there I saw the padlock was missing."

"Maybe it wasn't broken into, maybe he just followed you in and forgot to put the lock back on when he left."

Sometimes Hans surprised me. Even the cop hadn't come to that simple conclusion.

"No, it was broken into."

"How can you be sure? Did you see someone else other than Cutter leaving the facility?"

I walked out of the office abruptly to see what the cop was doing. I saw him sitting in the driver's seat with the door open, talking into the radio again. When he saw me, he asked, "Any luck this time?"

"No, I just left a message."

"Okay, the investigative unit and dog will be here within the hour. Let me know if and when he calls back. I'll hang around for a little while."

"No problem."

Hans was standing behind me as I turned around.

"What are you doing?" I felt like shoving him back inside the office.

"What are they going to do?" Hans looked over my shoulder at the cop car.

"They're going to bring in the dogs and the forensics people."

"Why? How can they be so sure that someone broke into the unit?"

"Hans, there's more to it than you think. Please—go back inside and we'll talk about it there." He was making me nervous with all these questions. I worried he'd start collaborating with the officer and that would be my unraveling.

"Ok. By the way, the accountant called, and he needs reports and stuff by noon today," Hans said.

"Already? What day is it?"

"It's the fifth."

"Great. I forgot all about that. I'm going to have to run them now."

I waved Hans off as he attempted to get more information about the break in, feigning that I was too busy trying to get the reports run. He wasn't a patient man. I could hear him squirming and tapping his feet the whole time I was working. When the second cruiser arrived a while later, I was immersed in accounts payable and receivable and receipts and deposits. The first officer got into the car, and they drove into the facility toward F Building.

"Should we lock down Cutter's code?" Hans asked.

I stapled a note to a small stack of spreadsheets as I answered, "Go ahead if you want to. I suppose it's a good idea so that we don't miss him."

Usually, whenever there was a reason we needed to speak to a tenant, whether to let them know their payment was overdue or if there was a problem with their unit or something, we would disable their access code so they would have to park on the street and walk inside using the pedestrian gate. Sometimes the tenant was curious enough to come to the office and ask why their code didn't work and sometimes they knew why and just bypassed the office on the way to their unit.

"So have you heard from Dana?"

"No, not since a few days ago."

"You guys must have had some fight."

"Yeah, we musta." I didn't know if the reason why I was so nonchalant about Dana was because I was in some sort of denial or because we had drifted apart so much the last few months that her absence was little more than a glitch in my day. During the day I would worry about it a little here and there, I would wonder what I should say to her and if I should call her. At night I would mostly think about Ellen. I was starting to fantasize about a life with her instead of wondering how to get my life back with Dana. I wasn't sure what exactly I was feeling about anything anymore. I just knew that my life had been spinning out of control for months, and on New Year's Eve it had finally slipped down the drain.

But the money would save me, if only a little. My thoughts kept coming back to the money. How much was in the bag? Was it all fifty-dollar bills? If so, how much would a bag full of fifties come to? Could I spend some of it tonight and go out to eat?

"Wow, what timing!" Hans blurted loudly.

"Huh?" I saw Hans looking out the window.

"Cutter's here."

He was approaching the office quickly from the pedestrian gate. He looked a little different from the last time I saw him. His hair was cropped closer to his head and looked a few shades darker. He had gotten some new sunglasses, and instead of his usual T-shirt and jeans, he was wearing gray Dockers and a black suede jacket. He ignored Hans as he entered the office and came straight up to the counter, facing me.

"My code's not working," said Cutter.

"There's a reason for that. Your unit was broken into this morning."

"Hey, were you here earlier?" Hans interjected, his expression timid but his voice booming from the other side of the office.

"It was what?" He leaned in closer and took off his sunglasses. "What do you mean it was broken into?"

"I got an alarm on it this morning. When I went there, I saw the padlock was missing. I saw a car leaving the facility—not yours—and I called the cops."

"And?" He looked like he wanted to lunge at me.

"And? They're back there now, checking it out, if you want to talk to them."

Without another word, he left the office and the premises the same way he had come in—without going back to his unit.

"What was that all about? How come he took off?"

"I don't know."

Actually, I did know. I knew exactly why. He didn't want anything to do with the police. Money or no money. Whatever he was involved in, it was serious enough that he wasn't going to risk a confrontation. That was fine with me. It would be just as well if he never came back again. "I'm going to run these reports over to the accountant. I'll be back in an hour."

As I was leaving, I heard Hans mumble to himself, "Yeah, I guess that makes sense now."

23

The Exchange?

My monthly visit to the accountant's office took me a while longer than I'd anticipated that day. His office was twenty minutes inland in a small cedarwood building that also housed two realtors and a dentist. When I arrived, he had a list of questions about the deposits and receipts, and I had to space my answers in between his incoming phone calls. I didn't mention that morning's incident to him, deciding not to risk jeopardizing my good fortune by unintentionally screwing up the story I had concocted for everyone. It didn't matter if I told him or not, anyway. Even though he was a close friend of the owner's, he couldn't care less about the day-to-day operations of the facility. Besides, I didn't want to engage him in any more conversation than was necessary and drag out the visit. I kept looking at my watch nervously, anxious to get back. I wasn't comfortable with Hans being in the office alone that morning and I was dying to know what the police had come up with, if anything.

By the time I returned to the office it was past noon. The police cruiser that had been parked in front of the office was now gone. Hans was sitting in the same spot as when I left, except now he was grazing on a small pile of corn chips and a sandwich.

"Sorry it took so long. So, what happened with the police?"

"Well," he put his sandwich down on the square of wax wrapping paper and rubbed his palms together to knock off the crumbs, "when they were done in Cutter's unit one of the officers came in to tell me that they had a positive on drugs, whatever that means, and that they would be in touch with you later. Then they both drove off in their respective cars. It's strange, because not a few minutes after the cops left, Cutter showed up again."

"You're kidding. Right after they left?"

"Yeah. He shows up, and he didn't even bother coming in here or anything. He went straight back to his unit."

"Ok." I remembered the zip tie the cop placed on the lock and wondered if, after the investigative unit was done, they had put another one on.

"He wasn't back there long. I wanted to go back there to see what he was doing but I had a customer in the office at the time. So I couldn't. I stayed here." Hans scratched his head.

"Right. So, what happened?"

"He came in here and started ranting and raving a little. Wanted to know if the police took anything out of his unit. I told him no, that I didn't think they did. I said that I saw them leaving and it didn't look like they had anything with them besides the usual police stuff, you know?"

"Uh huh. But why would he think the police took it? His unit was broken into. Duh!"

"I don't know. He looked real pissed. Didn't say much else. Asked for you, though."

"He did? Why?"

"He asked where you were." Hans lowered his voice to imitate Cutter's. "'Where's the property manager? I need to talk to him.' I told him you had to take some reports over to the accountant, and you'd be back later."

"Wonderful." I rubbed my eyes with my thumb and forefinger. "So, what else happened? Did the police call back?"

"Yeah. And you know, they asked for you too. I told them you weren't here. They asked if Cutter had been in or called, and I said yeah, he had. I told them how he had shown up twice. Once before you left and the second time—you know." He took a swallow out of his can of Coke and nodded at me.

"Right."

"They were *very* interested in the fact that he took off the first time, when they were in his unit. They asked me all kinds of questions about that."

"Hans?"

"Yeah?"

"Who's 'they'? Were you on a conference call or something?"

"Huh? No. What do you mean?"

I shook my head. "Nothing. Go on."

"I wrote down a number we're supposed to call if he shows up again. I put it over there next to the other computer."

"Fine. Listen, why don't you take a break for lunch."

"I am."

"No, I know. But why don't you go out for a cigarette or something. Get out of here for a while."

He shrugged, neatly packing up the remnants of his lunch back into the wax paper and putting it into the little refrigerator we had in the back storage closet. As soon as he left, I walked over to the door that joined the office to my apartment and tried the knob. It turned, and the door popped open. I had forgotten to lock it. I rushed upstairs to check if the duffel bag was still where I had left it. It was. I even unzipped it to make sure the money was still in it. It was.

I locked the door behind me this time as I returned downstairs to the office. The phone was ringing. I picked up.

"Is this Mr. Bailey?" The caller was male.

"Yes?"

"This is Officer Fillmore. I came out there this morning on that burglarized unit."

It's not even one o'clock, I thought, *and they're already calling back? Something is up.*

"We ran prints. The prints we found on the car were identified as belonging to a Michael Adams. Now, we can't be sure this is your tenant, obviously. But it's a pretty safe bet since his prints dominated."

"Michael Adams?"

"Yes. And Mr. Bailey? I must inform you that this man is considered very dangerous. He is wanted by the FBI for drug trafficking and murder. Because of this we are now turning the case over to federal agents. Michael Adams is one of the FBI's most wanted and, Mr. Bailey, I must stress that he is a very dangerous man."

I sat down hard on the gray swivel chair and gripped the armrest.

"If he tries to contact you in any way, please do not say anything to him. We are going to send an unmarked unit out there to keep a watch on the place for a while. If by any chance he shows up again, do nothing until you are sure he's gone. Don't try to call the police while he's around. We are going to have your facility staked out, so if he does show up, we'll know and we'll take care of it. Do not let on that you know anything about his identity. Do you understand?"

"Yeah." I stared at a spot on the wall across the office. "But why would he come back?"

"We don't know. Apparently this guy's M.O. is to use old cars for drug smuggling and transporting and also to use storage facilities as a means for the drug exchange."

"Exchange?"

"Yes. We have a theory that the burglary incident this morning may not have been a burglary at all. It might have just been a simple drug exchange that somehow got botched up. Perhaps the party that entered the unit forgot to replace the lock."

My brain was still stuck on his previous statement. "What do you mean, exchange?"

"I mean, Mr. Adams may have left drugs in the car and the person who entered the unit this morning took the drugs in exchange for cash. Unfortunately, we didn't find either in the car, so we don't really know what happened. Maybe the person was spooked and didn't leave what they were supposed to leave. Or maybe there weren't any drugs in there. I don't know. Maybe they took the drugs and didn't leave the money.

In any case, we doubt—now that we have become involved—that Mr. Adams will be making any more visits to your facility. I am very surprised, as a matter of fact, that he came back a *second* time. He was obviously very motivated by whatever had been in that car to risk being seen and arrested. He must have been parked on the street, waiting for us to leave, too, since he showed up within minutes of our departure, according to your assistant manager."

I heard a scratching behind me and nearly jumped out of the chair. It was only a tree branch outside, swaying from the wind and knocking against the window.

"Mr. Bailey? You still there?"

"Yeah." I could barely make a sound from my dry mouth.

"We'll be in touch. And one more thing," he added, "whatever you do, don't go into the unit. We've re-secured it, so there's no need for you to do anything to it. Alright?"

"Sure. No problem."

No problem? That was a crock. I was a sitting duck.

24

The Rat

A customer came in right before six o'clock that evening to rent a unit. I would have told her to come back the next day, that it was too late to begin any new transactions, but Hans was the one who helped her, and he gladly began the task of signing on a new account. My thoughts had been churning in dread all afternoon and all I wanted to do was go upstairs, count the money, and decide my next move. I kept imagining Cutter—Michael Adams—showing up and sticking a gun in my face, demanding I return the money. I was listening for the click of the pedestrian gate all afternoon, my stomach in tight knots.

When 6:15 came and went, I cut into Hans's cheerfully useless and time consuming conversation with the new customer and told him to go home, that I would take over and complete the transaction. He dismissed me with his eyes and resumed his chatter until I pulled the customer's application out of his hands.

"What are you in such a hurry for?"

"It's after six and I want to go home. I've had a long day."

"Then go home. I'll finish up. Don't worry."

"Hans," I glared at him, "just go. I mean it."

The middle-aged woman who had been sitting in a padded chair in front of Hans's desk looked up at me fearfully and I immediately regretted my tone. I smiled at her but that didn't seem to help.

"Geez, what's eating away at you today?" Hans retrieved his jacket and the uneaten portion of his lunch from the storage closet and made his way toward the door. "I hope you're in a better mood tomorrow."

It was already dark outside. I watched him leave, his body lit up for a while by the glow of the hundred-watt photo-sensitive lamp that was mounted outside above the entrance. When he got beyond the gate, I couldn't see him anymore. He was swallowed up by the dark.

"I can show you where your unit is, but the facility is only open until seven p.m. Are you going to need a while to put in whatever you're storing?"

"Oh, don't worry about that." She fondled the handle of her brown leather purse. "The moving people are going to show up tomorrow with the truck. I just wanted to arrange this tonight since my husband and I will be busy tomorrow. I don't even need to see the unit."

"Alright. Just be sure to give the movers your code for the gate and come back later and change it, okay?"

"Sure, that sounds fine."

Relieved that I didn't have to do anything else, I gave her a copy of her contract and walked her out to her car. I had to lock up the pedestrian gate now that Hans was gone. Walking across the driveway, I felt oddly vulnerable. I looked around. The facility was tucked away in the middle of a residential area off the busy main street that ran through the center of town. I went through the gate and crested the top of the driveway, glancing in both directions at the cars that were parked on both sides of the street. An unmarked car was supposed to be staking the place out— so where was it? I could only see inside a half dozen cars that were backlit by the streetlight, and all of them appeared empty. It was too dark in the other direction to tell anything. I saw a minivan parked across the street under the ragged fronds of a dwarf palm tree. Was that the stakeout car?

I walked back and locked the gate behind me, contemplating whether I should just lock down the entire facility a few minutes early that night. I had a good reason—a wanted and dangerous criminal might be lurking in the shadows ready to slit my throat. I quickly walked through the entire facility to check if anyone other than customers was still there. I didn't see any cars parked in the driveways. Everything seemed quiet. When I returned to the office I shut the front gate down with a few keystrokes on the computer before I headed upstairs.

How long would it be before Michael Adams got in touch with his contact and figured out what really happened to the money? I had no idea how trustworthy he considered the VW Jetta guy, but I supposed that he considered him trustworthy enough to make an unsupervised exchange. Would he think that the police took the money? What if he had contacts in the police department somehow who would tell him nothing was found in the car? How long after that before he would put two and two together and know I took his money? He knew I had seen him putting something into the trunk a while ago. He would remember that. He would make the connection.

Perhaps he already knew I took the money. Perhaps the only thing keeping him at bay was knowing that the place was being staked out. Maybe he was waiting for me to leave so he could follow me to a place where he could torture the information out of me before he kills me. I shuddered.

As I crouched down in the small space of the closet in front of the duffel bag, I caught a whiff of myself. I hadn't showered since the previous day and I was getting ripe. I knew I had to figure out what I was going to do before I worried about such things as showers and food. I pulled the bag into the center of the spare bedroom/office. I closed the blinds and clicked on the desk lamp.

A shrill ringing filled the room and I lurched back against the wall. It was the phone, and I stared at it in horror. What if it was Adams? I let it ring until the answering machine in the kitchen picked up. I listened breathlessly to the message.

"David?" It was Dana. "David, are you home? Pick up if you are."

Her voice was almost comforting. I picked up the extension in the office and answered, "I'm here. Hi."

"Hi." There was no warmth in her voice. "I'm calling because I want to come by and get a few more things tomorrow."

"Oh." I realized in that moment that I had forgotten she had moved out. I stood over the duffel bag, thinking.

She paused, perhaps waiting for me to say more. I felt almost obligated to say something apologetic to her. I hadn't spoken to her since she left, and now that I had her on the phone, my mind was a complete blank. "What do you have to get?"

"Some of my books, my CDs, stuff like that. I just wanted to, ah, kind of warn you that I was coming."

"Why? What do you mean warn me?"

"I don't want to show up tomorrow morning and find some woman sprawled out on our bed, David."

"Oh, for God's sake! There's NO WOMAN. What the hell are you thinking, Dana?"

"I don't know. How should I know what you've been doing since I left?"

"You really have the wrong idea about me, you know."

"Fine. Whatever. I'll be by tomorrow before noon." She hung up.

I shook my head and sat down on the floor in front of the bag. I unzipped it and began taking the stacks of cash out. There were some stacks of fifty-dollar bills, but most of the stacks were hundreds. I began to arrange them accordingly. When I had a pile of ten stacks, I decided to count how many bills were in each before proceeding. I took one of the stacks of hundreds and peeled apart the paper band holding it together. I lay the bills one by one on the carpet and mouthed the numbers as I counted.

"Seventeen, eighteen, nineteen...." I was mesmerized by the procedure. When I was done with the bundle, I calculated that there were a hundred bills of a hundred dollars in each bundle, which meant that each stack of hundreds was ten thousand dollars. Looking at the bulky bag, I knew already that there was a lot more money in it than I had originally thought. Much, much more.

I began counting the bills in the few stacks of fifties when I heard an urgent knocking at the side door downstairs.

"Who the—?" I crammed the bundles back in the bag and stood up, kicking the bag furiously back into the closet.

I stealthily made my way through the dark apartment to the windows facing the street and the driveway to see if by chance I could see any cars parked there. There weren't any cars. Everything was as it had been when I locked up the facility. The knocking continued, louder this time.

It was Adams. I just knew it. If I didn't answer the door, he'd probably either bust the glass in or pick the lock. I went into the bedroom closet and took my 9mm Glock out of its hiding place inside a shoe box that was on the closet shelf. I had kept it loaded but with the safety on. With my right arm extended down and the gun at my side, I looked out the bedroom window from between the slats of the white vinyl blinds. I couldn't see who was standing there, since the doorway was inset a couple of feet into the building below me.

The knocking continued. Whoever it was must have known I was home, and they weren't giving up. I stayed close to the wall as I made my way down the dark, carpeted stairway. The porch light wasn't on outside, but I could make out a shape through the curtain because of the ambient light from the driveway. There was no way to tell who it was, except that it seemed only to be one person.

As I reached the bottom of the stairs, I slowly and quietly neared the door. The gun was in my right hand and pressed tightly against my outer thigh. I kept my body away from the front of the door as much as possible as I pushed aside the curtain to see who it was.

Mrs. Vaughn's ruddy visage filled the window. With relief washing over me, I unlocked the door and threw it open. "What in the world are you DOING here this time of night? The facility is closed!"

"What took you so long to answer the door?"

"For God's sake, you scared the bejesus out of me." My breath came in spurts as if I had just finished a run.

"Can I come in? I want to talk to you."

"Talk to me?" I flicked the switch and turned on the porch light. "Why are you here? You're not supposed to be in here after seven."

She entered the small hallway at the foot of the stairs, and I turned on the stairwell light. A dozen moths and flies began to buzz around the porch light, so I closed the door behind her. "What's the problem, Mrs. Vaughn? And why are you in here so late? Did I lock you in? Do you want me to let you out?"

"No, you didn't lock me in. I've been staying here for a while now."

"You've been what? You mean you've been sleeping in your unit?"

I was aware that I was still gripping the gun at my side but that she hadn't glanced down in that direction, yet. I tucked my arm and the gun behind my back.

"Yes, as a matter of fact, I have been."

"You're not allowed to do that."

"Oh, you know, I am so sick of your you-can't-do-this, you-can't-do-that. I really am. I'm done deferring to men."

"Excuse me?"

"That's right! That jerk husband of mine had me almost under lock and key the last ten years. I was sick of it! I decided to move out."

"So, what—now you're going to live in a storage unit?" It was almost comical, her rationale.

"No, you idiot. This is temporary! I've put a deposit down on one of those apartments in the senior complex down the road. But I can't move in until the fifteenth. And I'm NOT staying with that jerk a day longer. I don't care if I have to live under a bridge."

"Don't you have anyone you can stay with?"

"I can't. When he caught on that I had slowly been moving my things out he went crazy. He's probably tracking me down at Stella's and Mary's and maybe even the Silverberg's. I think if he caught up with me, he'd kill me." Despite what she was saying, her tone was far from apprehensive. She squinted at me and sighed. "Anyway, it doesn't matter. I get the feeling I won't be staying here another day."

"Damn skippy you're not."

"I think you're going to help me out." I saw her lip curve slightly upward.

"I am? How's that?"

"I need a little cash. Say—oh—five hundred dollars. That should tide me over until the fifteenth."

I didn't believe what I was hearing. "Are you asking to borrow money from me?"

"Not asking. Telling."

I took a step backward away from her. "I don't understand."

"I saw you this morning. I saw what you did."

"What?" My lip quivered.

"I saw you taking something out of that man's garage this morning. A bag." Her lip was definitely upturned now. She had a big, obvious smirk on her face. "Now, I don't know what it was that you stole, and I don't really care." She extended her index finger and jabbed me in the chest. "But I'm sure the police would be very interested to know the type of shenanigans you're pulling around here."

"I didn't take anything out of the unit." I hoped she was bluffing.

"Baloney! I saw you go in, and I saw you leave. I know! I saw you!"

I gripped the gun harder. The tiny hallway was beginning to spin.

"So I strongly suggest, young man, that you provide me with that five hundred dollars, or else I'm going to go straight to the police department—"

"I don't have any money. I'm broke. What the hell do you want me to do?"

She stared at me, and I almost wondered if she knew about the money in the duffel bag. "I don't care. Borrow it from the cash register if you have to. I'm done fooling around with this place. And YOU. Now cough it up!"

I thought for a second. How much money was in the cash register? Certainly not five hundred dollars. The last thing I wanted to do was take the money out of the duffel bag. If she didn't know what had been in the bag I took, it wouldn't take her long to make the connection when I came down from my apartment with a fist full of hundred-dollar bills.

"Ok, I tell you what. I'll meet you out by the front door and I'll see what I can do."

"That's better." She marched outside and turned the corner toward the front of the building. I unlocked the door I was leaning against and entered the office, turning on the lights. Where had the old bag been hiding this morning? She must have been peeking out from one of the entry doors to F Building. Putting the gun down on the counter and out of view, I unlocked the cash register and counted out six twenties and eleven tens onto the counter. Mrs. Vaughn stood with her face against the glass of the front door, watching me. I waved the cash at her. She nodded.

"This is all I can give you right this minute," I whispered apologetically as I opened the front door and shoved the bills into her wrinkled fist. "It's two hundred thirty dollars. If you want to wait, I'll make a trip to the teller machine at the bank and get a cash advance on my credit card or something." I lied to buy myself some time.

"How long will that take?"

"Not long. Forty-five minutes? Is that okay?"

She shook her head but answered, "Yes. I'll wait. But no more than an hour. I mean it! Or else I'm going to the police."

"Fine."

I went back upstairs and directly back to the bag. I had to get out of here, and fast. How much money did I have?

I dumped the whole stack of cash on to the carpet again and quickly arranged the bundles in a row as I counted. When I was done, I found myself unable to calculate the math. I reached into a drawer in the desk next to me and got out a calculator. One hundred times one hundred is ten thousand. I punched in a one and four zeros and the "X" key and then a seven and a five.

Seven hundred fifty thousand? Could that be right? I had only counted the one hundred-dollar bills. There were a few stacks of fifties too.

"Oh, Jesus."

I double-checked the math again and began throwing the money back into the bag. No wonder Adams had risked a second trip. No wonder he is one of the most wanted on the FBI list. This was a lot of money. It was an insane amount of money.

That was the point when I knew I had to leave the apartment. I had to leave the apartment, the facility, the city, the state. I had to leave and take the money and never look back. If I was to survive another day, another hour, I couldn't risk another minute in there. If Adams got a hold of me, he'd kill me. If the police found out about me, I'd land in jail.

Going against all instinct to pack or take one more look around or grab any valuables, I grabbed only my wallet, my car keys, and the bag full of over three-quarters of a million in cash. I got into the Saab that I had fortunately parked inside my garage and drove away into the night.

25

Tom

Tom's house was the last one on a short street abutting the canyon. I had been watching my rearview mirror the entire drive over, making sure no one had been following me. I was pretty sure no one had; when I made the turn off my street I didn't see any cars behind me. Now that I was parked on Tom's driveway I let the engine idle while I craned my head to see if any headlights appeared down the road. There weren't any. I turned off the ignition and leaned my head against the seat, feeling remarkably better than I had fifteen minutes ago.

Originally I had debated just driving north on Interstate 5 until I could figure out what I was going to do. But I didn't get far before I figured out that the idea was flawed—a road trip was out of the question in the Saab. If Mrs. Vaughn followed up on her threat, I would be a wanted man. And I had seen enough movies to know that driving your own vehicle under those circumstances was almost always a mistake. It didn't help that my tags had expired a month ago, making my car a cop magnet.

So, I had driven to Tom's house. I trusted him. He would help me think through this problem. I got out of the car and looked at the bag, which I'd stuffed on the floor behind the front seat. I thought about bringing it in with me but remembered that Tom's girlfriend Lynda might be home, as well, and I wasn't sure that was a good idea. I didn't feel good about leaving it in the car, either. It bothered me to think that if I went inside, I couldn't keep an eye on it. After hedging for a few minutes, I decided that the better idea would be to lock up the Saab and see if Tom was home before I started lugging a suspiciously bulky bag around.

Tom answered the door, a toothpick in the corner of his mouth and his hand in the pocket of his pants. "David? Hey, what's up?" He stepped aside and motioned me in. I stood in the foyer, looking for Lynda. The formal living room was warmly lit by a corner lamp. A television boomed from the den on the opposite end of the house. Tom's dog, an Australian shepherd mix named Sparks, walked up and nosed my knee. I reached down with my fingertips and scratched his head.

"I need to talk to you. I'm in big trouble."

"Why? What happened?"

Lynda shuffled in from the den and stood next to Tom. She smiled, almost unsurprised to see me. "Hi David, what brings you here?"

"Just came by to run something by Tom."

Tom inspected my apparently disheveled appearance and gently put his arm around Lynda. "Honey, do you mind if I talk to David for a while? Just go ahead and watch the video without me."

Lynda frowned in concern and nodded. "Sure, that's okay. David, would you like something to drink? Some iced tea?"

"No, thank you."

"Okay, David. Good to see you again. C'mon, Sparks." Lynda rounded up the dog and ambled back to the den. Tom waited until she had gone before he spoke again. "You look like shit. What's going on?"

I plopped down on the living room couch and rubbed the stubble on my chin with the back of my hand. "I think I need to get out of town tonight."

"Out of town? Why? Is Dana coming down on you?"

"No, she's out of the picture."

"Wait—hold on. I think I need a drink first." He retrieved a couple of cold beers from the kitchen and came back shaking his head. "For some reason I just knew this was coming," he laughed. "What did you do, kill her?"

I pulled back the tab and took a sip of beer. "Pfft! I wish it were that simple. Actually, she left a few days ago. Unrelated event."

I told him everything that had happened that day, from the time I went to investigate the unit alarm to the incident with Mrs. Vaughn. What I didn't tell him was exactly how much money was sitting in the Saab. He didn't ask. He listened intently, rubbing off condensation on the side of the beer can with his thumb and nodding.

"Can Lynda hear us?"

"Hmmm?" He looked over his shoulder. "Oh! No, don't worry. You can't hear anything from this end of the house when you're in there watching T.V. Besides, don't worry about Lynda. She's not a snoop."

"OK. I just don't want to involve any more people than I have to, obviously. I feel a little bad involving you, but I need your advice."

"Don't feel bad about involving me." He leaned forward, putting his elbows on his knees. "What's with that old woman anyway, what's-her-name? Mrs. Fawn?"

"Vaughn? I don't know. I think she hates me."

"Why did you give her the money? I would have told her to get lost."

"I don't know why. I wasn't thinking. I just wanted to get rid of her and buy myself some time."

"Yeah, but I bet if you threatened to beat the crap out of her if she opened her mouth she would have just slinked away."

"Maybe. But she is the lesser of my concerns. Obviously I don't want to be arrested, but I am more worried about Michael Adams."

"As you should be. You did the right thing by getting the hell out of there when you did. If the police got a hold of you, then you might not have any way out. Adams might have his cronies all over the federal prison system in this state, for all you know."

"I thought about staying with someone for a while, maybe my brother in Phoenix, but I don't want to do that—it would be too easy to track me there and then what? I can't risk putting my family in danger."

"Absolutely."

"Maybe I should just go to the airport and hop a plane somewhere."

"Look, first of all, you can't be hanging around the airport buying up plane tickets with cash and looking like you do. That's first. You need a passport if you want to leave the country. Do you have a passport?"

"No."

"Obviously you can't be traveling under your real name. And another thing that you should worry about are all the security cameras at the airport. Even if you used a fake identity your face would be plastered all over video."

"Right. I didn't think about that."

"Don't worry about it. I have an idea about that."

"Good. That's one more than I've had all night. So, what's my next step here?"

"First of all, you're absolutely right. You need to get out of here, and fast. Did you make sure you weren't followed when you came out here?"

"I'm sure I wasn't."

"Good. Hang on for a second. I'm going to get something, and let Lynda know I'm taking off for a while."

I listened to the faint tick-tock sound of a grandfather clock behind me as I waited for Tom to return. It began to lull me, and I relaxed deeper into the cushions of the sage green velvet couch. Tom's house was tastefully and warmly furnished, and I had always wondered if the décor was left over from his first marriage or if he had re-done it after his ex-wife had moved out. Tom had been divorced three years, but I had only started coming over to his house after we became friends a couple of years ago.

My eyes closed with my head nestled in the big soft cushions. I was almost asleep when Tom's voice filled the room, jerking me awake.

"Alright. First thing you're going to do is bring that bag of cash inside and leave it here. Where we're going it's best not to bring it. We'll come back for it later, obviously." Tom was standing next to the front door with a medium-sized suitcase.

"What's in there?"

"You'll find out soon enough. Now, about the money—take about a thousand out. You'll need it. Then you're going to follow me in your car. You're going to park it somewhere a few miles away from here, at the Target or something. Leave it unlocked with the keys in the ignition. It'll be neatly disposed of in a few days. Then you and I are going to go for a little ride."

I yawned, almost too relaxed to move. "Where are we going?"

"Mexico. I know someone there who can help you."

26

South of the Border

Interstate 5 began in Washington state and ended at the border between California and Mexico. The interesting thing about the border checkpoint in San Ysidro was that the patrol on the way into Mexico consisted of a half dozen bored Mexican agents nodding at cars as they drove by. There were no questions asked, no documents checked, no inquiries whatsoever. One didn't even have to stop. Thus, the line to get into Mexico was almost non-existent. But the line to get out would sometimes stretch a half mile long and last anywhere from a twenty-minute to a grueling four-hour wait.

Tom veered off the main road that ran through the center of Tijuana's tourist district—Avenida Revolución. Less than ten minutes after we had crossed the border, we were driving along an unlit two-lane highway heading south, away from town. We followed behind an old Toyota with Baja California license plates a few miles before it turned off onto a dirt road, its taillights illuminating the plumes of dirt kicked up by its tires. Faint lights sprinkled the dark valleys in between canyons. Along the way there were a few small stores and businesses—squat, run down stucco buildings with dirty windows and hand painted signage. Cars glided haphazardly through intersections without stop signs or traffic lights. When

I cracked open the window, the ever-present rancid smell of car exhaust filled my nostrils.

"How far is this, where we're going? Where *are* we going, anyway?" I asked Tom.

"A few miles more. I hope I can still remember how to get there. It's been a while."

"So, who is this guy and how do you know him?"

"Carlos? Carlos and I go way back."

We slowed down as a pickup truck full of teenaged boys pulled out in front of us, seemingly from nowhere. They huddled in the back, unsmiling, the cold January air whipping through their dark hair.

"When I was a freshman in college," he continued, "I came down here from UC Davis for spring break. I drove down with a couple of my friends. We were all underage, and of course we heard about all the trouble you can get into down here without having to be twenty one."

"Trouble is right." I remembered my last trip to Mexico when I was in college. I came with a couple of female friends, and we drove down to Rosarita Beach, about fifty miles south of the border along the ocean. We had gotten chased by the Federales for illegally lighting off firecrackers on the beach. I had helped the girls up over a fence and in my haste to follow closely behind had gotten my sneaker stuck in the chain-link at the top and had fallen awkwardly to the ground, dislocating my shoulder. "Wait—I didn't know you went to Davis."

"I did. I didn't graduate, though. What happened on that spring break pretty much screwed things up for me, big time." Tom flicked off the radio, which had been producing nothing but intermittent static for the past fifteen minutes. "The two guys I had come down with were interested in getting fucked up as soon as we got here. We found a sleazy hotel in town where we parked our car and rented a couple of rooms for like twenty bucks, then hit the main drag, looking for action.

Josh had some weird fetish for sleazy women I guess, because all he kept talking about the whole way down from Sacramento was how he was going to fuck the shit out of some Tijuana hooker. Karl and I didn't want to have anything to do with that, but we did end up following Josh into a back-alley strip joint off Revolution Avenue where they had some bad color photos pasted by the entrance of a woman sucking off a mule."

"Oh yeah, I think I've seen those places," I chuckled.

"Josh got sorta picked up by this tall, slightly homely hooker who could barely speak English. She gave him a hand job right there in the bar and then when we left, she followed us outside. Josh said he wanted to take her back to the hotel room and we told him that wasn't a good idea, for a lot of reasons besides the obvious."

"I think I know where this is going."

"Do you?"

"Yeah, because I've seen the kind of women who hang around those strip bars. They're not women. They're transvestites."

Tom nodded.

"So, this hooker was a man in drag?"

"Yeah, but we didn't figure that out until later. He followed us down a few blocks, but it was all very suspicious because he kept looking around, acting very jumpy. He convinced Josh to walk down one of the side streets with him, and he did, maybe expecting to get a blow job in the alley or whatever. We followed, keeping a bit of distance, when Josh and Prince Charming slipped into this dark, sunken entryway of a building. Karl and I stood there, waiting and smoking cigarettes, when suddenly this car pulls up in front of us and three big Mexicans jump out and start beating the shit out of us.

They took our wallets and sped off, Prince Charming in tow."

"So how did Josh figure out that it was a guy?"

"Why? Because he got an awful bruising from him. Apparently the guy was only feigning not being able to speak English. He told Josh exactly who he was before he gave him a black eye."

"Ouch. That must have been brutal."

"No kidding. So, after that we were screwed. No money, no documents, no nothin'. We schlepped back to our hotel room feeling fortunate that at least we still had the car keys."

My stomach lurched in hunger. I hadn't eaten anything since that morning's bagel and coffee, and I didn't see any Taco Bells or Burger

Kings anywhere nearby. As a matter of fact, the landscape was beginning to look devoid of any signs of civilization.

"We were going to just spend the night and leave in the morning, but Karl said he found some bills in his pocket, about fifteen or twenty bucks, so we decided to head back to the main drag for a few drinks and some music."

"You guys weren't too worried about having just been mugged and slapped around?"

"It wasn't so bad. Besides, we had driven nearly twelve hours to get that far. We didn't want to just turn around and go back right away.

So anyway, we had been in this one bar for a while when I spotted Prince Charming in a corner booth, snuggling against some middle-aged, sloshed gringo."

"Uh oh."

"Yeah, uh oh is right. I went right up to the son of a bitch and decked him, demanded he fork over whatever he had on him. It wasn't but a few minutes later I was being cuffed and mauled by the Federales and stuffed into the back one of their putzy little cop cars."

"What happened to your friends?"

"I don't know. I didn't see them again until a year later when I finally got out of jail."

"You were thrown in jail?"

"You got it. For assault and robbery. I tried to explain that the guy had robbed us first, but of course there was no proof of that. I was screwed, big time. I spent almost a year in the jail here near Tijuana. It was the most horrific year of my life. There was only one reason I stayed alive in that hell hole."

"Carlos?"

"He saved my life. More than once, I might add. We've kept in touch over the years. He has a place up in Burbank, but he comes down here once in a while to visit with family and to do some business." Tom slowed the car and squinted at the road up ahead. "I think we're almost there."

"So, is that why you didn't finish school and why you couldn't get into the Academy? Because of the year you spent down here?"

"You got it. Whole life down the toilet because of some stupid mistake I made one night. That's the way it goes sometimes, doesn't it?"

I hope he wasn't referring to me. My life hadn't been heading in a good direction anyway, but I certainly hoped it wasn't going completely down the drain after tonight. I braced myself against the dash as Tom slowed the truck to a crawl through the gouged out muddy road that wound around the side of a canyon. The bouncing of the truck's headlights afforded us brief glimpses of the homemade shanties on either side of the dirt road. Some were better constructed than others, some were made of what looked like scrap construction materials, and some were made of plaster and stone. Trash was scattered across the dirt road and in front of the shacks. A child no more than five years old scurried in front of us, his eyes ablaze with mischief.

In addition to my hunger pangs, the bouncing of the truck punished my overfull bladder and all I could think of was getting out to take a whiz. "How much farther?"

"Not much. Just up the road a quarter of a mile."

The quality of the housing began to improve a little. I even saw lights on inside some of the houses, probably the result of an outdoor generator providing electricity. Cars were parked on dirt driveways—Fords and Oldsmobiles and Hondas and Volkswagens. I was amazed because some of the cars looked like they were worth five times more than the house. We pulled abruptly in front of a two-story white stucco house. The lights were on downstairs and cast a glow through the drawn blue curtains. A chorus of barking dogs greeted us from the fenced area on the side of the house as we approached the front door, which was marred and dirty.

A woman's voice asked timidly, "Quien es?"

"Rosa, es Tomás. Carlos está en la casa?"

"O, sí. Uno momento, por favor."

The door opened a minute later and a short pudgy man wearing gym shorts and a white tank top invited us in. He looked from me to Tom and back to me again. "Tom, hey, what's going on?"

"We're in need of your services, bud. This is my friend, David."

We shook hands and followed him deeper into the house. The ceilings seemed unusually low, and the rooms were small. The television was on in the living room and an older couple looking to be in their sixties were watching the news in Spanish. The house was cluttered but clean. Rosa sat in a nearby chair, sewing. She smiled at me as we walked past.

We followed Carlos up a flight of stairs to the second story. I had a difficult time with the climb. The stairs were narrow and seemed unevenly spaced, so I kept tripping every other step and had to hold on to the wall to keep from falling into Tom's ass.

"Walk much these days?" Tom chided.

"Shut up."

We were in a room filled with computer equipment and desks. Reams of paper were shoved up against the walls, and an area of the room was curtained off from ceiling to floor. Carlos turned on another desk lamp and motioned for us to have a seat in an old, worn-out loveseat that looked like it was from the sixties with its mustard yellow floral fabric.

"David needs new ID. Driver's license, passport. Probably doesn't need a social security card. Passport is the most important."

"How soon?"

"Right now. Tonight, if that's possible."

"Sí, I can do that. No problem."

Tom got up off the loveseat. "I gotta get something out of the truck. I'll be right back."

Carlos eyed me curiously. "Are you the David who runs the mini storage?"

"That's me."

Carlos nodded. Tom must have mentioned me.

"You have a bathroom I can use?"

"Down the hall."

Now all I need is a shower and a hot meal, I thought as I felt my way down the tiny corridor. I wonder if I could impose on Rosa to whip up an omelet for me? Or a burrito? I found the bathroom and almost began giggling at my predicament. In a few hours I should be getting started on my paper route. Oh well. I felt bad for all of two seconds before I remembered spending my last three hundred dollars to fix the Saab so the customer prima donnas could sleep in until seven a.m. *It'll sure be quiet on San Miguel Way this morning, ya bastards,* I thought.

The bathroom smelled funny. I aimed for the bowl in the dark and quickly zipped back up when I had finished. I wondered where I would be pissing this time tomorrow night. A posh hotel room or a community latrine?

Tom brought in the mystery suitcase from his truck and we inspected its contents. Inside were a variety of wigs, fake beards and moustaches, a dozen flesh-colored silicone noses, and a spectrum of makeup vials. I took out one of the noses and stuck it on my face. "Are we going to play Secret Agent Man with this stuff?"

"We're going to make you pretty, David. Pretty for the camera. You can't be going around in public with that ugly mug of yours. That just won't do."

I selected a blonde wig out of the case and tried it on. "Is it me?"

"No, that's all wrong for your coloring. You need darker hair. Actually, we're going to make you sorta balding, so you look older."

Carlos seemed fascinated by the suitcase's contents. "Where'd you get all this stuff? This is great."

"Remember that storage unit I bought out in LA?" Tom asked me.

"Oh, the movie studio unit? This is out of there? Cool."

We experimented with a combination of moustaches, wigs, beards, and noses until we decided the most convincing disguise was a balding man in his late thirties with a big, black, bushy moustache. With my two days' worth of stubble, however, I looked like a terrorist. Carlos shook his head and directed me back into the funky smelling bathroom to shave. There was only one razor to choose from, and it looked like it had some mileage on it already. I rinsed it under the stream of hot water and tapped it a few times against the basin of the sink to expel the accumulation of whiskers before bringing it to my face. I was slow and methodical with the dull blade, but still managed to nick myself a couple of times right under my chin.

Now instead of looking like a middle-aged terrorist, I looked like a middle-aged man with a bad case of razor burn. I inspected the fake passport. My new name for airport security was Robert Pollack. Carlos confiscated all my credit cards and my driver's license and four hours later my wallet was filled with my new identity.

Before we left, Carlos reminded me, "Just don't forget, the credit card is only good for a few days. Use it wisely. The limit is ten thousand dollars."

I thought about how many miles away ten thousand dollars would get me.

27

∽

Flying Blind

The traffic was bumper to bumper on I-5 on the way to Lindberg Field International Airport that morning and I sat uncomfortably shifting around in the passenger seat. I had stuffed half the money in a pair of thick tights that I had squeezed into under some tan baggy corduroys Tom gave me. The other half was in a suitcase under my feet, along with a change of clothing and some toiletries.

He stopped in front of the American Airlines sign, and I stumbled out of the truck. He grasped my hand, shaking it briefly. "Good luck. Be careful. I wish I could say 'drop me a line' when you get there, but I'm not sure that's such a good idea. At least not for a while."

"Thanks for all your help. I really appreciate it. You saved my life."

I raised my hand up to my forehead in a mock salute as he drove away. Inside the terminal I checked the departure information on the black and white monitors next to the American Airlines counter. I stepped up to the ticket agent and laid out my forged identity and credit card on the counter. "I need to purchase a ticket."

"Where to, sir?"

"Your nine fifteen flight to Hartford, Connecticut."

***

201

I was flying blind, taking a chance that Ellen would be around, that she would be able to meet with me, that she would actually want to. We had talked about our feelings for each other and about wanting to see each other face to face someday, but it's one thing to daydream about someone from the relative comfort of your familiar life and quite another when you are actually contemplating calling the person up one afternoon to say, "I'm just down the street at the Marriott. Can you come over?"

It was fortunate that I had Ellen's work and home number memorized, since I had not taken my address book or anything else with me from the house except my wallet and the money. I had never been in Hartford before. Hell—I had never been west of the Mississippi River before. So when the taxi driver dropped me off in front of the downtown Marriott, I was feeling slightly disoriented. I also knew I had to hurry up and check in so I could call Ellen before she left work for the day. With the cross-country flight and the three-hour time difference, it was already past four o'clock.

When I was finally inside the room and alone, the first thing I did was strip down to my underwear. I pulled the cash out of my pants pockets, my shirt pocket, my jacket pockets. I shoved off the tights stuffed full of sweaty money. It had been an insufferably long flight with over three hundred thousand dollars stuffed inside my clothes like ticking. I scratched myself all over with glee, relieved to feel fresh air on my skin again. I peeled off the fake moustache carefully, knowing I would have to replace it for the flight out in a day or two. When I took off the skull cap and wig, my hair remained plastered flat on my head. I studied myself in the mirror. I looked like one of the characters in the Weeble Village set, but with long red scratch marks all over my skin. I yanked off the fake nose and lay down on the firm bed with the telephone on my chest.

Things were hitting the fan back in San Diego by now. Hans would have come to work and noticed the cash drawer depleted of large bills. Perhaps Mrs. Vaughn had already gone to the police the night before, and so the cops were swarming around the facility like maggots this morning, looking for clues to my whereabouts. The self-storage owner would be notified of my untimely departure. I sighed. Taking his money and leaving him in a lurch was the one thing I felt really bad about. He certainly didn't deserve this from me. He had always been a very generous and caring man.

I dialed Ellen's number without picking up the receiver. I was nervous. I felt a little foolish, too. She would probably think I was a psycho, showing up on her doorstep out of the blue. I had to find a way to tell her from the start about my predicament so that she wouldn't freak out about my being in Connecticut.

I knew the company where she worked, and I knew that she worked in downtown Hartford, but I wasn't quite sure where, exactly. For all I knew, she could have been in one of the offices across the street, finishing up her day and thinking of me. I walked over to the hotel room window. I was on the seventeenth floor. I couldn't tell what the building across the street was. It looked like an office building of some sort. It was hard to tell exactly.

"OK, stop dorking around and call her," I said to myself out loud.

I picked up the receiver and dialed her number. It didn't occur to me what I would do if her voicemail kicked in. Fortunately, she answered on the first ring, and I didn't have to worry.

"This is Ellen Roth. May I help you?"

"Hey, you. You almost ready to go home?"

"David, how weird!"

"What's weird?"

"I just called you not five minutes ago. Hans said you weren't there."

"I'm NOT there, hon." I smiled. God, it was good to hear her voice. "You were thinking of me five minutes ago?" I teased, still composing how I was going to break my news to her.

"Yes, I was. I'm always thinking of you, you know that."

"I know. I love that. Me too, girl."

"So where are you, in your apartment playing hooky? Hans sounded bizarre, by the way. Like he had something he wanted to tell me but couldn't."

"I bet. I'm surprised he was able to keep his mouth shut."

"What do you mean?"

"Ellen, I need to tell you something, but I don't want you to freak out."

"OK—"

"Are you sitting down?"

The amusement in her voice faded. "David, what's going on? Are you alright?" she whispered.

"I've got myself into quite a jam. I had to leave San Diego. It's a bit of a long and complicated story but suffice it to say that I messed with the wrong people and I had to get out of town before someone came to rub me out."

"What? Oh my god, are you going to be alright?"

"I think so. I think so, yes."

"So, where are you?"

"You sure you won't freak out?"

"Why would I freak out?"

"Just tell me you won't get the wrong idea. I mean—"

"WHERE ARE YOU?"

"I'm in Hartford."

"Oh, Jesus."

"You're freaking out."

"No, I'm not."

"Yes, you are."

"Where in Hartford? Where?"

"I'm at the downtown Marriott."

I waited through the long pause that followed, struggling to swallow the lump in my throat. "I wanted to see you. I'll probably leave the country in a day or two, but I wanted to see you first."

"You don't have to explain, you goof. I'm glad you came out here. I am just a little bit in shock."

"I know. I can tell."

"I'm just trying to figure something out. I want to come over there after work to talk to you, but I have to make some arrangements first. What room are you in?"

"Seventeen twelve."

"Okay, let me call you right back. Okay?"

I put the phone down and ran my fingers through my greasy hair. I was going to make a great first impression on her with the bags under my eyes and my funky B.O., not to mention my nappy hair. Whatever arrangements she was making, I hoped they meant she wouldn't show up at least for another hour, so I could make myself presentable.

The phone rang and I did a belly flop on the bed before I picked it up.

"I'll be there in about an hour and a half. Is that okay?"

"Perfect."

"I'll meet you in the lobby."

"That sounds good."

"Great. See you then."

"But, wait!"

"What?"

"How will you know it's me? We've never met. Those pictures I emailed you could have been all fake. Some college buddy of mine but not me. For all you know I could be some hideous midget with a hunchback and a big hairy mole on my nose." I sneered in amusement.

"Don't be a goofball, David."

***

The Marriott had an overpriced men's clothier in the lobby where I bought eight hundred dollars worth of dress shirts, slacks, shoes, and a couple sweaters. I laid down the most I had ever paid for a pair of shoes—$450 for leather loafers, made in Italy, and $650 for an elegant brown tweed coat. I was definitely overdressed for the occasion. The weather in Connecticut was below freezing, and all I had for warmth was a thin nylon jacket and a few inches of paper insulation, compliments of the Federal Reserve.

The sales clerk looked like he was going to shoot his load right there at the cash register as he counted the two thousand or so in cash that I handed over for the purchase. When I returned to my room, the steak dinner I had ordered from room service had arrived, and I drooled in anticipation as I changed into my new clothes. Outside it had turned dark, and I could see my reflection in the window as I buttoned up the pewter-colored long-sleeved shirt I had selected to wear that evening. I hadn't bought new clothes in at least six months, and as I tucked the shirt into my new slacks I noticed by the way they were fitting that I had forgotten to buy the next size down. The last month or two must have really taken its toll on me.

As I went to pull the drapes closed, I looked out at the busy street below, teeming with rush hour commuters. Steam rose out of the gutters and hovered over the icy sidewalks. The red and white of car headlights reflected a hundred times in the glass of the surrounding buildings. I put my hand on the cold glass of the window and watched cars drive into the underground parking of the hotel directly below my window, seventeen stories down. Which one of those cars would be Ellen's? I didn't even know what kind of car she drove. I didn't know so many basic things about her. I didn't know what kind of clothes she wore or what kind of food she liked or if she was the kind of person who looked you in the eye when she talked to you. But on the other hand, I knew things about her that no one else did. I knew her insecurities. I knew her strengths and her fears. I knew what she dreamed about at night. I knew what it was that made her happy, and why.

I ate while watching the local news, growing increasingly aware of the time. What if she was already here? What if she had gotten here earlier than expected? Would she just wait in the lobby until I showed up, or would she come to my room? Why hadn't she suggested we meet in my room in the first place? I knew why. It was because, even though we felt like we knew each other so well, even though we felt so close, there was still that speck of mistrust. There was still that hint of trepidation because, after all, we had never really met.

Seeing the weather map of a region I wasn't used to seeing on the television and hearing news stories of towns whose names I had never heard before reminded me again that I had left behind familiarity. I had left behind everything and everyone I knew. For the first time in my life

I didn't know what I would be doing the next day. I didn't know where I would be in a week or a month. I hadn't even stopped to think about where I would go after Hartford yet, either.

I replaced the stainless-steel lid on my dinner plate and turned off the T.V. I wasn't completely without direction. I knew where I was supposed to be in five minutes. I grabbed the room key off the dresser and made my way down to the hotel lobby to finally meet the woman of my dreams.

28

More Like Nastassja Kinski

When she stepped inside the front doors, I almost didn't recognize her. Her hair was longer than I had thought it would be. It was straight and thick and black, and hung straight down around her long neck. She was wearing a gray trench coat and heels. Even from across the lobby I could see the tinge of red on her cheeks from the cold outside. She slowed her pace as she entered farther into the lobby and then stopped and looked around. I had settled into an upholstered chair near the elevators, and I waited for her to spot me before I stood up.

Her eyes locked on me, but she didn't move right away. Her expression softened and she smiled. As I stood up and walked toward her, her eyes didn't leave mine, and her body didn't budge an inch until I was within a few feet of her. She reached out her arms and we embraced for a long time without saying a word. Her coat was still cold, and I thought I felt her shiver. I caught my breath and hugged her tighter before stepping back.

"I'm so glad you came. Thank you," I whispered.

She studied my face while she gripped my hands in hers. "Oh God, is it really you? I can't believe you're here." She shook her head and smiled.

"Let's go sit down over there." I gestured to a couch nearby. "Or do you want to go sit in the bar and have a drink?"

"A drink is just what I need. Let's do the bar."

We entered the small bar that adjoined the hotel restaurant. There were only three other patrons there; two businessmen having a quiet conversation and a fat, balding man sitting at the barstool, watching his cocktail napkin. I helped Ellen out of her coat, and we settled into a corner booth.

"I had to go pick up Pete from daycare. I left him with my neighbor who sits for us occasionally. Jack's out of town this week." She pulled her hair back out of her face and adjusted the delicate charm that hung from a fine gold chain around her neck.

"What would you like to drink before I tell you my sad story?"

"I know! I can't wait to hear it. How about a glass of white wine?"

"Done."

As I stood at the bar, waiting for the order, I stole a glance at Ellen, who sat serenely in the booth with her arms crossed on the tabletop. She was so beautiful. There were things I hadn't noticed about her from the few photos she had emailed me. For instance, the fact that her fingers were long and delicate, and she had a wonderful profile. Or how sexy her ankles looked in her brown suede heels.

I handed her the glass of wine and sat across from her, watching her take a sip. Her lips were ripe strawberries and I wanted to kiss them. "Your photos don't do you justice, you know. I thought at first that you reminded me of Courtney Cox, but now that I see you in person, I think you look more like Nastassja Kinski."

"Nastassja Kinski? Wow, thanks." Her smile was wide and her cheeks glowed pinker. "I was just thinking the same thing about you. That you're so much more handsome in person, I mean. Your eyes are so intense."

"You should see me in my disguise."

She raised an eyebrow.

"I had to set up a new identity so that I wouldn't leave a trace of my whereabouts. I had Tom—you remember Tom—set me up with someone who got me a new passport. For the passport photo I posed as a balding man in his late thirties with a big ugly nose."

"Disguises and fake IDs? What kind of mess did you get yourself into? Is the mob after you? Did you rob a bank?"

For the next hour, I explained to Ellen everything that had happened. Toward the end of the story, we found ourselves speaking more quietly and looking over our shoulders to make sure no one was eavesdropping.

"Do you really think the police would have charged you with burglary? What if you had found a way to put the money back?"

"I didn't want to take that risk. Even if I put the money back, or if the police decided to cut me some slack, what would Cutter, ah, Adams have done if he caught on that I had ripped him off?"

"You think he would have risked getting close to the cops in order to get his vengeance on you?"

"The guy is a little crazy, who knows what he would have done? Besides, it's too late now to go back and change things. I took money out of the cash drawer to pay off Mrs. Vaughn, so I'm out of a job, even if Adams gets arrested and I don't."

"So, what are you going to do? Where are you going to go?"

"I don't know yet. I'll figure it out in the next day or two, though."

Ellen gestured for me to lean in closer across the table. "So, how much?" she whispered. "How much money do you have?"

"Seven hundred and fifty thousand."

"What?!"

I saw the bartender glance over at our booth. "Shhhhh."

"Are you serious?"

"Dead."

"Well then, I don't blame you for leaving. I would have done the same thing in your position."

"Exactly. What did I have to stick around for?"

"Here's the beauty of the situation, in my opinion."

"There's a beautiful side?"

"Yeah, there is. I think that as long as you are smart and lay low for a while, at least a year or two, that you'll be fine. I just don't think the FBI or the police or whoever will spend too much time and resources trying to find you. Hell, it's possible that they might not even know you took the money. Maybe Mrs. Vaughn was bluffing that she would turn you in." She finished her wine and continued. "I don't think Adams is going to waste too much of his time trying to find you. He's probably not as connected as you think he is."

"You're probably right. But I don't want to lull myself into a false sense of security and end up dead in a dark alley somewhere."

"Of course not." She looked at her watch. "You know, I have to leave soon to pick up Pete and put him to bed."

"I know. I wish I could meet him."

"You can. But not tonight, obviously."

"That wouldn't look too good."

"No."

"What are you doing tomorrow?"

"Tomorrow, hmmm." She grinned, the sexiest I'd seen her all night. "I'm picking you up tomorrow, bright and early. Say, seven thirty?"

"Where are we going?"

"My favorite place in the world. You'll see."

"I hate surprises."

"No you don't. You love surprises. You'll love this one, too. I promise." She stood up and retrieved her coat. "I'll come knocking on your door."

"I can't wait."

I walked her out to the parking garage and to her car, which turned out to be a white Land Rover. She pressed the remote button on her key ring and the car chirped to life.

"Wow, fancy," I teased.

She stood with her back against the driver's door and reached out to play with one of my shirt buttons, her eyes cast down bashfully. I took her hand in mine and brought it up to my lips, kissing her fingertips before I bent down and kissed her mouth. I felt my body come alive as she threw her arms around my neck and sucked on my tongue hungrily. My hands were lost in her hair as I tasted her, our chests pressed tightly together.

She sighed softly as my lips detached from hers and I began kissing her chin and working my way up to her earlobes. "David, we'd better stop or else I'm not going to be able to leave tonight."

"Mmmm." Her ears were soft and smelled of lavender.

"You have no idea how weak you make me," she murmured.

I went back to kissing her fingertips and then let her get into the Land Rover. She rolled down her window and I kissed her one more time. "I'll see you tomorrow. Sleep tight."

As I watched her Rover pull away, it occurred to me that I probably wouldn't sleep at all that night.

29

What Borders Connecticut?

We drove east along I-8 toward New York and Pennsylvania. The traffic was light and Ellen kept the speedometer at a steady sixty-five. It was a cold morning, and the sky was overcast and drab. I had packed my suitcase that morning and checked out before we had left. Ellen had taken one look at my expensive leather shoes and shook her head.

"Those won't do. We'll have to stop by somewhere and get you some hiking shoes or something."

"We're going hiking in this weather?"

"You Californians. You make it sound as if acid is pouring out of the sky."

"It almost feels that way."

The interstate out of Connecticut cut through miles and miles of forest and hills. I sat back quietly, mesmerized by the deciduous landscape. "You haven't told me yet where we're going."

"We're going to a place I haven't been to in years. It's an old three hundred-acre mountaintop estate in the Catskills in the north-easternmost corner of Pennsylvania. I called last night to make sure the people who own it still operate it as a bed and breakfast. The place is wonderful. They have miles of trails weaving through the forest, and views of the Delaware River. There's a beautiful Victorian town a few miles down the hill, too."

"Sounds very romantic."

"I suppose it does," she put her hand on my leg, "but since you've never been to this part of the country before, I wanted to show it off a little to you."

"You love living here, don't you?"

"I do. Very much. There's something about New England. I feel like I belong here. No matter where I go in the world, I always miss Connecticut." She adjusted the heat controls. "Where I grew up, you know—in Ohio, it was in this drab subdivision outside of Cleveland. When I graduated from high school I couldn't wait to get out to college. I applied to about a dozen places, but I was accepted into Boston University with a full scholarship. I was so lucky."

"And you've never looked back?"

"To Ohio? I'll never move back there. I hated it there. I visit my parents there at least a couple of times a year. My brother and sister have moved away, too."

"Right. One lives in Ann Arbor and the other in—where was it?"

"My sister lives in Cape Cod. She married a really nice guy, and they started their own investment company."

"Where did you meet Jack? I don't think you ever told me."

"He used to work at my company, straight out of law school."

We had unceremoniously crossed the New York-Connecticut border. I flipped open the glove box and looked under the owner's manual but there was nothing else there.

"Looking for something?"

"I was hoping you had a Rand McNally or something."

"Why? I know where I'm going."

"That makes one of us. I have suddenly become painfully aware that my knowledge of United States geography is very poor. I didn't even know that Connecticut bordered New York."

Ellen laughed out loud.

"I'm going to have to take a crash course in world geography if I'm going to decide where to go. This is why they tell you to pay attention in grade school when they're teaching you that stuff, you know. In case you're ever on the lam."

"David, I meant to ask you last night—."

"Hmm?"

"Have you spoken with Dana? Does she know what happened?"

"No. She has no idea what happened. She actually called me the night I left, to warn me that she was coming over to get some more things out of the apartment. She was worried she'd find another woman in bed with me."

Ellen kept her eyes straight at the road ahead. "She doesn't seem like she's too motivated to patch things up. Not that it matters now, I guess. Or does it?"

"No, it doesn't matter. That phone call made me realize that I had been living under a fog of self-delusion for a long time when it comes to Dana. I thought she would always trust me, always give me the benefit of the doubt. Perhaps she had been right about me in a way."

"Right about what?"

"Look at me. Look what I'm doing. What I've done. What I will probably do a little later." I looked to see Ellen's reaction to my last sentence. Either she had none or didn't understand what I meant. "I am not an upstanding icon of integrity, now am I?"

"You have a lot of integrity. Don't say that."

"Those few days she was gone, I thought about what to do to make her understand. I thought about asking her to come back. But the reason I didn't do anything in that regard was maybe because I didn't *want* her back. Dana and I were wrong for each other from the first day we met. I just never had time to think that through. I never had a week to myself to think about things. From the moment we met, we spent almost every day together.

First we worked together, then we dated, then we moved in together. At first I was high on the euphoria of being in love with her. Then when that died down it was five years of going through the motions. Somewhere along the way I fell out of love with her. It could have been a year ago, it could have been two weeks ago. I have no idea. That's the problem. I have no idea when things went wrong, exactly."

"What do you think she'll do when she finds out you're missing?"

"Get pissed because me being gone means I stuck her with the creditors."

"No, c'mon. Seriously."

"I *am* serious. I am trying to imagine Dana feeling bad or missing me, and I can't. Sometimes I used to wonder if she was capable of true warmth, true love. Even when I felt closest to her, she always had this far-away look in her eye. She always seemed to be thinking about something other than what was happening at the moment."

"Emotionally absent?"

"Yes, exactly."

"I guess there's more than one way to be absent from a marriage. You can be absent physically or you can be absent emotionally."

"You can. Absolutely. But let's not talk about that right now." I extended my arm over Ellen's shoulders and shifted over in my seat so I could kiss her cheek. "Because in all honesty, that entire week I was home by myself, there was only one woman I wanted to be with."

"Oh, really?" Ellen smiled slightly and blushed. "Tell me who."

"I'm looking at her beautiful face right this second."

***

The estate was named Evergreen Glen and was a few miles off the interstate in northeastern Pennsylvania at the toes of the Catskill moun-tains. Ellen knew every turn by heart, and I asked her how many times she had been here, and with whom.

"It's been a while. Several years, I think. The last time I was here was with my sister and her husband for a fall foliage weekend when they were visiting right after Pete was born. Before that, I came up here a lot when I was in college."

"Have you ever been up here with Jack?"

"No, I haven't. He doesn't like staying at bed and breakfasts. He's not much into going out of town these days, anyway. He travels so much that he actually thinks hanging out at home is a vacation."

She turned into a narrow, paved road that sliced through a thick wooded area, and the Land Rover dropped down a gear to pull up the hill. Snow that looked to be at least a few days old covered the pine trees in clumps and blanketed the surrounding forest. I was tempted to roll the window down to smell the fresh, pine-scented air. We drove out onto a clearing and Ellen turned into a long driveway that led up to a sprawling ranch surrounded by junipers and shrubs and bare maple trees. We drove by two parked cars and a small hand painted sign that read, "Welcome, Guests! Please pull in here."

"Aren't we a little early for check-in?" The digital clock on the console read 9:18 a.m.

"No, not at all. They know we're coming this early, and they've welcomed us to join them for a big breakfast. You're going to love it, too. The owners are this old German couple and their specialties are apple fritters with lots of Vermont maple syrup and butter."

My stomach tugged and I began salivating at the thought. I hadn't even thought about breakfast or eating up until that point because I had been mesmerized by Ellen and the idea that she was sitting within inches of me. I stepped out onto the driveway and stretched. It was cold but the air was moist and fragrant. The distant squeal of a bird echoed behind me.

We were welcomed inside by a tall woman with very short gray hair, wearing a colorful apron. We followed her inside the richly decorated house. A tremendous oil painting of the estate as it looks in the summer hung above the fireplace mantle. A stuffed elk head greeted us in the large dining room, where a long table set for twelve was cheerfully filled with pastries, vases of dried flowers, and steaming plates of sausages and fritters. Two other couples were at the table who greeted us as we sat down where the hostess suggested.

"I welcome our returning guest, Ellen, and her husband—I'm sorry, I don't know your name?" The German woman had a thick Bavarian accent and her R's vibrated off her tongue.

"Husband?" I felt Ellen poke me under the table. "My name is David."

"Welcome, Ellen and David. How is that baby boy of yours, that cute fellow?"

I poured myself some coffee from a carafe and kicked Ellen back.

"He's just fine, thank you," Ellen said. "He's staying with friends while we take a little break."

"How lovely. We hope you enjoy your time with us."

I felt Ellen's hand coil around my upper thigh under the tablecloth.

"Yes, we can't wait to see our room and get settled in." I choked out between big gulps of strong hot coffee.

30

Getting Warmer

We were given the key to our suite, which turned out to be the re-modeled stablemaster's quarters located down the slope from the main house at the end of a narrow flagstone path. The suite was small and sparsely furnished with a dining room, kitchen, a sitting area just off the front entrance, a large bedroom, and an adjoining bathroom. I put down my suitcase and took off my coat, feeling the chill of the underheated quarters bite into my skin.

"Brrr. You see a thermostat around here?"

"It's over there, I think. There's also some firewood around the back, if I remember correctly."

I came back with a stack of logs under my arm and began arranging them in the fireplace in the bedroom. Ellen found some matches in the kitchen, and in a matter of minutes I was able to kindle up a pretty good blaze.

Ellen was still wearing her jacket, her arms wrapped tightly around her torso. I spread her arms apart gently and began unzipping her parka slowly and deliberately while I leaned in to kiss her.

"You going to keep me warm?" her breath was soft on my cheek.

"I'm going to make you warm inside and out."

She sighed out a low groan as I slipped my arms under the warmth of her coat and pushed it off her body, letting it fall to the floor. She was wearing a low-cut cable knit sweater over her jeans, the same color as her hair, making it hard to tell where her hair ended and the sweater began. I licked the creamy skin of her cleavage right below the arch of the delicate herringbone gold chain that circled her long neck. Her fingers weaved through my hair as I dropped to my knees and lifted up her sweater, kissing her belly.

I felt her breathing quicken as lifted the sweater up over her breasts, revealing a red lace bra. Goosebumps spread across her torso at the moment my hands found her taut, dark nipples through the silky fabric.

When I stood back up to lift the sweater off her completely, her eyes were closed and her lips were parted slightly. I took her face in my hands and kissed the corner of each eyelid, kissed her long black lashes that fanned out across her cheek. She murmured my name over and over as I bent down to kiss her neck while my hands worked to free her breasts from the bra.

All at once we were on the bed, entangled in each other's limbs, my mouth and hands and eyes full of her. She kicked off her jeans and I straddled her, my elbows above her shoulders. I took a minute to catch my breath and look into her blue eyes.

"God, you are so beautiful," I whispered, as the tip of my nose touched hers.

She lifted her hands over her head and grabbed the top edge of the headboard as I nuzzled the soft underside of her upper arms. She arched her back beneath me, spreading her legs apart and grinding her lower torso into mine. I sat back slowly, my fingertips running down her long body beneath me. I watched the way her breasts undulated as she wrapped her legs around my hips and arched her back over and over. My fingers found their mark and curved up under the thin seam of her panties. My head was filled with the singular thought of tasting her.

I shifted down onto the bed between her long legs. As my tongue languidly glided in and out of her soft folds and her slippery warmth, the sound of her moans coursed through my body.

I cannot even remember how many times she came or how many

times I came or even if either of us crested the peak at all that day. I just know one thing—that was the day I lost myself inside of Ellen Roth. I had forgotten where I was or who I was supposed to be or where I was supposed to go. I had become disoriented with love for a woman who, up to that point, I had only known from afar. Who, up to that point, had only been a long stream of words and pictures in the margins of my life.

When the morning was over and our bodies were spent, I lay under the covers with her, watching the way the gentle curve of her shoulder rose and fell ever so slightly with each breath. My new life had started that day, and my first and only thought was that I didn't want to spend the rest of it without her.

***

We made a quick jaunt into town to the nearby Walmart so that I could buy myself some appropriate shoes to wear on a hike through the snow-packed forest. Ellen wanted to take me on her favorite trail, and despite my protests about getting lost in the woods, I ended up looking forward to a long walk in the brisk air. A fog had settled in my brain, and I felt like I was functioning in slow motion.

The trail was well trampled by previous guests of the inn, and easy to follow. We had packed a thermos full of hot chocolate and some sandwiches in case we got hungry later. The clouds had not dissipated at all, but appeared to have gotten thicker and grayer since we had arrived at the inn. The acrid smell of moss, wet leaves, and pine permeated the air. We dodged boulders and fallen tree trunks, and panted through a thigh-burning climb up a slope that seemed to go on for half a mile, at least.

My month-long gig with the paper route had put me in the best shape I had been in years and I felt invigorated by the climb. Ellen was having no trouble keeping up with me, and I was impressed. Whenever I looked back, she was right behind me, her eyes glimmering up at me and her head cocked, almost challenging me.

"I thought you said you were a couch potato." I took three big steps around a large rock and paused, turning around to extend my hand out to Ellen. "Liar."

"OK, you caught me. I'm not as sedentary as I led you to believe. I like to bike ride a lot, and since Jack is away so often, I end up pulling Pete along in the trailer. That's always double the workout."

"Great. You sleep with someone and suddenly the pristine façade begins to flake away and the lies rear their ugly heads."

"Real bitch, ain't it?" Ellen scooped up a small wad of ice and snow and thrust it at my head. She missed, but only by an inch or two.

"Aren't you worried about Jack calling you late in the evening and not finding you home?" I knew that Ellen had planned this outing as an overnight stay and my paranoid nature was beginning to kick in.

"No."

"Why not?"

"He hardly ever calls me, and if he did happen to call late at night, he probably would think I was over at a friend's house or something. Or not answering the phone. Or online, and the call waiting was disabled."

"Sounds like he trusts you and wouldn't have any reason to be suspicious." I thought about my last night with Dana and the way she had so easily believed all the untruths about me. I thought about how shocked I was to realize that she hadn't trusted me at all.

Ellen stiffened and dropped back a few steps, letting go of my hand. It took me a few seconds before I realized my blunder. "I'm sorry, I wasn't thinking. I didn't mean it that way."

"Don't apologize. You're absolutely right, after all. He *does* trust me. That's why this is so confusing for me." She sat down on the weather-worn bark of a downed tree, avoiding my eyes. "Even though I had never even kissed another man since I met Jack— until now—I feel so totally reckless. It's as if this entire relationship between us has grown without my regard for consequence or what he would think or what is the right thing to do. I've run headfirst into it without even a glimmer of guilt or remorse.

"I've felt this shift in my marriage since shortly after you and I began to get close. It seemed that the more my feelings for you grew, the less intimate I was with my husband, and the more I found excuses to be irritated with him. I knew the reason why. I knew what was happening and I did nothing to stop it." Her eyes finally locked on mine. "I didn't want to stop it. I couldn't. Why is that?"

I sat next to her and grasped her hand with both of mine, squeezing it. "I don't know. Maybe we needed each other and didn't even know it."

"That's exactly what it feels like. I ask myself, if I didn't need you before I met you, why is it that I need you so much now? What have you changed in me that makes you so necessary?"

"Girl, you are trying to answer the question that has no answer. Believe me, people have tried to make sense out of this stuff. It's yet to be accomplished." I began to feel clammy and stood back up. "We'd better hustle it up or we won't make it back before it gets dark."

A few minutes later we crested the hill and Ellen pointed down through the trees at the valley below. "See there? That's the Delaware River."

It was barely discernable through the mist that moved silently through the trees in the surrounding hills.

"But we're nowhere near Delaware," I joked. "Or are we?"

Ellen smacked my arm gently. "What were you doing during geography period in grade school?"

"Daydreaming about girls? What else?" I leaned into her.

The gray-soaked clouds seemed to drop down to brush the tips of the evergreens around us. Just as we began to follow the crest of the hill the wind kicked up, and seemingly from nowhere it began to snow. Big, chunky clusters of snow swirled around us. I stopped and looked straight up, dizzy when I saw the flakes rush down around me from the sky. Ellen's hand brushed my arm and she gently tugged at my wrist.

"Why are you stopping?"

"It's snowing." I could feel her cool hand in mine, my gaze still focused upward.

"I know."

"I've never seen it snow."

"You've never seen it snow? But—"

I smiled at her, then kissed a flake off her eyebrow. "I grew up in California, remember? The few times I went up into the mountains, into the Sierra Nevadas, I saw snow on the ground, but I've never actually seen it snow. Until now."

"My David; so deprived." She pressed her chest into mine and wrapped her arms around me, her face inches from mine. "How will you ever make up for it?"

"I don't know. But the possibilities are endless now, aren't they?"

"Mmhmm."

She rested her head in the crook of my neck. I smelled her hair, now wet with fresh snow. "It's so quiet all of a sudden. Do you notice?"

"Yes, the snow sort of blocks everything out. Isn't it nice?"

More than just a lack of sound, the air felt muffled somehow. It was as if someone had stuck pillows on the side of my head. "Nice, but I bet you're cold. Maybe we should go."

"No, let's stay for a bit. Watch it snow together. I'm fine. You're keeping me warm." She poked a finger into my belly before she added, "Just like you promised."

Our breathing became synchronized, and we rocked slightly as I held her against me. Nothing mattered to me at that moment except her. I had momentarily forgotten that just a week ago I had been lying next to another woman, that I was in fact still married. I had forgotten that I was on the run, that I no longer had a place that was home.

I brought my hand up to the side of her face and followed the soft curves of her cheek to the corners of her lips. She pulled back a little to look up at me as I traced the outer edges of her lips with my finger. Her eyes welled with tears, whether from the cold or from something else, I couldn't tell. I pressed my forehead against hers and blurted, "I am so in love with you." My eyes closed almost reflexively, and I kissed her, tasting her again briefly.

"And I'm in love with you, David Bailey."

As soon as the words left her lips I willed her to say them again and again and again. They were droplets of water for my parched soul, and I couldn't get quenched fast enough. But she didn't say them again. She just leaned into me tighter and we stood there, silently looking at the snow falling. I replayed the words for myself instead and let their warmth wash over me.

31

The Proposition

The snow fell steadily throughout most of the rest of the afternoon and into the evening, worrying us about being able to drive out the next morning. We had a long, relaxed dinner in town that night. The hostess seated us right next to the window where we could watch the street become stifled with the snow. Christmas decorations were still up everywhere, and the snow enhanced the illusion that I had been transported back in time, before the holidays.

By the time we returned to the inn the snow had stopped and we didn't worry anymore about having to leave that night. I lit a big fire in the hearth, and we made love by the flickering yellow light that filled the bedroom. We slowed down this time, our initial urgency for each other satiated earlier that day. I moved inside her in long, deliberate strokes, until I couldn't tell where my body ended and hers began. I watched the way her expression changed from relaxation to one that almost resembled pain and back again.

We lay tangled in the bedcovers and sheets and the dew of our sweat, panting for what seemed like a long time when we were done. My mind raced with questions, and even though I felt both exhausted and comfortable, I couldn't seem to slip into sleep.

I tightened my embrace around her, whispering, "I have to figure out what I'm going to do tomorrow. Where I'm going to go."

Ellen lay on my chest, unmoving and quiet.

"Tell me about the most remote place you've ever been."

I almost thought she wasn't going to answer, and I wondered if she was asleep. Just as I was about to ask again, she answered softly, "Fiji."

"You've been to Fiji?"

"Mmhm. After I graduated from college. I went with a girlfriend. It was almost on a whim. Her grandparents had given her ten thousand dollars as a graduation gift, and she decided to spend it on a trip to Fiji. She paid my way so I could go with her."

"Wow. So how was Fiji?"

"Fiji is—Fiji is very exotic. It's incredibly beautiful. You can live your life barefoot, literally and figuratively. There are a lot of English-speaking tourists who go there from Australia and New Zealand. Not many Americans, though. It's very isolated, very remote."

I listened to her breathe for a long time, her head resting on my chest as I stroked her hair. I waited for the words to form in my head, and I did a lot of editing before I spoke again.

"Come with me to Fiji."

She moved to prop herself up, and looked at me as if she were searching my face for an answer. "Fiji is on the other side of the world, David. In more ways than the obvious."

"That's why it sounds so perfect."

"Why can't you stay here? No one knows you're here. You've got your fake identity. You've got the money. I could help you invest it. You could lay low for a very long time."

"I can't, sweetheart. I just can't."

"Why?"

"If anyone got into my things after I left, into my email, into the office phone records, they'll know about you."

She bit her lower lip and watched me intently.

"This would be the first place they'd come looking for me. Where you are. I'm not worried about myself so much. But I could never put you in that sort of danger, that sort of trouble."

"We could be very careful. Not see each other for a while."

I sat up against the headboard and took her face in my hands. "Ellen, I couldn't live with myself if I did anything to hurt you, if my sloppiness ruined your life or worse, got you killed. I would rather not see you ever again than risk that."

"Don't say that. Don't say I won't ever see you again." Her eyes filled with tears.

"Then come with me. You and Pete. I'll take care of the both of you, I promise." I watched as tiny drops formed in the corners of her eyes and trickled in wet streaks down her cheeks. She struggled against it and tried to compose herself. "I know you can't answer me now, and that's okay. That's fine."

"It's just not that simple."

"I know, I know it's not. Of course it's not."

"But I can't bear the thought of you leaving."

"Then come with me." I pulled her to me as she finally surrendered herself to the tears and sobbed wetly into my neck.

Neither one of us slept that night. We lay in each other's arms watching the flames die down and the shadows dance and change across the walls and the ceiling as morning neared, each of us struggling silently with our own ghosts.

***

The sky had cleared overnight, and the veil of gray clouds were gone. The white of the fresh snow was almost blinding in its intensity. The air was crisp and dry. We trampled carefully up the flagstone path with our bags after checking out, joking and laughing and doing everything we could to avoid talking about what was foremost on our minds. After another gloriously fattening German breakfast, we set off for the drive back.

The friend that Ellen left Pete with was under the impression that she was on a short business trip to Boston and would be home this afternoon to pick up Pete, so our time together had a curfew. I felt the minutes slipping away in a blur. I thought about staying to the end of the week but knew that was dangerous and stupid, especially if the only reason I was going to stay was to spend more time with Ellen. If anyone came looking for me in the next few days, they would be sure to find me through her.

Pennsylvania was gone, and as we ripped across the interstate towards Connecticut, I ran through the list of things I needed to do to prepare for the long plane ride ahead of me. I would need to fly west again, to Los Angeles most likely, where I could catch a flight to Honolulu and then ultimately Fiji. I dreaded all the layovers and the strain of carrying a bulky load of money stuffed in my clothes again, but knew it was small punishment.

"I'm going to need to check into a hotel or something so that I can put my disguise back on and stash the money in my clothes for the trip."

"OK, we'll find one along the way."

I already knew the answer to what I was about to ask. It had been searing a hole in my heart all morning. "You're not coming with me, are you?"

"No, David. I can't. I can't just disappear out of my life. I certainly can't do it in one day."

"I realize that. It doesn't have to be today, or this week. I can lay low for a while, wait for you. How much time do you think you'll need?" I imagined spending a month shacked up at a hotel in Boston or New York or somewhere nearby until Ellen was able to get things together.

"The timing isn't the issue."

"What's the issue? Tell me. For months now you've been talking about how unhappy you are in your marriage, how you've been wondering if you want to leave Jack."

Ellen gripped the steering wheel tighter and said nothing.

"Well? What's the story? Do you still love him? Is that it?"

"David, if we left, I wouldn't just be leaving Jack. I'd be leaving my job. Hell, I'd be leaving my career. There's not much use for a marketing analyst in Fiji."

"I know that. Fiji is just an idea. A start. We can go anywhere. We can go to Australia, New Zealand..."

"But the most important thing is that if we left, I'd be taking my son away from his father, his grandparents, his entire family. Would we be able to come back? If not, what would I do? Fly across the globe once a year with him so that he could spend Christmas with his dad, the entire time paranoid about someone catching on about you, everyone asking me questions I can't answer? What kind of life is that for a little boy? I can't do that to him. I can't do that to Jack, either. He doesn't deserve that."

"You're right. I've been totally fucking naïve." I tried unsuccessfully to keep my tone neutral, but failed. The statement was razor sharp with anger. I wasn't angry at her so much as I was angry at myself and the entire situation. I hadn't even considered how Ellen would leave the country without leaving a trail.

"No, you haven't been naïve. I feel good knowing that you want to be with me. If you found a way in which you could stay in Connecticut, I would do just about anything to help you. I don't want to be away from you either, David."

"I can't stay here. I told you why last night."

"And I can't go with you."

I fought against the painful lump that was forming in my throat. I rolled down the window halfway, leaned out slightly, and let the cold air lap at my forehead. The faint lyrics of a Sheryl Crow song emanated from the car speakers, the radio volume turned just one notch above nothing.

"Hypothetically," I said, "if I stayed here, would you leave Jack and be with me?"

"Don't ask questions like that."

"Why not?"

"Because you're NOT going to stay here. Now you're just fishing around."

"So? I just want to know, would you leave him?"

"Why do you want to know so badly?"

"Why don't you answer the question?"

"Are you jealous of Jack, is that it? Do you want me to say that I don't love him, that I've never loved him? Would that make it all better for you?"

The conversation was getting out of control, fast. I didn't want to fight with her. The last thing I wanted was for her to be angry with me. I scrambled for a way to turn things around. I reached over and turned up the radio, catching the last few seconds of *Winding Road* by Sheryl Crow.

"I'm not jealous of Jack. I'm sorry if I've made you upset."

"I'm not upset, I'm just—frustrated, dammit. All of a sudden I'm faced with the dilemma that it's all or nothing. It's either you and nothing, or it's everything and not you."

"I'm looking at it more like—it's a chance for a new life. Something that can turn out to be really wonderful. I'm not trying to take you away from what you love. Or don't love. Or whatever."

"I can't. I just can't. I'm sorry."

"Ellen?" I put my hand in her hair and nudged the back of her neck, inviting her to look at me. She pressed her lips together tightly and kept her eyes on the road. "Please let's not do this. I understand why you can't come. I'm trying to accept it. It's just that I feel like I've lost everything, and you're the only thing I have left."

"But you haven't lost everything! You have a lot more than you think. It may not seem like that right now, but you have something inside you that will get you through all this, with or without me. You'll get through it, and you'll have more than you started with. I know you will. I know that about you."

I closed my eyes for a second. The glare of daylight was suddenly too painful.

"Right now," she continued, "the thought of you building a new life on your own and me not being able to share every single minute of it with you is tearing me up inside. It's killing me to see that hurt in your eyes and I know the hurt is going to be there a while, for both of us. Despite that, I know you'll be happy. I feel that deep inside me with such certainty, David."

"You really believe in me, don't you?" I asked.

Her eyes feel on me briefly, a flash of deep glacier blue as she whispered, "I've always believed in you."

32

∾

Meanwhile, Back in Fiji

The house I'm renting from Adelle is about a mile from the beach, situated in a tangle of island vegetation and palm trees, and directly behind a small food market. Although it does have electricity, it doesn't have the modern amenities of air conditioning and central heating (the latter not being very necessary, as the climate doesn't fluctuate much above or below balmy). The back porch has an entrance that leads into the kitchen, a simple area of counterspace flanked by a modest refrigerator on one side and a porcelain sink on the other. The stove, an ancient-looking scarred relic, is across from the sink, and runs on propane. I leave the door to the porch open to let in some more light and air. I turn on a portable fan I bought to help me through the oppressive heat that is inescapable this time of the year.

I don't spend too much time here, fortunately. I am either working at the resort bar or hanging out at Adelle's perfectly climatized house, playing cards or watching Australian programming off the satellite dish that he has hooked up to his television. His place is near the shore and not too far from his resort, the Salay Plantation. He spent a small fortune building it seven years ago when he first arrived in Fiji. It is a plantation-style design, with a wrap-around, covered deck and the largest room in the house being the ocean-facing living room. He built it with five bedrooms to accommodate visits from his siblings and his nieces and nephews who fly in once a year from New Zealand, where Adelle is originally from. He moved to the states after high school to attend Yale on a full scholarship. After receiving his master's in finance, he lived in New York, working on Wall Street until he was thirty-five, at which time he had accumulated enough wealth to come to the islands and buy a way of life.

I put the laptop on the square table that divides the kitchen and begin frying up some breakfast. Later, before my shift at the bar, I plan to take the laptop to Adelle's and plug it into his phone line in order to send the email message. I consider, too, the possibility of writing my brother and letting him know I'm okay. Fortunately, I still remember his email address because of its simplicity and hope that it's still valid. He'll probably be pissed as hell that I didn't get in touch with him earlier, if he even believes that I'm alive. Maybe he'll know something about what went down at the self-storage after I left. Maybe he'll also know what happened to Dana.

I've often wondered what direction her life had taken after I left. A permanent tinge of guilt clouded my thoughts of her. Some days I couldn't even remember why I felt such animosity towards her after I left San Diego. Instead, the beach here would often remind me of the times we used to pack a lunch and spend the day lounging in the sands of the Pacific shore. Sleeping alone would often remind me of the years I shared a bed with her and the comfort and warmth I took in her body. Once when I was watching a rerun of her favorite Seinfeld episode at Adelle's house an odd melancholy overtook me. I had loved her once, and I know that I had failed her in some ways. I found myself desperately hoping that she had found what she was looking for, finally, and that she was happy.

I boiled some water for coffee and threw a few pieces of fish into the hot oil of the cast iron skillet. Despite the past life that haunted me, I hadn't become a complete mope and isolationist. A few months ago I stood in my kitchen as I was standing now, frying up the same fish and eggs breakfast for a beautiful twenty-year-old blonde who was here vacationing with her parents and sister. They had come into the bar, and as I served them their drinks I couldn't keep my eyes off her. Dressed in a short yellow skirt and a white tank top, she shamelessly flaunted her long, tan legs. Although her hair was the color of sand, her eyes were dark, and her skin was a golden caramel. We had been flirting with our eyes all night. She waited around until my shift was over and we ended up on the beach, making out like teenagers by the glow of the moon. Eventually she and I found our way into my bed before sunrise, her taunt, tanned body under mine. I clutched at her in a half daze, and when my eyes were closed there was a brief moment when I thought I was with Ellen. We only spent that one night together. She left later that day, back to the States with her family.

Footsteps pounded the old wood of the porch, and as I turned to look over my shoulder I saw the lean silhouette of my friend Poseci fill the doorway. Poseci was the bartender at the Salay.

"Bula! What's for breakfast?"

"Christ, don't you ever get your own?" I joked with him, already pulling an extra plate out of the cupboard.

"Why should I when you're such a good cook?" Poseci's accent was smoothed out and replaced by the short-clipped sounds of Australian English. He poured more water into the tea kettle and made himself comfortable in one of two kitchen chairs.

"You really need to find yourself a wife, my friend," I told him.

"I'm trying, believe me. I have a date later tonight with that new desk clerk that started last week."

"Oh, that's right. You've got today off." I divided up the eggs and fish onto two plates and joined him at the table.

"Yeah, but I promised Adelle I'd go to Viti Levu today to order up some more liquor and some glasses. You want to come?"

"I don't know. I've got something I have to do today before my shift."

"Where'd you get this computer?" Poseci opened the laptop and began clicking the keys, trying to bring it to life. "Is this yours?"

"Yeah, it's mine."

"I didn't know you had a computer. How long have you had it?"

"Not long. And stop fondling it; you'll break it."

He rolled his index finger over the track ball and with his other hand brought up a forkful of food to his mouth. "Nice. What do you need a computer for? You going to start looking at dirty pictures on the internet? Don't you need a phone for that?" He snorted as he flipped the lid closed and wagged his eyebrows at me. "If I knew you were that desperate, I'd have set you up with Marla's sister the other night."

"It has nothing to do with that, and forget Marla's sister. If she looks anything like Marla, I think I'll stick to rubbin' it out on my own, thank you very much."

"Suit yourself," he pointed his fork at me and added, "but sometimes you can't be so damn picky."

"Not for what you do with them, no. I guess you can't."

The tea kettle started its throaty whistle. Poseci sprang up and doused the cup of tea leaves he had prepared with the steamy water. He shook his head as he walked the kettle back to the stove. "I don't know what happened to you back in the States, my friend, but you really need to loosen up. A year on the island and look at you, all bunched up like someone stuck a sugar cane up your ass, *still*."

I thought about the email I was going to send later and the possible response that it might invoke. "Give it a day or two. I might be a whole new man."

33

Dawn

I rode my bicycle to Adelle's house with the laptop snugly stowed inside a backpack. The road was rutted and still muddy from a rainstorm a couple of nights ago. It seemed almost ludicrous that I had gone to such lengths to get in touch with Ellen. A few months ago I had asked Adelle if I could use his phone for a call to the United States. My request was immediately followed by an implication that I needed him to be as discreet as possible when he got his bill for the call. No questions, no call backs, no inquiries to the person I called. Adelle looked horrified that I would even suspect he would be that nosey and left the room, giving me privacy.

I wasn't expecting to talk to Ellen when I called her work number. It was the middle of the night in Connecticut. I was curious if she was still working there and most importantly, I wanted to hear her voice. When the number finally connected, I was greeted by a man's voice, asking me to please leave a message so that he may return my call as soon as possible.

I wasn't sure what to make of that. Had Ellen quit her job or gotten a new extension or promotion? Although I knew the name of the company where she worked, I didn't know the main number, so I would have to make several calls before I could speak to someone who could answer that question for me. The last thing I wanted to do was call her house. I couldn't do it in the middle of the night, and I didn't want to risk anyone being home during the day. My frustrations had prompted me to think about emailing her instead.

I pedaled harder up the last mile of road before Adelle's driveway. The sun was beginning to get hot already that morning, and sweat formed wet patches on my shirt. Despite it being almost Christmas, it was summertime in Fiji. I leaned the bike against a tree to shade it, not wanting to burn my thighs on the black vinyl on my return home.

I found the spare key to the villa in its usual hiding place behind the flowerpot on the porch in case Adelle wasn't home. Even though he had told me several times to just walk in even if he was home, I always liked to knock first. The house seemed quiet, and the salty aroma of ocean filled the air as I waited a few seconds after rapping on the adjacent window. Just as I was about to insert the key into the lock, the door swung open, and I stood facing a beautiful woman I hadn't seen before.

Momentarily stumped, I stuttered out, "Hi. I'm David. Uh—is Adelle home?"

"Oh yeah! David." She stepped aside and motioned me in. "He said you were going to come over to use the phone." She had a melodic Australian accent.

I took my backpack off as I entered the house, fascinated by the woman's long, whiskey-colored hair. It hung straight down around her shoulders and to the center of her back. She was tall, about my height, and when she spoke to me our eyes locked at the same level.

"I'm Dawn, Adelle's cousin." She extended her hand out to me. "I'm here for a few weeks on holiday."

"Nice to meet you." I squeezed her hand gently as my eyes followed the shiny flickering of the gold hoops that decorated her earlobes.

Dawn followed me into the kitchen, where I set out the laptop and booted it up. I unplugged the phone wire from the back of the cordless phone and inserted it into the back of the computer.

"Adelle's mentioned you."

"Has he? All good, I hope."

"He said you were his American friend with a secret past."

I coughed into my fist and glanced over at her, surprised to see the look of suppressed amusement on her face. "Really? That's fascinating. I don't have a secret past."

"Sure, you do. That's why you're emailing your letter instead of just calling the person."

I opened the file that I wanted to send and collapsed the window down, feeling slightly exposed.

"You think? People email all the time. That doesn't mean there's a conspiracy going on, or that they're trying to hide something."

"Perhaps, in the real world."

"It's no big deal. It's just that I don't know how else to contact this person these days." I cleared my throat.

She brushed my arm with her fingertips. "I see I'm making you uncomfortable. I'm sorry. I'll leave now." She winked at me and ambled over to the living room. Her feet were bare and she was wearing a beaded ankle bracelet around her foot.

"Not at all." I heard the familiar beep and clang of the modem dialing up. "So, how long have you been here?"

"I just got here yesterday. This is my first time here, actually. On the islands."

"Where are you from?"

"I live in Sydney. Where are you from?"

"I'm from California."

"No kidding! What part?"

The modem connected to the ISP, and I addressed the note before sending it. "Southern California."

"Nice! I've been there a few times. I like San Diego, especially. It reminds me a lot of Sydney in a way."

"I've never been to Australia."

"But you've been to San Diego?"

"Yes, I lived there."

"Really? Did you grow up there, too?"

"Yes, I did."

I realized with slight irritation that Dawn managed to pry more out of me in ten minutes than Adelle had in the year I had known him. I folded the laptop back down and replaced the phone wire.

"I'm finished. I'll be out of your hair."

"Oh, please, don't rush off. I am enjoying your company." She beamed at me.

"Thank you for saying that. But I have to start my shift soon at the resort."

"Ah. Well, how about this? How about I extend an invitation for you to come over for dinner some night soon when you're not working? I'll cook up one of my Australian specialties for you and Adelle."

I thought for a second. "I've got the next couple days off. So, how about tomorrow?"

"Perfect." She followed me back out to the front door. "I look forward to seeing that sexy bum again tomorrow."

"What?" I paused at the doorway.

"I said, I look forward to seeing you at seven p.m. tomorrow."

"That's NOT what you said the first time."

She blew me a kiss as I stepped off the porch. "It's the tropical air. It has a way of distorting things, doesn't it?"

I snickered as I climbed back onto the bike and rode away.

34

What To Do with the Money

The aroma of chili greeted me at the doorway, along with Dawn, who had pinned her hair up in a fat knot at the top of her head for the occasion. I handed her the collection of tropical flowers and a bottle of white wine I had bought at the market adjacent to my house. She twirled back around toward the kitchen, and her flowing, thin dress left a trail of colors in my brain. She was still barefoot, and still had the beaded ankle bracelet adorning her slender foot.

"Smells great. You made chili?"

"The Australian kind. It's Dinkum chili. I think you'll like it."

"I'm sure I will. I can't remember the last time I ate chili." My stomach growled as I leaned up against the wide counter that surrounded the kitchen. "Hey, Adelle."

"So, how do you like my cousin?" he asked. "I heard you two met yesterday."

"Yes, I had the pleasure." I accepted a glass of wine from Adelle as I watched Dawn bustling around the stove, mixing and stirring and shaking containers of spices over the steaming pots. She had taken the little gold hoops out of her earlobes, I noticed, and replaced them with small turquoise studs, the color of which matched her dress. My eyes wandered to the hem of the dress, which rested closely against her shapely bronzed thigh, just about three inches above her knee.

She was well into her second sentence before I realized she was talking to me. "Dinner will be ready in about half an hour. Maybe we should go out on the deck with our drinks while the whole lot simmers?"

"Let's," I smiled.

"Oh, by the way?" Dawn twirled away from the stove and faced me.

"Yes?"

Adelle had cleared all the vegetation in front of the house so there was a clear view to the beach, only a few hundred feet away.

"Did you bring your laptop with you tonight?"

"No, I didn't. Why?"

"I wanted to go online and check on some tour schedules for tomorrow over on Viti Levu. I'm in the mood to go sailing and snorkeling."

"Forget taking a tour. I'll take you. I've got tomorrow off."

"Really? You wouldn't mind, then?" Dawn's eyebrows shot up.

"I would love to." I smiled at her.

Adelle brought out a plate of appetizers and we sat around the big wooden table, sipping our drinks.

"So why are you living here in Fiji, David?" Dawn asked me.

Adelle started rubbing at the condensation on his wine glass. "Uh oh. Don't start asking him those questions or he's going to bolt out of here like a rabbit." He chuckled to himself.

"Give me a break, Adelle." I leaned back in the padded chair.

"Well? Why are you here?"

"My life was going totally shitty, and I decided to get away from it all, that's why."

"What were you doing back in the States?"

"I was a property manager."

"Oh, how awful!" Dawn grimaced, her small nose wrinkling.

"What's awful? Being a property manager?"

"Yes. That sounds like an awfully boring job."

"It was."

"So instead, you decided to fly across the world, shack up in one of Adelle's huts and become a cocktail waiter?"

I busted out laughing, spilling some of my wine on my shirt. "Well, of course, it's a little more complicated than that."

"My god, I sure do hope so!" She touched the soft area of skin right between her breasts, rubbing her middle fingertip over a cluster of brown freckles. "I see you're wearing a wedding ring. Are you married?"

I had forgotten all about my wedding band. I looked at my left hand and at the ring as if surprised to see it there. "Oh, that." I lay my hand on my thigh and under the table, out of sight. "No. I'm divorced."

"And you're still wearing a ring? That's odd."

"Christ, Dawn. What it is this, the inquisition?" Adelle popped a shrimp appetizer into his mouth.

"No, it's not. It's just that David fascinates me. I want to know all about him." She winked at me, and this time I felt a warm rush in my face when she did. "Besides, I ask because when I got divorced the first thing I did was toss my ring out."

"It just hasn't crossed my mind. I'm so used to the ring. I suppose I should take it off." I rotated the ring with my right index finger and thumb. It felt like it would be too small to get past my knuckle. "So, you're divorced?"

"A long time ago. I got married too young. You know how it goes."

Later that evening, after we had gorged ourselves on Dawn's Australian chili, I took Adelle aside in the living room over a strong cup of brandy-laced coffee. I had decided earlier that day that I would begin investing some of the cash, as long as I could do it through alternative channels where I didn't have to produce proof of who I was. I asked him if he could help me in that regard, and he looked at me soberly for a while before he answered.

"I was wondering when you were going to ask me to help you with that."

"You were?"

He asked me how much I was wanting to invest, and I hesitated before answering. It wasn't so much that I didn't want him to know how much cash I was hiding; it was more that I wasn't sure how much of it I wanted to part with.

"About seven hundred thousand."

He didn't blink. He nodded at me slowly and sighed. "I think I can help you. I've got some friends in Hong Kong who can do something with the money. Your risk will be minimal. Maybe we can split the funds up a little, too. Make it so you can have some cash available, so it's not all tied up."

"That would be great." I wished I could have asked Adelle about this earlier, but I really didn't feel it was the right time until that day. I knew I could trust him, and I needed to do something with all that money before it all got eaten by some tropical beetle. I had to give it a value on paper, or risk losing it all.

I threw my bike into the back of Adelle's truck and he drove me back to my house. I sat for a while at the table in the kitchen with just the dim light of the sixty-watt bulb above the sink lighting the cramped space. I sat staring at the laptop. I had sent two emails the day before—one to Ellen and one to my brother, Greg. I felt both anxious and uncertain. I wasn't sure I had done the right thing writing either one of them. If Ellen didn't respond, or if she had bad news, I would have to feel the searing burn of hurt yet again. On the other hand, what if her situation had changed? What if she would be able to at least come see me for a while—stay with me for a week, a month, longer?

I would have to wait until morning to find out.

Meanwhile, I let the repetitive sound of the water dripping out of the kitchen faucet lull me into drowsiness. I fell into bed with my clothes on, and as I dozed off into a solid sleep, the vision of black hair, red hair, blue eyes, green eyes, turquoise earrings, and freckles danced around and tangled in my consciousness.

35

❧

The Rumor of My Death

This time, I had to use the key to get into Adelle's. It was early enough in the morning that he was still on his daily run. Dawn wasn't anywhere in sight—probably still sleeping. I set my laptop on the kitchen counter and poured myself a glass of water while I waited for it to boot up. I was hoping to have some privacy for at least a little while, until Adelle returned or Dawn heard me rummaging around and woke up.

There was a letter for me. It was from Greg.

My God, my brain is still spinning. I thought you were dead.

I can't believe I'm reading what I'm reading! Where are you at? Why don't you call me? You have no idea how relieved I am that you're still hanging in there, little brother. If you were here right now I'd either give you a congratulatory slap on the back or I'd kick your ass. Or both.

A few days after you disappeared I had a visit from some feds. They came around to the house while we were eating dinner. They said that they were looking for you, that you inadvertently got involved with some wanted felon and that you were missing. The look on my face must have told them everything, because they looked dissapointed even before I told them I had no idea what was going

245

on or where you were—that the last I'd heard from you was a few weeks prior and you seemed to be doing okay. When I called your number after they left, I got your answering machine and I left a message for Dana, since I had no idea that you two had split up.

When I didn't hear back from her I called to the self storage, and the guy who answered gave me the rundown again of what had been happening. He told me that Dana was gone, that you had disappeared without so much as a clue. He claimed that he was made manager now that you were gone, and it struck me as odd that he focused on that point more than anything else. It also seemed a little weird that the owner would have promoted him, because that guy didn't seem altogether with it, if you know what I mean.

I flew out to San Diego a couple days later. I racked my brain trying to remember Dana's maiden name and finally when I did, I was able to track down her parents' house in Rancho Bernardo. She had found out what happened to you from the cops when she went to pick up some of her things the day after you left. They had the apartment all cordoned off and wouldn't let her anywhere near, which freaked her out.

She and I went down to the police station and asked again if we could go into your apartment, which they agreed to. They said that they had some theories about what happened to you. They thought maybe that Adams guy got a hold of you. He was still at large. They speculated that you might have had something to do with the theft of his money, too. But it confused them why you seemed to have left so abruptly, and, if you did have the guy's money, why you would have taken money out of the cash register at the self storage.

Dana and I looked through the apartment together. Everything was as you had left it. You even had some meat defrosting (by then, decaying) in the sink. All your clothes were there. Everything was there except your wallet, which is no big mystery since you keep that in your pocket. We went through your files on the computer, but couldn't find any clues. We tried to get into your email online but had no *luck cracking your password. Your car was gone, and the police had put out a search for it in hopes that it might lead to some answers.*

The police and the FBI interrogated us pretty thoroughly. Dana said she had called you that night, and that everything seemed normal. They said that they ran phone records on both the home and office lines and that no outgoing calls had been placed from either line that night. Only one incoming call was received—and that was from Dana.

Dana mentioned a friend of yours named Tom. She thought maybe he would know something. But he seemed as surprised by the whole thing as we had been.

I didn't know what to think or what to do when I finally flew back to Phoenix a couple days later. Oh, and there is one thing I forgot to mention earlier—the last person to see you that night. Apparently some lady who was still at her unit that night said she talked to you and had seen you driving off. She said that you had reprimanded her for being in the facility after hours and that you said you were leaving and would be back shortly, but that you never came back.

I thought about hiring my own private investigator, but squashed the idea a week later when I got a call from the Encinitas police. They had found your car. It was parked on a dirt shoulder off a side road in Descanso. They found traces of blood in there, which turned out to be your blood type. The keys were still in it, and had your finger-prints all over them. Your case had shifted from a missing persons to a possible homicide.

I tried to understand why in the hell you would be driving through Descanso. We didn't know anyone in Descanso. But the police said that the car was completely out of gas, and they thought maybe you had been trying to outrun someone and had been afraid to stop. They speculated that if you had the guy's money in your car, you would not have wanted to go to the police for help, either.

The money was never found. Michael Adams was never found. You were never found. After a few months I started to think that you might be dead after all, although I had some nagging doubts.

Dana was a wreck. She said that her last conversation with you was antagonistic and she felt awful about it. But she must have gotten over it quite quickly, because the last I heard she was living with some guy in La Jolla. She hired a lawyer to get you pronounced legally dead or permanently missing or something so she could get married again.

In your letter, you had written that you were out of the country. I would love to know where you went, though I understand if you can't tell me right now. The feds and police say they are still investigating your case. Of course, you can never be sure if they are just saying that out of professional courtesy and obligation to the family, or if they really are still keeping your case active. I spoke with your friend Tom about that one day over the phone, and he seemed to think that the case has been chucked out the backdoor. He seemed to be convinced that although they're still looking for the drug dealer, they've pretty much concluded that you were just one of a long line of victims. I can understand why you would be leery of coming back anywhere near California, however, in case he was still looking for you.

Now that I think about it, there was one time a while ago when my wife mentioned that she had seen someone parked down the street from our house, sitting in a car and reading the paper. It was a couple weeks after I had come back from San Diego. It could have been the feds. It could have been completely unrelated. Who knows? Or it could have been someone else altogether, looking for you.

You have no idea how relieved I am that you're alive and seem to be doing okay. What are you going to do now? What are your plans? You said you were working at some resort, but you didn't say what you were doing. Call me at work sometime if you can. Let me know if there is anything I can do to help you, anything at all. I am not going to tell anyone that I heard from you unless you request me to.

Take care, bro.

I composed my reply:

Greg,

I am very sorry to have put you through all that business about my alleged disappearance. It seems to me, however, that my impulsiveness may have paid off as far as the police are concerned. I think it's absolutely likely that they are no longer looking for me, which is a tremendous relief. As for Michael Adams, I have no idea what to think about him. But I think I'm going to lay low for a little while longer. For that reason, I don't want to tell you yet where I am. Not until I know for sure that I won't be putting myself or anyone else in danger.

I appreciate that you won't tell anyone that you've heard from me. As far as Dana is concerned, especially, I don't want her to know I'm alive. I don't think she'll be discreet if she knows where to find me since it seems to be in her interest to expedite a quick severance of any ties with our marriage. That's fine with me. Let her think I'm dead. Let her get that judgement. It's probably better that way. She seems no worse for wear, from what you've written.

I'll be in touch. Maybe by this time next Christmas we can have a family get-together on me. What do you think? I hope you like hot, humid weather in December.

I signed off and rolled the track ball around with my thumb. So, Tom had taken my car and staged it to look like someone had killed me. There were traces of blood in the car, and although it was impossible that it was *my* blood, it was my blood type. How did he pull that off? How did he know my blood type? I thought back to my last night in San Diego and our road trip into the back canyons of Tijuana. I couldn't remember him sticking a pin in me or anything like—wait! At Carlos's house, when I shaved with his shitty Bic razor before slipping into my disguise. It dawned on me with absolute certainty that I had cut myself shaving, and that I ended up wiping off the blood with some toilet paper. Tom must have made plans in his head to stage the scene with my Saab while we drove back to his house. Maybe after I left, he called Carlos and asked him to save his trash. I shook my head. Tom definitely missed his calling.

He would have made a great investigator. I wondered if I could get a hold of him somehow to tell him how much I appreciated everything he had done for me.

I heard the back door open, and when I turned, expecting to see Adelle, I was greeted by Dawn instead.

"Sending another email today?" she panted. She was wearing a tank top and athletic shorts and was drenched in sweat. She had obviously been running.

"I thought you were sleeping."

"Sleeping? Nah, I joined Adelle on his run this morning. I beat him by at least a half a mile on the last stretch, too."

"I'm impressed. Adelle's a solid runner. I've joined him a few times myself."

"Really? How come you're not running this morning?"

"I don't know. I'm a little low on motivation these days."

She grabbed one of the kitchen towels and began wiping her brow and neck. She then lifted her tank top, revealing a white sports bra, and began to wipe the sweat from her belly and from between her breasts. She paced the kitchen, taking deep breaths.

"Haven't you ever heard of a cool down?"

"A what?"

"You shouldn't just come to a dead stop like this after sprinting. It's not good for you."

"I like jumping into the shower all hot like this, though."

She made one more pass at her neck and threw the towel at me. I dodged it, watching it land instead on a container full of spatulas and various cooking utensils. "Lovely. Remind me never to eat here again."

She walked up to me with a smirk on her face, and for a split second I thought she was going to kiss me. Instead, she leaned over me to take the towel off the spatulas before gliding around the corner and upstairs toward the bathroom.

"Are we still on for snorkeling and such?" she called down from the hallway upstairs.

"You bet. You want me to wait while you get ready or come back later?"

"Why don't you use some of those utensils I soiled and whip us up an omelet? I'll be down in twenty minutes."

As I cracked the eggs, watching the yolks wiggle around in the large glass bowl, I found myself thinking of the restrained curves under Dawn's bra. Her bra had been soaked with perspiration and her nipples hardened as soon as the chill of the air conditioning made contact with them. The thought made me hazy, and I found myself standing perfectly still in the middle of the kitchen with a fork in one hand and the bowl of yolks in the other.

"Jesus, you need to get laid, and soon, or else you're going to be useless," I mumbled to myself, just as I heard Adelle kicking off his sneakers at the back door.

"That girl's gonna kill me before she goes back home, I tell ya." Adelle's face was redder than I had ever seen it. He bent down to stretch out.

"I see you've finally met your match."

"Yes, I suppose." He placed his hand against the wall and lifted his leg behind him to stretch out his quads. "And from the way she's been talking about you all morning, I'm thinking you've finally met yours."

36

Fortune Tellers & Fish

The large rubber raft slowed when it approached the edge of the reef and the guide instructed us to keep close to the boat as he handed us our gear. Up ahead in the mouth of the lagoon, the tops of the palm trees stretched up the slope of the island and swayed in waves like grass in the wind. I could barely make out several small bures, or guest huts, that were tucked in at the tree line at the back of the beach.

I helped Dawn with her mask so it wouldn't tug and tangle her hair, which she had woven into one large braid. Her skin smelled faintly of coconut suntan lotion. We lowered ourselves off the raft and into the sapphire water. It was hard to judge how deep it was, the ripples distorting the pink and white corals under our feet.

In the warm suspension of the tropical water, surrounded by hundreds of jewel-colored fish, I felt calm and finally free of the vague impediment that had been dragging me down for the past year. The thought that I had somehow gotten away with something kept washing across my consciousness. Tom was certain that the police had terminated the investigation. If he was certain, that must mean that it was true. I had the feeling that Tom knew more than he could tell Greg.

Even if I knew that Michael Adams was no longer a danger, I knew at that moment that I didn't want to go back. At least not to San Diego. I had grown to love this part of the world, with its easy pace and its beauty and its colors and scents. I knew I had to begin thinking more seriously about what I wanted to do with the rest of my life. I knew for sure I didn't want to spend it serving drinks to tourists.

Dawn's arm brushed mine, and I followed her down a valley of corals. The ocean floor dropped a few feet and we swam up on a large basin filled with a kaleidoscope of sea anemones and schools of small purple- and yellow-striped fish. We circled the basin slowly, exploring every recess and hollow. Although I had gone snorkeling off Taveuni Island before, I was enjoying it again through Dawn's eyes.

When we came up for air for the last time that afternoon, I donned the scuba mask and floated on my back in the water for a while, feeling the sun begin to dry my exposed skin. My mind bounced off an endless stream of memories before it settled on one that snapped me out of my daydreaming. I flailed my arms and began to tread in the salty surf, looking for Dawn. I saw her head bob a few feet away, her air tube skimming the surface of the water. I splashed at it, trying to get her attention.

"What?! What?" she gasped for air, shaking the water out of her face. "Did some fish swim up your trunks? What?!"

I kicked my way closer to her. "Do you believe in fortune tellers?"

"Fortune tellers? No. Why? Did you see one floating in the reef?"

"C'mon, be serious!" I smacked some water her way. "I just remembered this tarot card reading I had a year ago."

"Oh, lordy." She rolled her eyes. A big droplet of water hung suspended from the tip of her nose.

"I thought it was bullshit, too. But she told me that I would be moving to another large of body of water within six months. I did. I moved here. She also said something about someone doing something sneaky behind my back at work, or something, and that was true, too."

"You sure you didn't subconsciously keep that in the back of your mind and *that's* why you moved here?"

"Doubt it." I shook my head. "It's wild, though, now that I remember it."

"Did she also tell you that you'd be meeting a gorgeous Australian redhead in Fiji who would pull your trunks off under the water while you were snorkeling and hide them in the reef?"

She dove under the surface and lunged for me, but I didn't move. I grinned madly and waited for the feel of her hands on my waist. Her fingers found the pull string of my swim trunks and I felt a small tug as she began unraveling my waistband.

She came up for air abruptly, her face inches from mine, her hands on my waist. "Why aren't you trying to get away?"

"Why would I want to miss out on such a nice fondling?" I licked off the new droplet of water that had formed on her nose. She didn't flinch.

"You're a strange one, you know that?" She began wading toward the raft. "I'm really going to enjoy getting to know you while I'm here."

37

And Everything Was Going So Well...

I watched the white bladed ceiling fan above Adelle's living room slice through the air silently while I reclined on the canvas sofa with a glass of beer. I was beginning to get drowsy sitting in the cool room after a day full of ocean and hot sun. After a quick shower, I retrieved the extra set of clothes I brought with me that morning, along with the laptop, feeling the tightness of sunburn on my shoulders as I pulled the cotton shirt over my head.

After snorkeling, Dawn and I had rented kayaks and paddled our way around the lagoons and beaches surrounding Taveuni for a couple of hours. Her energy and enthusiasm were contagious. But now that she was upstairs showering, I quickly felt the energy drain out of my body. I wanted to take a nap. But I knew that as soon as Dawn got dressed, we'd be out the door again. I had asked her out to a restaurant on the other side of the island to watch the sun set and to eat the best food in the South Pacific.

I got up and fired up the laptop, realizing that I hadn't thought of Ellen since that morning when I saw that I had mail and hoped it had been from her. When I connected to the Internet and saw again that I

255

had another letter, my heart pounded frantically in my chest. I pushed the laptop farther onto the counter and leaned on my elbows in front of it, taking a deep breath.

How I've waited for you. How I've missed you. You have no idea.

David, as I sit here reading your email for perhaps the tenth time, I am left with such an ache in my soul. At the same time, I am so happy to know that you are living, surviving, thriving on that beautiful island. Not a day has gone by that I haven't imagined you there, under the stars of the southern hemisphere, wondering what you were doing, what you were thinking, what you were dreaming. Some days I could see your face so clearly, smiling at me and telling me that you were doing fine, and some days I would panic because I started forgetting what you look like.

The day you left—the second my eyes lost sight of you when you made the bend down that hallway and into the plane—my heart filled with such pain and loneliness. I began walking back to the parking lot, but about midway through the terminal I stopped and turned around. I started running toward your gate. I wanted to catch you, to tell you that that I had changed my mind, that I was going to go with you after all, and that you should take another flight so I could pack.

But when I got there, your plane had already left the gate. I stood at the window, in a state of restrained hysteria, watching your plane taxi the runway. I thought about following you to Fiji. I almost bought a ticket before I left the airport, but my determination had left me as quickly as it had overtaken me.

For the next few weeks I was a zombie. I jumped every time the phone rang at work or at home. I checked my email at least ten times a day. I was a woman obsessed. I both anticipated and feared hearing from you. I knew that if you called or wrote, asking me again to join you, that I would drop everything to be with you. Why couldn't I have told you that while you were still with me? Why did I hesitate? I knew the answer, of course. The answer had not changed. What had changed was the way I felt like doubling over in regret when I woke up every morning without you.

When Jack came home from his business trips we were like strangers living in the same house. He would bury his attention in his contracts and law books and I would try to keep myself busy with Pete or in the kitchen or just zoning in front of the television. Reading was completely out of the question. Every time I would sit down to read anything my concentration would be all over the place and inevitably I would think of you. An hour later, I would find myself on the same page I had started on. For some reason, baking made me feel better. I had never baked so many cookies and cupcakes as I had last winter. Isn't that funny?

I would go to the bookstore every so often to browse through books on Fiji. I would wonder what island you were living on. I would speculate, looking at the photos in the books, and even contemplated calling some of the resorts to see if they knew anything about a thirty-year-old dark-haired American who was living there. But I didn't do it. I didn't want to risk it, for your sake, in case anyone was still watching me.

On Valentine's Day, Jack had planned an elaborate night on the town for us, which both surprised me and filled me with guilt. We were at a low point in our relationship; I didn't even care if he was home or not, or whether we spent time together or not. I knew I had to make some sort of decision about my marriage and face up to the consequences. At the restaurant that night Jack had told me how sorry he was that he had been away so much and how he wanted to let me know that Pete and I were foremost in his thoughts always, and if I could just hang in there a little while longer...

It was hard to get out what I had to say. I told him how unhappy I had become, how our marriage wasn't working at all for me. I told him that I needed some time apart from him in order to sort things out in my mind. I told him that I wanted to go away for a while, to leave Bridgeport.

I never mentioned you. It was hard to explain what had been

tearing me up inside so many months without telling him about you, but I managed it. Besides, I knew the main reason I was having that conversation with Jack had less to do with you than it had to do with having an absentee husband for almost two years.

He was completely in shock that night. He said that he knew that his trips were a source of irritation sometimes, but had no idea I was that unhappy. He had taken my hand, and that night was the first time I had ever seen him cry. Later at home that night, he held me so tightly, as if he was afraid I'd slip out of his grasp and out of his life forever.

Three days later when he was scheduled to fly out to New York to oversee negotiations for his biggest client, he didn't go. He called his office and told them he needed to take a leave of absence. When he got off the phone, he told me he was not going back, ever. He said that his job was not worth losing me and Pete. He was going to stay and work things out with me. I was horrified, because I knew how much his job meant to him. I begged him to reconsider, but he wouldn't budge.

He found a job in Bridgeport. The salary was better, the perks were better, and the best part was that it involved almost no travel. Faced with this new situation, I felt at odds. Now that I had what I had wanted for so long—a husband who was home every night, I wasn't sure I wanted it anymore.

But Jack wouldn't give up. He begged me to go to counseling with him, and I did. It was something I didn't want to do at first, knowing that it would be difficult, if not impossible, for me to be completely honest. I went, regardless. It turned out to be a good thing. When I was ready to discuss my feelings for you with the therapist, I was able to do it without Jack in the room.

This was a long, grueling process. He and I went twice a week for six months, until I could say that I was willing to work things out, that I wanted to be with him after all. I hadn't heard from you in so long, and you were beginning to become more of a sad memory than the deep wound that you had been, back in January. I started losing hope that I would ever hear from you. I was trying to be realistic.

Of course, you'd probably met someone else by now. Here I was, struggling against the man who loved me deeply, holding out for a man who wouldn't even write me or call me. I felt like a fool.

Things are so different now. Jack and I have the kind of marriage we had when we were first together. We take road trips on weekends and we spend our weeknights at home doing family things—cooking or playing games with Pete or just talking. It's been wonderful. This year for Christmas Jack surprised us with a family vacation to California (Los Angeles and San Diego, yes—don't laugh). We're going to leave in a few days.

And now comes the hard part, the part that I can barely make myself write.

The hardest part about it is knowing that I had been wrong about what you had been thinking this entire year. All those times I thought you had forgotten me, that maybe you had found someone else—you hadn't. You had in fact kept me foremost in your heart the whole time. I wondered if I should even write you at all, considering what I have to tell you. But I knew that you deserved the truth from me, no matter what. It's the fair thing to do.

David, we can't write each other the way we used to. We can't know each other anymore. It's not good for either one of us. I've worked so hard this year to get you out of my heart and to work things out with Jack. I've finally gotten to a place that feels right again. Already, after reading only one letter from you, the old feelings are starting to come back. I can't let that happen. I can't imagine what it would be like if we wrote each other every day again, like we used to.

Even though you seem tormented by your past, your life seems very peaceful otherwise. You've found a good friend whom you can trust. You live in one of the most beautiful places on Earth. In some limited way, you still write. Don't ever stop writing! You have a lifetime of possibilities ahead of you, my dear David.

I know that by writing this, I have hurt you twice, and I am so sorry. I hope you'll find it in your heart to forgive me someday. Take care of yourself, stay as optimistic and strong as you always were.

> *I won't tell you to forget about me, because I know that I will never forget you.*
> *Ellen*

I had to force myself to slow down and read the words again, because in my initial excitement I barreled sloppily through the sentences, not really registering what she was saying. When I finally got through the letter again the second time, I closed my eyes and whispered simply, "No."

38

The Road Beneath My Feet

Ellen,

This will be my last letter to you, I promise.

Something has happened since you wrote me back two weeks ago. I've started writing again. No, not the scribbled journal entries that were just a way to pass time since I got here. I mean, I have started a new book. This book won't be the three-year struggle that the first one was. I won't be sitting at the keyboard trying to find motivation for a story that I thought was important, but that soon became a chore, rather than a pleasure. This is a book where the story is clamoring to get out. I know exactly what will happen at every turn. I am writing about what happened to me in the last year and a half. I am writing about you. I'm writing about us.

I have met a woman who was pivotal in my decision to do this. She is Adelle's cousin and she has been here the last few weeks on vacation. As it turns out, she is an editor at a major publishing firm in Australia. I was feeling so reckless and depressed the day you wrote me that I told her everything. When I finished, she became very excited about the story and absolutely ecstatic when she heard I was a writer. She said that her company has been searching for exactly this sort of contemporary story. She is going to help me edit it when I'm finished and assist me through the publishing process. I am hoping this book will be the starting point to a lifelong career in writing. Oh, by the way, her name is Dawn. She is wonderful, I think you'd like her.

I am no longer working at the resort. As a matter of fact, I quit the day after you had written. I am using the money to support myself while I finish the book. I have been putting in full days of writing. Some days I have to practically force myself to stop and eat something. I feel so awake and alive, you know? I'd forgotten how much I love to write.

Things do have a way of happening very fast, don't they? They have a way of changing before you know it. When I read your letter, for example, I felt like my life had slipped through my fingers while I wasn't paying attention.

In a way, I did let life slip through my fingers. I had gotten so distracted by the details that I lost sight of the big picture.

Despite the fact that the landscape had not been exactly to my liking, and that I had strayed from what it was that I loved to do, the road never left the bottom of my feet. It had been there all along, solid and unwavering as I absentmindedly chugged along. When I look ahead, I see that the road has a purpose, it has a destination. All the places I have been, all the people I've known and loved, have led me to this juncture, to this fate.

You had been right about me all along, my love. You told me that there was something in me that no one could take away, that would always be there, no matter what.

You were right.

39

The Last Word

April, 2001

I bought a house recently. It isn't a large house, but it's comfortable and has a good chunk of property surrounding it. The smell of eucalyptus is perpetually in the air. Some days when I sit out on the back deck with my laptop, the rustle of the long-leafed trees reminds me of being on the balcony at the self-storage apartment. If I concentrate just a little, I'm able to convince myself that I can hear the surf crashing against the sandstone cliffs a half a mile away.

I'm almost done with my second novel. This one is only semi-nonfiction. My main character is a high-ranking federal agent with a secret past—he spent time in a Mexican prison when he was twenty years old. His unlikely prelude to law enforcement has provided him with invaluable insight into, and contacts with, the underbelly of Los Angeles.

This book is a long thank-you note to Tom.

Dawn likes spending time in my new house even more than I do. She says that she feels more at home here, and so has taken it upon herself to rearrange my drawers and closets and even the refrigerator to make herself more comfortable. I let her do all this, of course. I have asked her to officially move in with me, but she insists that the real estate market is stagnant, and she can't sell her house quite yet. I know better. There is nothing wrong with the real estate market. It's just Dawn's way of playing both sides of the relationship fence. It's just one more way she never ceases to amuse me.

I decided to add this epilogue in the second printing of this book after something that happened not too long after it hit the shelves in the States. Dawn brought a letter home from her office that was addressed to my pen name and mailed to the publishing house, care of the editor. As soon as I saw the envelope, I knew who it was from. I recognized the uneven handwriting. It was from Dana.

She began the letter quite formally at first, even hesitantly. "My name is Dana. I picked up your book last week at the Barnes & Noble and I haven't been able to put it down since." At first I was in awe of the unlikely coincidence that Dana had actually found my book on the shelf and purchased it. It wasn't a frontrunner on the New York Times list or anything. I wondered if she had coincidentally picked it up, or if instead someone had told her about it, or perhaps mailed it to her.

After the initial introductory bullshit, she cut right to the chase. *Your book is about me*, she wrote. *It's about me and my former husband. I know your name isn't Robert Pollack. It's David Bailey.*

The letter was so odd—it was almost as if she was trying to convince herself of the facts as she was writing them. Instead of just saying, *Hi David, I know it's you.* She spent an entire page making a case for how I was really her former (deceased) husband.

She didn't know what to make of the whole Ellen thing. *Was this true*, she had asked herself? *Or was this a fiction in order to make the book more interesting?* She said that when she got to the part about me stashing Ellen's card into one of my writing notebooks, she drove to her parents' house where she had stored a lot of my old things in the garage and had gone through the boxes that came out of my office.

Right there, she wrote, *in the notebook you mentioned, I found that card with the dog on the front. The name signed on the card was different than your character's name, obviously, but I realized that your relationship with "Ellen" had been real. I vaguely remembered some woman you were in contact with over the Internet, but I didn't put two and two together until that very moment.*

There were other issues in the book besides my online romance with Ellen that were a revelation to her. Dana finally read the truth about Alicia. I was surprised to read that she was apologizing for having doubted me. Apparently, she and Alicia had a falling out after I left. Alicia took the news of my disappearance rather hard, Dana said, and had felt that her lie had in some way contributed to what happened. She was probably right. If Dana was still with me that day, I probably wouldn't have taken the money.

Dana also apologized for being so critical and unsupportive of my dream to write. She didn't really mean it when she said I sucked, she was just trying to hurt me. I didn't really care whether or not she liked my writing anyway. Her taste in literature never went beyond the TV Guide.

She closed her letter by saying that she was married and expecting a child. Things were going well. Her husband owned a restaurant in La Jolla and was planning on expanding to a location downtown in San Diego in the near future. She promised me that she wouldn't tell anyone about discovering me in Australia, because she didn't want to spoil how well everything was going for her in her new marriage.

She thought about me often, she wrote. She missed me a lot. But she acknowledged that in some ways we were all wrong for each other from the start. She had been angry about the whole Ellen thing at first, but understood that in some ways she and I had drifted apart long before Ellen and I met online. *What can I say?* she wrote, *She was a better friend to you than I ever was.*

There had been a postscript, written very close to the bottom edge of the paper in tiny print so it would all fit. *It's funny though, how even though I rushed to judgement about you and Alicia, I didn't want to believe the whole Ellen thing when I was reading about it. If it hadn't been for that card I found, I probably would still be thinking it was all something you had made up for the sake of the story. I guess I just didn't want to believe you could ever love anyone else.*

I kept Dana's letter, just as I had kept Ellen's card. I didn't know why

I kept it, but I did. I guess old habits die hard. It's stashed away in one of the hanging file folders in the filing cabinet of my office. I hate to be sentimental in my situation, but I can't bear to throw it out.

I don't plan on ever writing Dana back, though. She'll be expecting me to, but I won't. But it'll be okay.

It's better that she has the last word, anyway, knowing Dana.

Margaret Emerson holds a master's degree in Ecopsychology and has written hundreds of self-help and relationship advice articles for psychotherapists, coaches, and personal development experts through her work as a ghostwriter and marketing copywriter. She's also the author of *The Mountain Paradox* and *Contemplative Hiking Along the Colorado Front Range.* She resides on a homestead in Ridgway, Colorado with her husband and enjoys hiking, fishing, and gardening.